THE PALE MOON
OF MORNING

Liam Lynch

WOLFHOUND PRESS

First published 1995 by
WOLFHOUND PRESS Ltd
68 Mountjoy Square
Dublin 1

Wolfhound Press receives financial assistance from the Arts Council/
An Chomhairle Ealaíon, Dublin.

The author wishes to acknowledge the assistance of
the Arts Council of Ireland

British Library Cataloguing in Publication Data
A catalogue record for this book is available from the British Library.

ISBN 0-86327-310-6

Cover illustration and design: Brian Finnegan
Typesetting: Wolfhound Press
Printed by the Guernsey Press Co Ltd, Guernsey, Channel Isles

THE PALE MOON
OF MORNING

In Memory of Breda

... the pale moon of morning
was co-existent with the risen sun ...

PART ONE

The sun was setting. A vast pink O in a pink washed sky, it hovered over the horizon of the plain he knew from geography as the great plain of Munster which swept from the south-eastern coast of Ireland to the western seaboard and the cold, choppy grey waters of the Atlantic. One of the most fertile plains in Europe, its bold green sweep went quite unchallenged by hill or hummock of any kind.

In the gathering darkness the train pulled into the small station. He leaned from his compartment window in the hope of recognising people who were to him mere sepia figures in a series of oil photographs. He thought: I'll recognise Veronica, and Veronica will recognise me. Forgetful of the fact that the photographs had been taken by some inept person forty years before.

It was highly unlikely those he sought had ever seen a photograph of him. Not Veronica. She was the one, he had always imagined, as a child, who would miraculously emerge from the print, and bring wealth, shower him with gifts, and above all waft him away to Farrighy House, of fabled beauty ... Sumptuous magnificence. Farrighy and what his mother termed 'his father's people'. Veronica was the one he chose to love because unlike the others in the photograph she didn't smile with the promiscuous abandon of the others. Those who smiled so freely. So madly. So glad. Veronica's eyes were sad. In a sense defeated. He knew that with the absolute certainty of the very young. That she had suffered. She would not spurn him. One of her eyes .... The left. Was imperfect. It seemed gashed. As if it had suffered physical injury. With a tolerance infrequent in him, he had chosen to overlook the blemish.

He alighted from the train conscious of the fact that he was wearing his Sunday-best suit; it was serviceable, somewhat shabby. His shoes were badly scuffed; shoddy. He clutched his heavy suitcase. Now he was on the very verge of despair, thinking again he had taken the wrong train, was getting off at the wrong station.

One or two people alighted to be greeted by friends on the platform. There was laughter. Then the small gatherings dispersed. The station was empty. In a nearby flowerbed asters, marigolds, snapdragons. All basked in the dim light. As though conscious of their riotous colour. Their beauty brazen.

The door to a small office opened. A uniformed railwayman peeked out. Popped back inside. He heard the man shout .... 'Oh to be sure. To be sure.' He glanced in despair at the tracks along which the small steam engine had gone pulling its reluctant, swaying carriages. The tracks appeared to coverage in the distant; then disappeared.

The door to the small office opened again. This time the railwayman, a cap on his head, stepped fully from the office, whistling loudly. Badly. Approached him, respectfully tipping the visor of his cap.

'Master Timothy Gates destination Farrighy care of the Phipps?'

He, nodded, his mouth too parched to speak.

'I thought as much,' the railman said good humouredly. 'Who else but yourself would be left here like a chick without its mother. Your ticket, Master Gates ... if you don't mind.'

He surrendered his ticket. It was carefully punched. Placed in the railwayman's uniform. 'Miss Phipps asked me to offer you her apologies. There was some trouble with the motor car. They'll be here shortly .... Well what do you think of that?' The railwayman looked at him with big trusting blue eyes tinted with pleasantry.

'Between ourselves there's always trouble with the Phipps. If it isn't this, it's that. If it isn't that — it's the other. Take them as they come, that's what I say. Otherwise they'd drive you stark raving mad ....' He paused. His eyelids flickered rapidly.

'Do you know something but I think you're a Christian that hasn't had a bite to eat all day ... and you're parched with thirst as well. Am I right?'

He thought it best not to encourage the man.

'The Phipps .... I heard my grandfather tell of the times when they were in the full of their grandeur. Balls and dances of every description. House guests. Shooting parties. God knows what else beside. And the finery ... beyond all .... Well, it's all gone now. All gone and no two ways about it.'

The railwayman sighed. Not exactly desolate at the family's fall from grace and favour. His ears practically bristled.

'That's them. Oh, that's them to be sure. They're coming in the trap. The motor must have broken down altogether. Not worth a damn the same motor when all is said and done. Fit only to stop a gap in a ditch.'

Timothy listened. Heard nothing. Then, faintly, the clop of horses hooves striking the tarred surface of the road. Unaccountably he felt sickened. Feared he would faint. Imagination, he realised, was one thing. Reality another. The railwayman kindly took his suitcase. He knew it was kindness. Not subservience. They went outside. A young towheaded man of animal good health smiled, taking Timothy's case from the railwayman. A mannish woman dressed in heavy chopped tweeds, stout brogues and what appeared to be a hunting cap sprouting a feather from some wild game, stood watching impassively. Her face was pale. A smear of red lipstick on her lips seemed a mere concession to gender rather than an effort to enhance her femininity. Goldrimmed glasses on a long black ribbon were perched on the bridge of her nose. The gold glinted coldly. Her eyes were deeply brown. Very large. Not particularly welcoming. Veronica's left eye was indeed imperfect. Not as noticeable as it had been in the photograph.

The fairheaded young man exchanged pleasantries with the railwayman. 'Sound man Billy .... How's the wife?'

'Good man, Gur. The wife and our offsprings are giving us no cause for concern. Well, no undue cause for concern.' The railwayman paused and lifting his cap, inclined his head toward the woman in tweed. 'Your goodself Miss Phipps. Glorious weather for the time of the year.'

'Glorious indeed, Mister O'Sullivan, glorious.'

Her voice was hard. Harsh. He thought of grinding millstones. He approached her unsure whether or not to extend his hand.

'I'm Miss Phipps,' she announced to him in clipped, short tones. She kept her hands firmly wedged into the deep pockets of her jacket.

'Veronica Phipps.' He knew that however he chose to address her it was never to be as Veronica.

'You must be Timothy.'

He nodded. She nodded shortly to the railwayman. Smiled as if by reflex. Turned on her heels. Walked away. The railwayman called 'Goodnight Miss Phipps. Safe home to all.'

The towheaded fellow smiling broadly laid a broad hand on his shoulder, applying slight pressure. Meaning to be friendly. Reassuring. Timothy smiled gratefully. Felt he could weep at so cold, so off-handed a welcome: from Veronica. Veronica the young lady who smiled less than the others in those old brown family photographs his mother treasured. She had never been over enthusiastic about 'his father's people'. Veronica who had suffered. Would not spurn him .... Had done so. Just now. Decidedly. He felt he could weep. Would weep. But not now. Later, in the shelter of his bedroom. No one would know. Or even guess. That he, a gangling youth of fourteen, could weep so. Did so. Frequently.

A splendid green-lacquered trap with a fine horse in harness stood outside the station gates. The sun had set.

Darkness had begun to seep in from all sides. In the glooming he could just discern what appeared to be a hooded figure, enveloped by a sweeping cloak. Its face turned from him, holding the reins of the trap. The hands were elongated. Deathly pale. Those of a woman. The horse pawed restlessly at some loose chippings. Miss Phipps turned to the young man.

'You'd better light those sidelights Bannion.'

Her voice was even harsher. Graceless. She mounted the metal step hanging from the back of the trap. Took her seat in the trap which had tilted noticeably the moment she put her foot on the step.

Bannion touched his forelocks respectfully. Then out of sight of Miss Phipps he scowled. Winked broadly. Conspiratorially. Watching, Timothy felt gratitude rush through him as though it were a soft benign tide of water coursing through his body. He assumed he was to follow but Miss Phipps alarmed cried, 'No. Bannion must get in first. To preserve the balance.' She snorted in what he could only assume was disgust.

Humiliated, he watched while Bannion lighted the candles in the lanterns attached to the sides of the trap at front. They gave little light. Sufficient to signal the approach of a horsedrawn vehicle. Little else. Or so he thought. In what light was shed he saw that the mane of the horse had been plaited with colourful ribbons. A few cornflowers were entwined with brazen effect. Bannion took his place in the trap opposite the hooded woman whose features he, Timothy, had not yet seen. Had she been ravished by some disease he wondered. Left foully disfigured that she should take such great pains to conceal her face? She was slight. Lightly built. Frail. Fragile. Breakable. Fragile of body. And of mind?

'You may climb in now,' Miss Phipps said, her voice if anything now irritated. 'Bring your suitcase with you.'

He did so. With difficulty. Miss Phipps herself slammed the door. Turned the safety catch. As if he were incapable of doing so. She rooted about in the pockets of her tweed jacket. Took out a cigarette case which glinted brightly for a moment as it caught the light of the candles burning in the lanterns. She jammed a cigarette between her lips with a total lack of ceremony. Took out a petrol lighter. Snapped it alight. A flare. The acrid smell of petrol. So alien to the scents of the night air which were a lovely compound of subtle smells. Miss Phipps inhaled deeply. Exhaled forcefully.

'Right Bannion. This isn't exactly the state opening of Parliament. I suggest you get on with it.'

Bannion acknowledged her implied command with a languid nod of his head. Bannion's eyes were bright. Harbouring at one and the same time mockery, irony. And, oddly, affection. There already existed, Timothy understood, a subtlety, a curiously balanced relationship between them. Bannion was no subservient yokel, but a free being of great spirit. Bannion and he would be close friends. The prospect pleased him.

Above, the darkness impacted further. Bats now skimmed low over the trap. He detested them for their filthy stealth, their rattish uncleanness. Bannion communicated slightly with the horse, only flickering the reins to signal command. The hooves beat rhythmically on the hard, tarred surface of the road. Miss Phipps' cigarette glowed brightly pink as she dragged avariciously on it ... Exhaling great gusts of smoke which strangely, he found companionable, almost pleasant.

'This,' she said disturbing the hitherto unbroken silence, 'This is my sister Philippa.'

The hooded figure bowed her hooded head. As if in veneration. Said nothing. His greeting thudded to its death. In the quiet. No willing hands to save it ....

'And this,' Miss Phipps announced, handsomely now, 'This is Gur Bannion. Known more commonly as Bannion. There are other more fitting epithets but we won't go into that just yet.' Bannion snorted quietly. Whished the whip gently on the horses flanks. A mere brush; as if sharing a joke with the horse. Timothy smiled. In the darkness he imagined Miss Phipps had smiled. She. Veronica of the photographs had not spurned him. Nor would she. Ever. Her tone of voice now told him so.

He nodded. Slipped into shallow sleep. Tired. Hungry. From time to time he jolted. Awake. Wondering if they had arrived. Once when he awakened, he saw the evening star. Emotion flooded him. Pain overwhelmed him. It — the evening star — had always been to him an object of private worship. The bright star of hope. Eternal. Self-perpetuating. Never failing. But had failed. On such a summer's night as this. He had been to the sea with O'Neill. His closest friend. The water had been cold. Invigorating. Their humour effervescent.

As they cycled home from the grey-green waters which had so stimulated them, swinging at each other, as they dangerously weaved among the traffic. Seeking to whip each other lightly on the back. They parted. By Fairview corner. O'Neill shearing left to the city tenements. Timothy turned right. Towards Drumcondra. The light on in the house. Nothing amiss. Or so it seemed. He recognised Monsignor Madden's car. Realised with a chill. That something was gravely amiss. Both killed. Killed instantly. Failure of the brakes. No one's fault. The will of God. The inscrutable will of God. Pray for them. Poor people. More sinned against. Than sinning. Prayer. The only solace. The only refuge. From such pain. Pray for them. The recently deceased. Amen. For those he had thought he had never loved. Amen. Or who he also believed had never loved him. Amen. The faithful souls. Departed. His parents. Both of them. At the same time. At the same time. In a motoring accident. Killed. Instantly. Painlessly. Amen. Amen. Amen. Unconsciously, he whimpered. Very. Nearly. Cried. Out. So acute the pain of remembering. The evening star. The worshipped star of hope. Which had shone that evening. Aeons ago. When his parents who mutually loathed each other with the terrible passion with which they had once loved. Had died. Been killed. He whimpered again. Bared his teeth. Almost. Cried. Out.

Miss Phipps leaned forward. Touched him gently on the shoulder. Waking him. 'We are nearly there Timothy. We're nearly at Farrighy.' The horse turned left. Between two unimposing gateposts. On one of which was painted not very prominently the name *Farrighy*.

But for the stars all was nearly deep dark. He was glad. He was weeping quietly. He knew. The others knew as much. They were too polite. Far too polite to let him know. The horses hooves beat a tattoo on pulverised stone. Above them now excluding the night sky of stars, the limbs of ancient trees entwined. With clarion spirit sounded the bark of a dog, raised in delirious welcome. It met them about half-way in the long straight drive. Its eyes blazing with delight, sparkling clearly in the darkness. It ran ahead, barking playfully, inhibiting the horse.

'Our rather stupid mongrel Tan,' Miss Phipps commented. Bannion uttered the vilest obscenities to the dog, quietly, in the tender tones of a lover. The driveway ceased abruptly. They swung onto a crescent of loose gravel. The house arched to their right. It was starkly, linearly, austerely, beautiful. Decidedly so. Above the doorway, at a landing window, a lamp burned brightly. In welcome, he assumed. He felt welcomed. Cheered by the sight of it.

'We have arrived,' Miss Phipps announced, and alighted from the car. Bannion also. Slipped quickly to the front where he stroked the horse's head. It pawed gently at the gravel beneath. Timothy alighted, taking his case. He stood by the trap door. Gave his hand to Philippa who did not speak as she alighted. Her voluminous cloak swept the gravel. Her head still hidden, she nodded as reverently as before. Ghostlike or like the very materialisation of death come to gather lives, as such a hooded figure might harvest arum lilies. Entered. Miss Phipps boomed.

'Leave your suitcase for Bannion. He will see to it provided he can wrench himself from his devotions to that worthless nag.'

Turning, she crunched the gravel as she moved to the open doorway. He hesitated, then followed. They entered the hall. On a niche in the wall a number of candles wedged firmly into silver holders. Philippa lighted two as she might for a religious ceremony. Guarding the light from a longstemmed match, tipped the candles. They took light. She blew the match out. With equal ceremony she deposited the spent matchstick in a small metal box on the ledge. She took a candle. Holding it at about waist level directly in front of her. Her other hand resting at her slender waist.

She approached them. Her features sharp. Her skin very white, her eyes dark. Dull. Vacant. Her hair was drawn harshly back above her head. Braided into a bun at the back. Attached to a white ribbon tied tightly about her head was a posy of primroses. They looked so real, so delicately made, he imagined he could smell their spring freshness.

'If I may be excused I'd like to go and change for dinner.' Her low voice lacked assertion. Miss Phipps watched her with such affection. He understood she rarely showed affection so freely to another.

'You have been simply topping,' she murmured. Leaning slightly forward, and to the side, she kissed Philippa on the forehead. 'You needn't join us for dinner if you feel it would be too much.'

Philippa smiled. Very sadly. A Victorian image of sorrow. She smiled, slightly. A smile which barely registered in the lines of her tight lips. Her stark eyes now shone beautifully. With an inclination of the head towards Timothy she turned. Processionally mounted the high staircase which curved up through the central well of the house. Darkly clothed she was soon in darkness, following the pallid light shed by the candle.

Miss Phipps sighed, dragging off the scarf she had worn loosely about her neck. Pink and cream white. Crimson. It flared in a splash of brazen colour as, catching the candle-light, it billowed out in its first short flight to the hall-table onto which it had been slung. Miss Phipps swept off her feathered hat. It too was slung onto the table. As were her gloves. One at a time. She fingered her cropped hair, glanced with a distinct lack of interest at her own image in the looking-glass above the table, and strode about the hallway with crescent impatience.

'Damn. That fellow .... Damn him to hell .... Horse's mane all bedecked with flowers and coloured ribbons like a milkman's tarty animal ....' She bared her teeth. Visibly ground them. Angry now. Anxious to swipe out at anything. Or anyone. Timothy knew no comment was wanted.

How silent it all is. How silent through and through. Silent. Even here in the hollow of the house. They had heard the crunch of gravel as Bannion led off the horse followed by the yelping dog still feverishly excited. Since then; silence.

Miss Phipps took a cigarette from her splendid case. Tapped its tip aggressively on the lid. Placed it between her smeared red lips. Lighted it. Drew heavily and held her breath for some seconds. She exhaled. Relaxing visibly.

'That damned useless lout. Why I tolerate his insufferable behaviour is quite beyond me. Do please excuse.' She turned her back on him and taking a handkerchief from her jacket pocket, wiped the lipstick from her lips. She bunched the handkerchief. Jammed it back into her jacket which he now saw was shapeless. Both the pockets hung heavily from constant rough treatment.

'Do forgive me. But I simply can't stand that vile stuff. My apologies.' She grimaced .... 'Horrible. Slime. That's all it is.'

They heard the steady throb of an engine slowly revving to life. Above them, suspended from the ceiling high up in the well of the house, a splendid brass lantern glimmered faintly. And then more steadily. More brightly.

Miss Phipps snorted. 'You see, Timothy, we have our own God-giver of light. Bannion .... The Prince of Light. I should warn you we generate our own electricity by means which are and always have been mysterious to everyone but my grandfather who originally installed the wretched thing. Bannion sees to it these days. Be warned. The damned thing is apt to fall at any time without warning which is why you will find candlesticks and boxes of matches on virtually every window ledge of the house. So if the lights fail, please don't panic. Stand perfectly still no matter where you might be. Then calmly feel your way to the nearest ledge. There you will find some matches and a candle. For God's sake don't panic or scream. And do make sure you place the spent match in the rather battered Oxo boxes you will also find on the ledge. Don't trample the match underfoot. This house is tinder dry. Should a fire break out we should all be like well-roasted fowl before we quite realised as much. And don't dare approach the generator in the disused stables. It is a monstrous thing with spinning fly-wheels of all kinds. The wheels have been known to break with terrible effect. For goodness sake please do as I say. The thing is wretchedly dangerous and Bannion who is at that stage of life during which one loves everyone and all things — he simply adores the contraption. You'll be given a tour of the place. Bannion will want to expose the machine himself for your adoration. It is one of the very many privileges he has appropriated to himself during his time with us. Though God knows what we should do without him.'

Her voice was soft ... with some regret. She turned abruptly. Faced him. Squaring her shoulders. All the better to do battle. He saw in her eyes the sharp glint of hostility he had seen when they had first met on the railway platform. Then, as now, ashamedly, he quailed.

'Come along. I think we should get some things straightened out. We'll both eat and sleep all the better once we thrash a few things about a bit.'

He followed her out into and along a flagged stoned corridor. Her brogues struck the stone with both precision and intimidating authority. Someone about to do battle on their chosen field. The corridor was unhappily cold. Institutional. Their footsteps rang loudly. Echoed a great deal. Died away. Miss Phipps threw open a stout door to the right. It had, he had time to notice, a dull brass plate stamped in black lettering: 'Office'.

In a commonplace fireplace a log fire blazed. Above, a vast painting of a harrowed-faced west of Ireland woman seeking to restrain her grief. Her hardfaced brother. Jaws clenched.

Eyes fierce with anger. Her aged parents. Watched as their daughter, a forlorn figure of fragile, sensitive beauty waved. Just as one assumed she was about to step into the currach which was to take her to the mainland where she would begin the journey to lifelong exile. The skies about her. The sea. Seabirds in flight. Trailing growths of seaweed. The stone-faced men who were to row the tender boat of light timber covered with seasoned hides. All appeared to scream their anguish. At the girl's terrible flight. Her parents' moments of great pain. And terror. And loss. To be borne in silence. As ordained. Miss Phipps saw he was glancing at it ....

'Simply hideous. But it does arouse some emotion when one first sees it. To what purpose I do not know ... it is called 'Parting' which you may have deduced by now ....' She sat behind a stoutly built, large desk. Strictly functional. To her left were shelves of ledgers in handsome bindings, stamped with gold lettering. He assumed they were the accounts of the estate covering a span of well over a hundred years. On the desk stood a green-painted tin canister. In it were sharpened pencils. Black. Puce. Red. Blue. The pencil parer sensibly close to, tied to a string which in turn attached to an iron weight. Veronica rarely lost things, mislaid them; or gave them away. Or, more tellingly, had them taken from her. She gestured to him to sit in a chair which had a pneumatic rubber cushion. He did so. Settling snugly into its wooden form. Firelight danced about on the ceiling. On the white-washed walls. He waited for her to switch on an electric lamp which stood on the desk. She did not do so. Nor did she light the candle in its holder which for him now represented Farrighy. Always would. They too were on the desk. The firelight danced on the glazed surface of her glasses. Light danced upon the lens as does sunlight on a clear undisturbed pool. It was impossible to see her eyes. To assess her feelings. To gauge her temper. To predict what she would say. Something Miss Phipps was quite aware of from long experience behind the desk.

'We do sympathise with you on the tragic death of your parents. I do assure you I remember them constantly in prayer.

A most fearful, bitter blow to fall on anyone still less on one as young as you.' The impact of her statement made in the same harsh tones in which she seemed to address everyone stunned him. He recoiled. As from a well aimed, well-calculated blow.

Her polite sympathy he had anticipated. Her assertion that she remembered them in prayer was wounding in its simple directness. He uttered a low cry of distress despite having steeled himself not to do so. Prayer and Miss Phipps seemed incongruous. Unreconcilable. Prayer and Veronica did not. Which facet of her character would predominate? and to what end? Miss Phipps toyed absently with the pencil sharpener ....

'There's — or rather there was a link between your father and my father's people. So weak as to hardly merit notice. So tenuous in legal terms as to be legally nonexistent. You have in law and in all good conscience no claim of any kind upon us. Or upon the estates of Farrighy. I don't say that to be hurtful. But to make it unmistakeably clear where exactly you stand, particularly in legal terms. I want no misunderstanding. I must repeat it. You have no claim against us. Or against what were my father's estates. And are now mine.'

She turned aside at the log in the fireplace which occasionally spluttered in renewing flame. She appeared to lapse into thought. In the still night the steady throb of the generator beat steadily. Evenly. Its constant pulsations were not at all as unpleasant as one might expect. Doors opened and closed in the recesses of the very big house. Footsteps sounded with all the incisiveness of bells being struck. Voices varied like dream voices. Shadows now more threatening danced wildly on the walls. A clock struck. What hour, he wondered, weak from exhaustion and lack of food. Miss Phipps stirred herself. She spoke. Her voice now more moderate.

'There is however a debt to be honoured. A matter of restitution between the affairs of your father and of my father.' She paused. Unaware of how she emphasised the words 'my father'. It was at once most bitter, most loving. Unforgetting. Unforgiving.

'The nature of this debt is unknown to me. But the fact that there is a debt, an obligation, is unmistakably clear from my father's papers. Papers which are now in my possession. I'm sorry I can't enlighten you further on the matter. It's all undoubtedly distressing in the extreme to you. We were informed of your parent's death by your father's solicitors. It took some considerable time to trace related papers. Hence the long delay in contacting you. Inviting you to come here .... And should you wish, in time, to remain here with us in Farrighy. My father was, I must tell you, a most eccentric man. That is putting the matter rather less bluntly than others might put it. He was selfish. Irresponsible. Regrettably not always a man of his word. He was, I assure you, not without honour. He was in some respects a man of the utmost honour. Poor father. His failings continue to flay us long after his death.' Her voice quavered. Shook. Slightly. She was, he saw, deeply affected.

'We at Farrighy will do everything to make your stay pleasant. But make no mistake you'll have to take us as you find us. And if you can't take us you may leave us and jolly good luck to you. If you can take us and I must admit we are rather hard to take then you hew wood, draw water like the rest of us. Farrighy is no mansion of leisure. We are not monied people. A penny to us is as it is to most other people. A penny. You will continue your secondary schooling at Tibraddenstown. There is an excellent teaching order there which conducts a day school with a very good reputation. They also have, I believe, a very high success rate. Our means here at Farrighy will not allow for your education at a good boarding school but if you show sufficient promise, and I believe you're above average in most subjects, it may be possible to let you attend Trinity in Dublin or some other university of your choice in Ireland.

Miss Phipps drew breath. Paused. Lit a cigarette with her usual lack of ceremony. A cloak chimed but did not strike. What hour, he again wondered. Numb with the hunger and fatigue. Miss Phipps continued.

'I'll be jolly hard on you. You'll have to cycle to Gerard's Cross which is some ten miles from here. There we have arranged with a man who runs a haulage firm doing business in and around Tibraddenstown to pick up and drop you at the school each morning. He will drive you back to Gerard's Cross each day after school providing he has business in the region. If he has no such business in the region you will have to cycle all the twenty miles from Tibraddenstown. Not by any means easy but then I've done it myself and so did my brothers David and Harold — now deceased. Hard but not difficult. And not all without its compensatory moments. Should you not qualify for university or should you fail to graduate from university you will be taken by the scruff of the neck and thrown out into the world. Make no mistake about that.' Her voice was. Hard. Pitiless. Truthful .... 'I've enough millstones about my neck without having another one round it. A hard neck I may have, but not quite as hard as that.'

An attempt at humour? He thought ... perhaps ... not really. He simply did not care.

Miss Phipps rose. Went to the fireplace, kicked the much reduced log to the back. Her hands wedged deeply in her shapeless pockets, with difficulty. Her lower lips curled. A clock chimed. Clearly. The dog barked. Its bark was yelpish. High with excitement and pleasure. It drew closer. Louder. Soon it was barking furiously outside. Pawing the door, demanding admission. Miss Phipps shouted.

'Oh do be quiet you stupid mongrel. Sit. And do be quiet.' She commanded. Outside, the dog obeyed, but whined softly. Miss Phipps approached.

'Timothy, I've been brutal and direct, perhaps unwarrantedly so. But you have to understand that while we will help all we can, there is very little help we can in very real terms give you. Time will help. But it won't ever quite assuage your grief as much as you might wish. Do forgive me my brutality. Welcome to Farrighy. Consider yourself one of our benighted family.'

She inclined her head and kissed him on either cheek. He

broke. Wept. More brokenly than he thought possible. His sense of humiliation was such that he knew he would never, quite, forgive her. For being there. For seeing, him. Weep. Like that.

Her voice was soft, dispassionate. 'Every evening the rugs in front of the fires are kicked aside into corners which you'll see have stone flooring about the hearth and fuelbox. Please always remember to do that every evening in your room and study and if you're the last out or leave a room at night. I think you have had enough for one day. I think it better that you eat alone. Here. I advise you against taking a bath. An unsupervised bath in your state of extreme fatigue would I believe be dangerous. I'll send Bridget to you shortly. She'll show you to your room. Please forgive my lack of tact. But I thought it best ....' Her voice trailed away. 'Goodnight .... Oh — should you hear a cry in the night. Do not be unduly alarmed .... Philippa's nerves aren't the best.'

With that she left him. Spent. He lay back exhausted by the events of a day which he saw with clarity would feature as a day of great moment in his life. Silence now settled. Strangely he had not noticed Miss Phipps' footsteps after she had left the room. They were, he understood, characterised by stout, ever present assertions. He had not thought her of being capable of moderating their tone. Somewhere a clock struck.

What hour he wondered and counted the strokes. Ten .... Eleven .... Twelve .... Twelve. Midnight. The bewitching hour of midnight when the graves yawn. And the dead come forth to unsettle the living. His parents. Both killed. Instantly. In a motor accident. The recently deceased. He started awake. Someone had knocked softly on the door. The dog barked. The door opened. A woman, back bent, with a rugged face and a crop of fine silver hair entered. She wore black, shapeless boots, a black dress, a white apron. A gold brooch on her dress, at the throat. Valuable, he thought. A smile hovered on her lips. Bridget he knew. Instantly loved her.

'I'm sorry to be disturbing you but I'm Bridget, Sir. Miss Veronica thought you would like something to eat before you went to bed. I thought it best if you had only something light to eat, Sir. It will rest easier on the stomach. You'll sleep better and please God, you won't dream.'

Wise woman. Lovely woman. Warm woman. Bridget. The Mary of the Gaels. How nice to live so unequivocally.

'Soup Sir. It's what Miss Veronica always recommends. And some brown bread and butter and thin strips of warm chicken and a few chopped runner-beans. Something light, Sir. To help you sleep.'

She was, he realised, holding a white cloth bunched in her right hand. There was no sign of food. Or the dog.

'I'll bring it now, Sir. It's outside. Tan will be licking his lips but never fear, he never touches food not given to him.' She turned, walked very slowly from the room, returned with a tray covered with crisp linen. Tan entered. Eyes wide in devout beggary. His tail thrashing wildly. His body waggling as he sought to ingratiate himself. So reap a reward. A splendid red-setter. His body sparkled with reflected light.

'Your supper, Sir ... and a cup of the finest water to be had in all Ireland. Taken from a spring down in the Culgey field at the end of the Quaker's walk. Miss Veronica wouldn't hear tell of anything else for herself.' She smiled. Enigmatically. Her eyes, he noticed, were unusually large. Deeply blue. Just like Bannion's.

'Take the soup and the few bites. You'll feel all the better for it.' He did so. Bridget nodded approval. 'It's a nice soup. Potatoes, the small pieces of chicken, nettles, the blob of butter. And just a dash of salt and pepper. Miss Veronica's mother taught me to make that. Handsome and very proud. But kind and faithful. She stood by you Sir if you know what I mean. She wasn't the kind that are all sunshine and roses. Then when things go wrong, go and pick the flesh off your very bones. You're liking that soup. I can see from your eyes.' She smiled with girlish delight. He nodded assent.

'I thought you would. And you'll like the food too and the good night's sleep and tomorrow .... We'll wait and see what tomorrow brings before having to deal with it. You'll like us here in Farrighy once you get used to us. We're all a bit odd but God-look-on-us we're harmless ....' She removed the empty bowl and slipped the plate of chicken, potatoes and vegetable before him.

'Miss Veronica is more bark than bite but I'd be lying if I didn't admit that she's the lady to bite if she has good cause to. Mind you it takes a lot to make her bite but by the merciful Jesus she can take lumps out of you with that mouth of hers. As for Miss Philippa, God love her, she has the odd manner. Don't try and make friends with her Sir. Wait and leave her make friends with you. A stouter friend nor a nicer lady you wouldn't meet in a week's walking. And Master Peter. Well, you'll have to take him as he comes. Be kind but stand your ground at the same time. He'll respect you in the long run.'

She paused and glanced at his plate. Her eyes shone with satisfaction. Delight. 'There you are. You have the plate near licked clean. Sure what did I tell you. The good cup of milk or if you'd prefer it tea. Though I have to tell you Sir, Miss Veronica disapproves very strongly of tea at all times. Still less before going to bed. But sure I'd drop for the want of it if it wasn't the last thing I had at night and the first thing in the morning.' She busied herself at the fire. Banking it down for the night. He poured himself some tea and sipped it slowly.

'Bring the cup of tea with you. I'll show you to your room.' She preceded him upstairs. The staircase was wooden. Quite without covering of any kind. Its steps dipped in the centre where they had worn down by long use. Some creaked noisily. He felt irrationally fearful as they advanced deeper into the upper reaches of the house. His room was warm and comfortable, but to his surprise without electricity. An oil lamp served for light. By his bed stood his battered suitcase. On the washstand stood a basin of steaming hot water. By it a bar of soap, and a towel. He was far too exhausted to wash. Bridget left him to undress. Saw that he was comfortably settled for the night. He fell asleep instantly. Slept deeply. Once he heard a scream of pain. Or thought he had. He awoke. The oil lamp was still burning though turned low. In the folds of an old leather armchair Bridget slept. Enfolded in blankets, one hand clutched her rosary. She kept vigil. He remembered. Prayed briefly. Wept. Felt infinitely grateful to the bright-eyed Bridget keeping faithful watch over a total stranger. When he awoke sunlight streamed through his bedroom window. So soft, sensual the light. Its fragile grey shadows. He experienced something akin to joy, believing it augured well for the future.

The chimes of the Protestant Church in Tibraddenstown sounded softly, faintly, in the twilight. Above them swallows darted high and low in the evening sky in what one could well imagine was their ordained response to beautifully orchestrated music they alone could hear. He had commented as much some weeks ago when first he saw what he took to be their ritual dance.

'Stuff and bloody nonsense,' Peter had retorted. 'The atmosphere pressure is high. They are feeding on insects. Twilight flies. Minute little flies. Something like a mosquito. Only it isn't. When the pressure is high it drives them down to within a few inches above the ground. That's why they skim so low at times. To feed. It's also a sign of rain. Beautiful bloody music has nothing to do with it.' Peter's voice was hard. Gleeful. 'Flannery told me as much. Incidentally Flannery says you're a Catholic shit from the slums of Dublin. Is that so?'

Miss Phipps had made clear that as he, Timothy, would be known to all as Timothy, that he could address Miss Philippa as Philippa, he would have to address her — Veronica — as Miss Phipps, at all times. She wished it so. Little did she bother about how that stung. A droplet of molten lead striking the surface of the face where it burns deeply before being shook aside. The arrangement clearly signalled his position within the family. Peter, all of twelve, addressed her as Veronica.

Timothy waited for Miss Phipps to check Peter's language. She simply continued to assemble on a round table a monstrous jigsaw puzzle. Everyone was forbidden to touch the puzzle even if they spotted where two or more pieces could cojoin. He, Timothy had not replied to the offence. He knew that he had in some way failed. Or disappointed them. In the way a runner balks at the hurdle. Or a horse at a difficult ditch. His form had been judged. Found wanting.

Philippa was bent over a piece of embroidery. A table cloth of exquisite colour, and design. She had it more than three quarters finished. Could soon expect to see the result of years of unrelenting servitude with needle and thread. About her shoulders was a dark brown shawl. Her dress was, as always, black. With ruffles at the wrists and throat which relieved the depressing dark colours that for him conjured up images of death. Usually she wore a brooch at her throat. More splendid than that worn by Bridget. Both brooches were the results of one man's craft, he thought. Or art. He estimated both were valuable. He thought it odd that gold and silver should be in common use in a household pauperised beyond redemption — if what Miss Phipps had so firmly informed him, that day two years ago when he had first arrived, was true.

Amber candles burned in the beautifully wrought branches of a silver candelabrum which stood on an old kitchen table placed out of doors many years ago. At one time it had been painted dark green but that paint had faded. Exposed to the elements the boards were now grey. Or whitish. Warped. Its endurance was considered by the family as little short of miraculous. Sometimes all waged amongst themselves that it would not survive a further winter. But endure it did. Known as Veronica's table, it stood unseen in a corner of the walled orchard where the grass grew high. The windfalls when crunched underfoot gave rise to a delicious smell. The trees were old. Gnarled. Despite neglect they bore handsome crops of small redstreaked apples which were very sweet. And light-green apples. Which were very bitter but superb for cooking. So negligent was Bannion about its care, it had when first seen all the appearances of an orchard long abandoned. Bannion who had the body of an ox and solid good health did not believe in undue exertion yet good naturedly undertook a series of multitudinous tasks far more complicated than one could expect of a hired hand. Bannion laboured hard. The bunched red apples seen against the dark greenery of the branches gave a fleeting expression of marvellous birds of paradise come to roost.

They had dined out of doors as Miss Phipps loved to do. Bridget and Nora, a strong country girl from nearby who helped Bridget, had taken all the dinner things. The family were now drinking the strong bitter coffee Miss Phipps favoured. Moths were flying low over the high grass. Some drawn to the flame burned their wings. Fell to the earth. Others more cautiously danced about the flames as butterflies might about a bush of many flowers. Miss Phipps was smoking. Her cigarettes smelled more strongly in the summer stillness. Peter had taken a rose from a silver dish of roses. Blood red. Strongly scented. Their leaves, velvet. Lovely to touch. He pulled absently at the petals scattering them about the tabletop. Miss Phipps gazed at him from the security of her reflective glasses. Peter sat beside her. The sharp candle flame lighting his handsome face to best advantage. His fair hair all but blazed in the reflected light.

Unconsciously Miss Phipps sighed deeply, and spoke. 'Birdy, are you being absurd? Needlework in this terrible light .... You are hazarding your sight. Think for a moment what life would be were you without sight?'

Philippa cocked her head like an inquisitive cocker spaniel. Bluntly she replied, 'I'd kill myself by drowning if that were to happen.' She returned to her embroidery, the others silenced by the shock of her statement. Philippa made few positive statements. All realised she was perfectly capable of such action. She raised her head. Smiled. Pleased at their reaction. Her eyes blazed brightly. With unstinting, unqualified hatred, she turned to Peter. 'Do stop doing that to the roses. You're picking them apart. How would you like to be picked apart like that?'

'They're only flowers. Flowers don't feel pain.'

'Is that so indeed?' Philippa asked. 'And who pray is your authority on this matter ...?'

'Flannery.' He replied promptly. Flannery was the only person other than himself whom Peter recognised as being of significance.

Philippa carefully wove a bright red thread into her cloth. 'Flannery thinks he knows everything. I admit he does know a great deal. But I doubt if his word is worth very much more than anyone else's in this matter. Flowers are living things. Pain is growth. Growth is pain. In all things. Humans, animals, birds, flowers, trees. I sometimes hear hay, corn heavily headed, other grain crops, cry as they fall before scythes. I assure you they do cry out. Very faintly ... very poignantly ... very much pained.'

Peter and she exchanged glances. Peter looked swiftly to Veronica who was now smoking the butt end of a cigarette. She smoked her cigarettes down to the last centimetre. One would have thought she would burn her lips. At times she held the nub between a thumb and forefinger. In precisely the way Bannion and other labourers did. Her fingers were stained brown. Once or twice she had used a cigarette holder of beautiful amber. Inlaid with silver. Tipped with jet. Thinking it as an affectation, she ceased to use it. From time to time she acknowledged her fingers were unsightly. Very unladylike. Removed as much of the stain as she could with a pumice stone. After some days of harsh self discipline she lapsed happily into her own slovenliness but never attaining so low a level as Flannery who declared squalor was the natural state of his soul. The inclination, however astonishing, was nevertheless present, unmistakably, in her unsuitably bright evening dress cut short at the sleeves. The material of the finest satin, cut to the mode of twenty years before. Splattered with the colours of flower beds at railway stations. She drew a shawl about her. Shivered slightly. She returned Peter's rather blank stare but remained quite impassive. Yet from experience Timothy realised they had communicated, as they often did, silently. Philippa bared her teeth. Half snarl. Half sneer. 'Come off it Peter. Don't turn to Veronica for help. As Flannery rightly says, she is in the last analysis a bigoted Catholic bitch.'

Peter's mouth opened. Gaped in astonishment. First at Philippa ... then at Veronica, then at him. Timothy. As if on an agreed signal, all drew breath sharply, held it as if they were being timed. Philippa smiled maliciously.

'Veronica's God is a God of hatred and malice. Hateful. Vengeful. In extreme. Pain, suffering, despair, horrid fear are all he has to offer. A crown of thorns is a rather painful headpiece. See how uneasily it rests on Veronica's brow. See how silently she suffers for the sins of the world. She is crowned with an invisible crown of thorns. Blood erupts from her wounds. Blood. Her horrible God demands the blood of not only Veronica but of all mankind.'

Peter gulped, gasped .... 'What?' Peter asked.

'God told me, Peter. That's how I know. God spoke to me as he does to everyone who will listen to him. We create God in our own image and likeness. Veronica's God speaks to her. That's why she flagellates her body. Lacerates her mind ... because God tells her. Her God is that kind of God. She prays, fasts from food, allows the filthy priests to daub her forehead with black ash. And her sins. In the gloom of a wooden box she confesses her sins to one of those filthy beetles in black. Those coarse drunkards who keep greyhounds. Train them to tear beautiful hares and rabbits to pieces. Reward their hounds' barbarities. These are the demands of Veronica's spiteful God ....' Philippa drew breath heavily. Her entire upperbody convulsed as she gasped. Her head jerked in a series of nervous moments like an ungainly swan swallowing too big a morsel. She bared her teeth. Snorted. Froth bubbled at the corners of her lips.

Veronica. Softly.

'Please don't do that Birdy. You will only succeed in making yourself ill. It is a beautiful summer's evening. We rarely get so beautiful an evening. Why not go with Peter to see the salmon in the river or go for a walk along the Quaker's Walk. Something pleasant like that.'

'Oh yes, Philippa, let's go to the river. Bannion said there were some beauties there today. We know where they shelter. Do let's go. Just you and I.' Peter's voice was high pitched. Concerned. Begging.

Philippa shook her head. Momentarily the flowers she had woven into her braided hair shone in the candlelight. She snorted rather than laughed.

'Now Peter, I do so much more beautiful things because my God is beautiful and tells me to do beautiful things. I gather flowers and entwine them in my hair. They are beautiful wild buds which rest lightly on my head. They do not draw blood. They demand nothing only perhaps that their beauty be admired. The sacrifice of my having picked them, caused them pain, is altogether undone. Haven't you noticed Timothy how I like to leave vases and crocks of flowers of all kinds around the house? Is that not more beautiful that laceration? Whispering one's sins to lice ridden clerics? Do I not sing? Beautifully ...?'

She paused. Mania rife in her eyes. Her hand jerked convulsively. She drew her shawl about her shoulders. Sang. Her voice long broken. Her faculty to sing long lost. She sang. Meaningless cant. Above in the darkened sky stars gathered. Shone. The air was fragrant with all the scents of a summer night. One could plainly smell the fresh waters of the river. It was at its lowest level. More moths, bigger than the others, were everywhere in flight. Some gathered like furies about the lighted candles as though intent on quenching them with breath. One dared too much. Ventured too close. Wings scorched, it fell heavily to the table where it entered its death-throes, wings drumming the table, it inscribed almost perfect circles on the boards. No one sought to kill it. Timothy thought to do so. Was far too timorous to do so. Philippa continued to sing. All silenced by her unlovely croak. Her head convulsed a few times. She fell silent, bowed her head, wept, pitifully. Peter wept also. More quietly. He turned aside to avoid being seen. Timothy felt he too could weep. Managed to keep his emotions under control. Miss Phipps stared at the candlelight. Her face frozen. Her voice betrayed no emotion but was pitched lower than usual.

'Timothy, please go and fetch a shawl for Miss Philippa. Ask Bridget to prepare her bed and some soup.'

Even as she spoke, Philippa, who was sitting on a rug spread beneath her, bowed low, spewed upon the wet, glistening grass. They heard the quiet crunch of gravel. Immediately recognised Bridget's shuffle as she emerged from the darkness, clothing draped across her arms.

'Ah my love, Miss Philippa I knew the day would have some effect on you sooner or later. Weren't you the foolish lady to be blatherskiting all over the place on such a warm day. Sure the sun was only killing ... and the heat like a furnace. Ah you ought to have more sense. I'm angry with you .... Aye. And annoyed no end.' She helped Philippa to her feet, wiping her mouth with a clean handkerchief .... 'The drop of something to take the bad taste away.' Philippa obliged by drinking a few sips from a cup of coffee held by Peter.

'There, now, stand straight while I wrap this round you.' 'This' was Philippa's massive cloak she liked to sweep about in so silently. And ominously. Bridget tut-tutted. Emitted other sounds of disapproval .... 'Sure. You're perished. So you are. Your forehead is that bit hot. Will you come along before you catch your death of cold ...?' Bridget turned to those at the table. 'Wasn't there one of you could see what was likely to happen in the day that was in it?'

Veronica spoke with contrition. 'So sorry, Bridget. Far too wrapped up in my own thoughts. Missed all the warning signals. Sorry Birdy. I should have known better.' To Philippa: 'Forgive me, love.' Bridget rounded angrily on Miss Phipps.

'Sorry! Well you may be sorry. You'll all fetch and carry for yourself tomorrow. I won't leave Miss Philippa's side ....' She snorted, glaring at Miss Phipps with undisguised anger. 'Sorrow never healed a wound that I ever heard of .... Sorry! Well you should be!'

Veronica accepted her chastisement in silence. Rose from her place at the table, approaching Philippa. Kissed her on the brow. Philippa clung to her. Weeping again.

'Why am I so hateful to you all .... Why do I behave so detestably?'

'Don't reproach yourself. I more than any understand. Bridget is right. It has been a very hot day. You have been over-stimulated. You must rest now. Bridget will sit with you.' She again kissed Philippa sadly on the brow. 'Goodnight Birdy. Sweet Birdy good-night.' She regained her seat at the table. Coughed harshly to conceal any sign of emotion. He, Timothy now knew her sufficiently well to realise that she was disturbed. Tempestuously so.

Folding Philippa to her body protectively, Bridget uttered endearments to her, led her away.

'Thank you Bridget .... And thank you for the shawl.' Veronica spoke through gritted teeth. Bridget had draped a shawl on the back of one of the benches. Bridget turned while still within the periphery of light and vision. Bunching her right hand she waved it threateningly at Miss Phipps.

'We have sinned. We have sinned. We have sinned exceedingly,' said Veronica. Her voice neither light nor jocular.

'Bridget .... May I come?' Peter's voice desperate. 'May I please, Bridget. Please, I shan't be in your way. Promise!'

Bridget's reply, her voice flaunting her rebellious state of mind: 'Do.'

Peter dashed up to Veronica and kissed her dutifully. He ran after Bridget and Philippa, now gone from the garden, their footsteps on the gravel marking their progress to the house. In a moment he also was lost from sight.

'Shall I leave Miss Phipps ...?'

'Do you wish to leave?' Blunt. Direct. Through clenched teeth.

'No. Not if you wish me to remain ....'

Veronica cocked her head inquisitively. Her glasses reflected distortingly the silver candleholder. The communion of candles. Their flames high. Elongated. Unmoved by any breeze. She turned aside. Sat in silence for some minutes. Rooted about in her handbag which was by her chair. Found her cigarettes. Lighted one. They smelt strongly. Unpleasant, at first. She inhaled deeply. Exhaled deeply. Spoke, curtly.

'I do wish to be alone but not yet. Drape that shawl about your shoulders or you will catch your death of cold.' She saw his hesitation. 'Go on. No one will see you .... We'll see anyone who approaches ....'

He draped the green shawl about his shoulders. It belonged to Philippa. Beautiful. A fine mixture of wool and silk. She esteemed it greatly. She usually gathered her flowers in it rather than in a wicker basket. Or simply carrying them in bunches, she would loop it round her waist. Gather the flowers. What foliage she needed to mix amongst the flowers to show them off to best advantage in vases placed all over the house. The low throb of the generator continued. So used had he become to it, he thought of it as a sound of silence .... An inherent part of the night's peace. Not a great intrusion.

'We shouldn't be sitting in this damp at all.' Miss Phipps commented. 'It really is deadly dangerous. But I've done so all my life. Father used to come here on evenings like this. Sit by candlelight. Reflect. He might have a cup of coffee or perhaps a whiskey. Simply sit. He was a very taciturn man. His silence was most eloquent. He was halting in speech. He found it impossible to express himself. No matter how deeply he felt. A touch of the shoulder. Slight pressure on an arm. That's how one knew Papps was aware of one's hurt. Or pain. Or ... disappointment. He let me join him. Alone of the three of us. He let me sit by him here. Keep him company.' Her voice was mellow. Its modulations spoke of love and loss. Both. Most bitter.

'Poor Papps. I rarely think of him now. He's been dead ....
What? Eleven, twelve years. Once I was faithful. Regularly
visited his grave in the cemetery at Knocklong. Now I never
go. I am however diligent in my prayers for him. As I am for
all my dead ....' She hesitated. Fractionally. 'I know you'll like
us Timothy. One doesn't have to ask. Bannion and Bridget tell
me you're a jolly good worker. Willing. But are you happy? I
think not. I know you've no close school friends. You never
speak of any. You never in fact speak of school at all. You are I
know now less grieved than you were by your parents' death,
but ... it ... distresses me to see you so much alone. You are
kind. And tolerant of Philippa. What you rightly see as her
great affliction. She likes you. No. Loves you. I know. Bridget
is fond of you. You help her in many ways while she delights
in pottering about doing the very necessary things one never
thinks about as having to be done. Very much appreciates
your company. You derive great pleasure from reading.
You're by nature a solitary person. But you must forgive me:
reading and walking are the refuge of the lonely. I think you're
alone far too much. You need a companion. A kindred spirit. A
friend of mine in Munich, one of a family with which I have
retained links from my convent days in Belgium, has written.
Asking if I could allow her son who is quite scholastically
brilliant but who has stretched himself too far, too quickly ....
Might come and stay with us .... I was only too happy to oblige.
So he and his mother Elizabetha will be coming next week. I
look to you for help in this matter. I think you'll find
Alexander — that is his name — good company. Certainly his
mother is a fine person indeed. Very fine. I have no reason to
believe Alexander will be anything less.'

Miss Phipps exhaled, tightly holding the tiny nub of her
cigarette between her thumb and forefinger. While foraging
about in her handbag for another. She was chain-smoking. A
clear sign of tension.

Nothing happened yet suddenly his perceptions were
immediately altered. It was dark. The air breezeless.
Somewhat heavy. It seemed one could smell clearly the

essence of all green-growing things. He shivered. Heard with his inner ears a bell tolling. Wondered fleetingly: why?

Alexander. He would very much like a friend named Alexander. It would alter his life.

'I think that would be marvellous. It would be nice to have someone to talk to. I think I'd like to meet Alexander.'

Miss Phipps lit another cigarette, drew deeply on it, nodded. She was smiling. He could readily distinguish in the draped woman of advanced age the smiling Veronica who as a young girl at convent school in Liege had not quite laughed with abandonment. The excess of the others' smiles. He had always loved her from the time she, a figure in a photograph, sepia tinted and with serrated edged, confronted him. Touched him deeply. Veronica. True image. Named after the only person among a multitude who saw the agony of Christ on the Via Doloroso and had stepped forward to wipe the brow of the man they thought of as a Jewish zealot. Crazy. Like so many others. In that hot naked land.

'I do rely on you very much in this matter, Timothy .... I know you shan't fail me. Be yourself. You're intelligent Timothy. Not without a certain wisdom despite your youth. Now I should like to be alone. I shan't stay for much longer. But I'd like a little solitude. I rarely get much of that. Please .... Quench all but one candle. Wasteful really. Burning candles out of doors. But I so like doing so.'

He did as she wished. Rose. Wishing to speak. Unable to do so. Muttered simply .... 'Thank you Miss Phipps.'

She nodded in what was both acknowledgement and dismissal. He turned to go. 'Timothy. Please call me Veronica.'

He nodded his gratitude. Could not speak. Raised his hand in salute. Veronica reciprocated somewhat. Then turned to stare at the night sky with its clusters of stars.

Wordlessly he slipped away.

PART TWO

Entering the kitchen he saw a fat pink-faced man seated in what was generally considered Veronica's chair. Though Veronica rarely occupied it. Should they dine in the kitchen, as they did most days, Veronica sat in the 'cook's' chair at the head of the table. In her absence Peter liked to occupy it and resented deeply if anyone sought to deprive him of the privilege. He particularly resented Timothy's occupancy. Timothy recognised the fat man as Lord Trawann, a disreputable friend of Flannery's. Fat and pudgy, his fat form was wedged into a suit of what was possibly fine silk interwoven with a coarser thread to give it body and resilience. His two close-set eyes peeked at the world from behind a pair of glasses. The lenses were perfectly round, and gave him the appearance of a comedian. His face was fat, his skin very pink. His hair silver grey. Rather sparse. His suit a delicate pearl blue. His shirt scarlet. His necktie white. And a white rose in his lapel. About him like a vapour hung the scent of many perfumes ably mixed. The rose, Timothy knew from experience, was perfect, without blemish, though it came from a garden more neglected than those of Farrighy. Lord Trawann gazed at him, his eyes bulging with terror. In his right hand, frozen halfway to his mouth, he held a butter biscuit on which was spread a generous layer of caviar. His look of terror changed to one of relief. He exhaled audibly. His eyes brightened.

'Oh Timothy. Timothy, my dear fellow …. What a relief to see you.' Clearly he had been expecting Veronica who had more than once forbidden him the house. 'Do sit down. Have some caviar or pate or champagne. Anything that takes your fancy. See there. Wild strawberries. From France. Dip in that red wine there which positively tastes like vinegar …. Touch them …. Just gently touch them to a few grains of sugar. They are simply unforgettable.' He waved his hands. Like an excited child confronted with too many delights.

Flannery, the sleeves of his oil-stained shirt turned up, sat eating generous helpings of everything and swilling champagne. 'Bobo,' he said, savagely. 'You're shouting or should I say squealing like a stuck pig.'

Lord Trawann struck his breast like a penitent. 'Oh forgive me, Timothy …. Dear Timothy forgive me …. I do rather shout. It is, I assure you, nothing but heightened sensibility. Nothing more. Forgive me my human frailty.' He paused. Gazed at him with all the innocent trust and appeal of a King Charles spaniel proffering spurious repentance.

'Have I sinned that you should shun me so?'

Timothy shook his head. Signifying no. Though he would rather have not done so. He crossed to where Bobo was now standing clutching a linen napkin like an antique nude holding a splayed hand to conceal its nakedness. He liked Bobo though he knew him to be corrupt. He took Bobo's plump, scented hand. Shook it. Repulsed by its excessive softness. Bobo seized his hand. Kissed it impulsively.

'There!' he squealed in positive ecstasy. 'I greet you as I would His Holiness the Pope. With the greatest deference and delighted homage. You have met Skipper?' Skipper, a thug dressed in the height of vulgar bad taste at immense expense, sprawled in a chair, his booted feet thrust forward, crossed at the ankles. He flaunted a gold cigarette holder which held scented Balkan cigarettes of a better quality than Veronica could afford. The young man — he could hardly have been in his mid-twenties — was conventionally handsome. Craft and greed despoiled his face. Riding on the flesh of the face what

35

lurked beneath. Supple, lithe, with a body of classical symmetrical beauty, he was essentially a thug of great violence. A sexual marauder who cared only for the conquest of the object, male or female, who aroused his passion. He was Bobo's procurer. Extorting generous payment for his services. Dark and sullen. He was now filing his nails. When Timothy entered he scarcely looked up. But nevertheless did. Smiled knowingly. Timothy feared and detested him.

Flannery's place was a decrepit three storey house of uncertain age, now ruinous. Flannery lived there oblivious of the surrounding squalor and filth. Scrupulous in personal hygiene, Flannery sported a naval dress — though he had been a flier — an aviator — during war — consisting of a navy-blue jacket emblazoned with an impressive badge of gold. And silver braid and heavy colourful threads. Flannery invariably wore a meticulously clean white shirt. (He had a few. Washed two every night. Slung them on the clothes lines which hung cradle-like above the kitchen range. The fire of which burned day and night.) Flannery flitted about Farrighy. Materialising everywhere at the most unexpected hours of day or night. Like a ghost whose haunting grounds it was. Sporting creaseless flannels. White tennis shoes which he painstakingly sought to keep white. He whitened them daily. Placed by the range to dry. There were other signs of Flannery's presence. The kitchen table littered with the debris of meals he had ingeniously created from the limited amount of food to hand. He cooked brilliantly. Sometimes undertook as a great favour to Veronica to cook sumptuous meals worthy of a first rate chef.

His tin of brilliantine. The oil-stained handtowels in the bathroom. The bath unwashed after use. All were signs of Flannery's presence. Shell shocked during the war he was subject to fits of terrible temper. Destructive rage. His tongue was sharp. Well honed. As a near perfect weapon to wound, and maim. For greater effect tipped with poison. Veronica he despised above all others. Bobo he held in high contempt describing him as a fat fowl ripe for the plucking. He humiliated him at every opportunity. Yet one sensed he feared

Bobo. Though why, no one could know.

Of an evening. When the garden scents were overpowering. The gardens at Flannery's place had been wild for generations. Splendid shrubs, rare and rarely scented which had once been cherished. Cared for with the utmost diligence. Were now wild thickets scarcely capable of penetration though Flannery annually cut a passage through them. Cleared an area beside the greenhouse which served as his studio. Which clearing he grandly termed the lawn. He loved his place passionately. Entrance into what he considered his private preserves he guarded jealously.

There of an evening in summer. The first summer of Timothy's stay at Farrighy. He, Timothy had seen Skipper embrace a lout from the village. Forced the trusting fellow into humiliating sexual submission. He was not unattractive. The lout. He was fair headed. Of heavy build. Slow in movement. While he and Skipper had kissed. The boy's eyes were bright. Luminous with both lust and love ... or so it seemed to Timothy watching some distance back. Too terrified to move and betray his presence .... Trustful above all, the lad's eyes. Large. Deeply brown. Trusting. When they had done the boy had smiled ashamedly at Skipper seeking affirmation that what they had done was not shameful. Skipper had beaten him with systematic brutality. Left him naked. Bloody. On the ground. Too weak to move. Timothy had shown himself when Skipper had gone. Tried to staunch the flow of blood from the young man's nose. Offering him his discarded clothes to hide his nakedness. Received a stunning blow to the jaw. Was spat upon. Fearful, he, Timothy, withdrew from the anger of the boy now totally despoiled. Enraged, Timothy kept silent. The bushes nearby shook, he heard a high pitched giggle. Chortling, Bobo emerged from the bushes. Not having seen Timothy. His hands grasped about his genitals. Skipper at Farrighy doorway. Smoking. Languidly. Nonchalantly. Triumph, viscous. In his eyes. Contorting his mouth. Bobo tittered even more. More highly. More skittishly than before.

Touched Skipper at the crotch. Grasped him by the arm. 'Exquisite emission. My pet. I've positively drenched myself. Thank you.' He kissed Skipper's hand. The gesture was mean. Sordid. More humiliating than if Bobo had grovelled at Skipper's feet.

Timothy had crept away. Sat for a long time in his room. His room in darkness. Horror and disgust rampant in his mind. But mingled among horror, disgust, was desire. Sexual excitement. Sexual want. He prayed. To no avail. Later in the early hours of the morning waking in his bed. To his great disgust. He succumbed. He loathed himself. Such a base desire in any man. Desire so base he had been warned in the confessional by his priest. It was a desire more base than any the beasts of the field experienced. And was therefore more detestable to God. The sinner must atone, repent, make reparation. He did so. Sincerely. But failed again. Often. More often than he cared to remember.

Now this summer evening, Skipper, his gold cigarette holder clenched between his teeth at the jaunty angle affected by Franklin Delan Roosevelt in so many newspaper photographs, barely glanced at him as he entered the kitchen. But glance he did. And smiled. Knowingly.

Bobo gushed. 'Do join us, Timothy. Timothy, *do* join us. I know we repulse you at times .... But we are only human .... Are we not?' Bobo glanced at him angling his head. Raising his eyes like Tan at his most appealing. Timothy gazed at the man who so repelled him. Even more than did Skipper. Skipper he realised was the means by which Bobo was capable of exercising such corruption. The fault he reasoned with immense theological exactitude was more Bobo's than Skipper's. Bobo was the most responsible. Yet he not only liked but was fond of the fat, pink fleshed man. They possibly had much more in common than he realised. How much in common he wanted to see. That, not self-relief, was his true offence. Against God. Against himself. He did not see it so clearly. Not then. As if mesmerised by a rising cobra he remained when instinct told him he should flee. Far. Bobo held a biscuit aloft encrusted with butter and caviar. Timothy opened his mouth. Bobo popped the piece inside. Even as he closed his mouth, relishing the delicious morsel, he realised the act was a parody of the act of receiving communion. Bobo, he realised, was not altogether unaware of the fact. Bobo tittered, waggling his thighs. Buttocks ....

'Oh Timothy, am I not sinful? Am I not wickedly sinful?' He laughed. Curiously. The fat man. Corrupt and corrupting. Laughed the laugh of a child innocent of all sin other than those which sprung from the childhood state itself. Bobo's smile vanished. His eyes widened in terror. His eyes darted about furtively.

'Timothy. Oh Timothy *do* tell me Miss Veronica isn't in the house.' He assured Bobo she was not. Nor was Philippa. Nor was Peter. Accompanied by Alexander and Elizabetha they were visiting a friend of the family some miles away. Bobo's eyes sparkled with relief.

'Such a Christian woman.' Bobo hissed serpentinely. 'Such a Christian woman.' Bobo managed to imbue the word 'Christian' with vilest undertones. Viler than any obscenity. He took Timothy by the arm. Squeezed affectionately .... 'You understand, Timothy .... You understand my need to touch the things I love. I have an overwhelming sense of the tactile. I *need* to reach out to touch ... flowers ... materials .... Everything I love and admire.' He tittered.

'Would you believe it Timothy, I was once ejected from the Uffizi Gallery in Florence? I couldn't help but *touch* the beautiful skins of those beautiful Renaissance young men in slit hose of the most gorgeous materials .... It was simply delightful. I felt I was communing with them. The beautiful young men .... You *know* of course, I have a little weakness in *that* respect?' His voice was girlishly coy. 'I felt I was communicating in the deepest sense of the word not just with them ... and Timothy, dear Timothy. Beauty *wounds* me so .... I was I felt, in direct *touch* with the gifted men who had an unerring eye for the beautiful male. I felt I couldn't have restrained myself with simply capturing their beauty of mind and spirit. I would have entwined the hair of their heads and the hair of their groins with glorious lilies. And roses. And herbs which not only smell beautiful but are beautiful to behold. But of course *that* would have been excessive. Excess is one of my frailties ... my besetting sins. They actually ejected me as a vandal from the gallery because I wanted to worship not only with my eyes and soul, but with my hands. I am rightly venerated by my friends for my humility. My modesty is the talk of the continents ... but I do have singularly beautiful hands ... and feet.' A squeeze of the plump hands. The fingers of which struck Timothy as being like ravenous, fat white maggots. He suppressed his revulsion.

'I do have beautiful hands and feet .... Have I not, Timothy?' Bobo extended his hands. Spread his fingers wide. On the forefinger of the right hand a pale blue diamond set in gold surround shone. On his left hand three lesser rings. Not without beauty. Of considerable value. Tightly embedded in the white flesh of the fingers. Bobo did have tiny hands and feet. They were not beautiful.

'You see I'm wearing what I call the crown jewels. I would have bedecked myself with jewellery if I were certain of seeing the already legendary Alexander. They tell me his eyes when happy sparkle like those Adonis ... and when saddened are as tender as the eyes of Saint John of the Cross .... Is that so, Timothy? Do his eyes mirror the very beauty of God as did the eyes of Saint John of the Cross?' Bobo was earnest .... Entreating. Eyes wild. With avid beggary. 'Timothy *do* tell ... is he so beautiful?'

When first they arrived at Farrighy, Alexander alighted from the trap glancing towards the doorway where Bridget, Peter and Timothy waited patiently. The evening fair. The sky somewhat overcast. An air of heightened expectancy. Veronica decided to use the trap and not 'Chugg' her squat Hungarian car with its unpronounceable name and the glorious coat of arms on the radiator ... said to be the Royal Arms of Hungary or so Flannery insisted ... motor making in Hungary being a state monopoly .... And Flannery when unwisely asked by Peter what the impressive wording coiled about the arms in fine red and green and silver enamel on the radiator meant ... answered .... 'Oh probably Mobile Fuck House for Virgins ....' At which childishness Peter chortled with delight ....

Elizabetha, a fair haired woman with dark eyes. The somewhat pallid complexion, the eyes, of one who was experiencing or had recently experienced the joys and misery of being in love with someone who did not fully reciprocate that love. Alighting from the trap embracing in her arms a bouquet of arum lilies ... the gift of Philippa ... presenting a picture of pre-Raphaelite holiness as, wrapped in furs of the finest quality she took Alexander's proffered hand. The perfect image of a woman aware of her remaining beauty. Alexander taking her gloved hand. Helping her alight. Glancing. Briefly, not with any great curiosity, towards the steps before the doorway. Where Bridget and Peter and he, Timothy waited. Light chaste and bright spilling from the house, in stark contrast to the evening he, Timothy, had arrived. Above the central doorway behind the large beautiful window which bridged two flights of stairs. The light that had been lighted on Timothy's arrival was shining brightly. But now the windows of some four or five other rooms spilled the rich yellow electric light from the generator which throbbed in the distance like a heart of great fidelity. Tan had been with them. Squatted on his haunches, his sleek flanks heaving with excitement as, barely containable, he awaited the return of Veronica, Philippa, Bannion. Usually for him, he stayed at the doorway when they heard the first distinct clops which marked the approach of the returning pony and trap. Veronica had decreed that Chugg her Hungarian car was to be shuttled into one of the outhouses. Its existence unmentioned or even hinted at. Why she was shy of her beloved sleek and lovely motor she hadn't said. They had taunted her good-humouredly at first. At first she endured their taunts good naturedly. But had snapped. Suddenly. She snapped 'enough'. They saw her quake with rage. She had stalked from the room. The matter was no longer referred to. Nor was the fact that some six of the rooms on the southern front of the house had been thoroughly cleaned. A beautiful drawing room with light-blue papered walls, and every other colour, where material was used in the furniture coverings, also in blue — a variation of that of the walls. Fires had been kept burning for weeks on end to dispel the slight dampness which had accumulated during their long vacancy. The windows unshuttered. Thrown open to light. Fresh air dispelling the feint not unsweet smell of mustiness. Nora, her mother and younger sister Mary became members of the team which under Veronica's direct control had restored the rooms to their former glory. Now blazing with light, with log fires burning in each suite, suitable for anyone even of the blood royal, awaiting Elizabetha Grossman and her only son Alexander. Quite arbitrarily Veronica decreed that Elizabetha should be Elizabetha to all but the servants. Alexander was always to be Alexander. Under no circumstances was he to be referred to or addressed as Alex.

Tan turned and thrashed about showing the infinite treachery of his nature. He fell in love with newcomers. Sought to attain as quickly as possible their love. Adulation. Having gained their love, he disdained it as he did the love of all others. His shining coat shone brightly in the evening of weak sunshine .... He seemed a blazoned bronze statue brought to life .... Elizabetha he conquered instantly but his courtship of Alexander had been a little more difficult. Then Alexander had succumbed. Smiled .... And squatting, pampered Tan now whining ... a mixture of delicious pleasure and pain. Timothy had been disappointed at his first sight of Alexander. For no accountable reason he had been expecting, perhaps hoping for, someone of Saxon beauty. Light-haired, more blue-eyed than Bannion, Alexander's hair was slightly fair. His eyes, expressive, unexceptional. His features distinct, showing the sharp underlying bone structure. He smiled. Suddenly Timothy saw Alexander was one of these rare humans of no particularly physical beauty suddenly proved beautiful by the grace and accord of their superior qualities of mind and being. He was tall, lithe. Slimly built. He helped Philippa and Veronica to alight. With them he turned and moved to the doorway. His smile wonderful. His movements graceful, his manner distinguished. Because he was of an age when young men fall in love with other young men, Timothy fell instantly in love with Alexander. Believing it to be innocent. Quite untainted — unattainable — the animal lusts of Skipper's kind. Alexander greeted him after being introduced by Veronica ....

'I have heard so much about you, Timothy. We will be good friends. True friends. That I feel in my blood.' His accent was purely English. English, Timothy was to learn later, was their family language. Had he not known Alexander was German he would have classed him as an English gentleman. By appearance, speech, and disposition. In as much as could so far be judged. Alexander's hand was warm .... Strong. Stronger than one would have expected from one so slightly built. Strength. Undoubted strength. Of mind and body. Alexander turned to Bridget who was toying shyly with the ends of her white apron. He laid his hands on her shoulder. Kissed her on the forehead .... 'Veronica has written so much about you over the years .... You are, you know ... after Philippa the love of her life. How nice to meet you at last.'

Bridget flushed. Abashed. In thrall to Alexander within moments of first meeting him. Peter, mouth agape with excitement was greeted. Stuttered his greeting in return. Elizabetha approached. Timothy realised that Alexander had taken precedence. Alexander not Elizabetha had been the first to come. Exchange greetings. He thought it strange. And significant. A cloud on so fair a night. A sign of things to come? Alexander passed into the hallway. Bridget there to take his heavy, cloaked coat from him.

Timothy greeted Elizabetha. Her smile sad, constrained. It mirrored no inner radiance as did Alexander's. Alexander signified inner warmth .... Living fire. She, Elizabetha by far the most beautiful woman Timothy had ever seen in his life, harboured spent embers ... waste ... suffering. In an excess of zeal impelled by Alexander's example he attempted to kiss her in greeting though she had extended only a gloved hand. She deflected her face at the last moment. They failed to touch.

'How kind.' She murmured. 'How very kind of you.' Her eyes focused elsewhere. He realised he had trespassed. Unforgivably. Veronica seeing his humiliation touched him on the arm. 'Well done, Timothy,' she whispered. 'Don't worry ... Elizabetha is tired from travelling. She has had immense difficulties at home .... Come along.' She called aloud with almost schoolgirl levity .... 'I don't know about anyone else but I'm dead with the hunger.' Her voice was uncharacteristically light. The piping voice of a young vivacious girl who realised she was not noticeably beautiful but possessed beauty of a kind nevertheless. It was, he realised, the voice of the Veronica he had first seen in photographs so many years ago. Had loved. Immediately. She led him inside to comfort him for so pointed a snub. Philippa followed. Her cloak now fuchsia coloured, lightened with flecks of white. Timothy saw how Philippa was relishing Elizabetha's humbling of him ....

The guests were shown to their rooms where they refreshed themselves before reassembling at the diningroom door. Ill-tempered, Flannery awaited them. He had not changed his dress for the occasion. Still wearing his blue blazer, shirt, flannels. He even wore his runners, recently whitened. The only visible concession to the occasion was a bright crimson cravat tucked inside the neck of the shirt. As a calculated insult to Veronica he had perfumed himself. So liberally it was immediately noticeable. He nodded his head in greeting. Keeping his hands behind his back. Alexander was nonplussed. He frowned. Not quite understanding what confronted him. His discomforture and that of Elizabetha pleased Flannery enormously. Veronica gritted her teeth. Refusing to glance at Flannery whom she introduced as Jonathan Flannery a distant cousin, 'usually addressed as Flannery'. Jonathan she assured her guests was a superb cook.

Had cooked a particularly delightful meal for them on this their first night at Farrighy.

Philippa came, took the arum lilies from Elizabetha. She took them as might a mother take a child from the arms of another to which it had been briefly entrusted as a privilege. Wraithlike Philippa withdrew, no one noticing her withdrawal.

Elizabetha warmed her hands at the fire though it was a warm evening. Everyone fussed about uncertain what to do. 'Jesus Christ,' Flannery snorted furiously. 'Will everyone seat themselves at the table before the bloody food goes off altogether.' Chastened, all meekly did so. They sat to a table of the utmost magnificence set with silver. Glass bowls of scented roses. An exquisite dinner service of blue and gold. Lighted candles. The flares of which rose in high tapering shapes undisturbed by breeze of any kind. He, Timothy, saw that Veronica, as herself might phrase it, had 'pulled all the stops out.'

'How very beautiful and how kind of you all to receive us so,' said Elizabetha. 'We feel honoured guests.' Alexander helping his mother seat herself at the table assented. 'Thank you Veronica. And thank you Philippa ... we are indeed honoured by such a beautiful display as well as by the kindness of you all ....' Veronica and Philippa having sat, Timothy and Alexander did so. Veronica blushed with pleasure .... Her voice was still piping, still excited.

'We rarely dine in such high estate I hasten to assure you. We usually grovel about in the kitchen for our food but tonight is so very special. Flannery has been kind enough to cook for us .... So I assure you, you are both twice honoured .... The pleasure of your company is our pleasant reward ....'

'Oh for shit sake Veronica do ring the bell. The food will spoil .... Another few minutes and it will sicken even a cat.' Veronica glanced at him. Smiled benignly while Elizabetha frowned. Looked to Veronica as if expecting her to censure Flannery for his crude language. She and Alexander exchanged puzzled glances. Flannery glared at Alexander on the lapel of whose jacket gleamed an enamelled pin. The swastika.

'Is that the damned crooked cross I see you wearing? Flannery was determined to be his most unpleasant.

'It is,' Alexander replied smiling. 'The German National Symbol. You, I see, wear a badge on the pocket of your jacket.' He pretended to peer at it from across the table. 'The National Emblem of Ireland no doubt ....' He pretended perplexity. 'Oh no ... I see clearly now it is a Crown. The English National Symbol ....'

'Bollix,' Flannery snorted. Alexander smiled as did Veronica. Indeed Veronica beamed with pleasure. Here she realised, as did Flannery, was someone who would not take to his heels at first signs of churlish bad manners such as the use of inexcusable language in the presence of ladies. Peter snorted. Smiled with delight at Flannery.

'One down Flannery.' Flannery's mouth twitched. He almost smiled.

Veronica rang the silver table bell. Bridget entered the room followed by Nora and her sister Mary, both dressed as their predecessors might well have been in the happier times at Farrighy. They bore trays laden with soup bowls. To everyone's relief managed to place the bowls before everyone without incident. Veronica relaxed. She was noticeably pleased with the evening's progress. Her eyes were bright. Merry. Timothy was surprised that she was capable of such merriment. In the library was a portrait photograph of Veronica, quite adult, wearing the white nunlike garb she had worn for her confirmation which she had explained one received much later in those years than one did now. She was ungainly. All in white. Flowers in her arms. Tiny waxen lilies woven into a circlet holding in position her rather plain white veil. Her eyes were merry .... Then. As now. Suppressed laughter hovered about her lips. Everyone ate the soup. Commented upon its excellence. Elizabetha asked for the recipe but Flannery shook his head ....

'Not likely sweetie .... My recipes are my recipes and I

intend taking them to my grave with me.'

Elizabetha was quite undisturbed. Like Alexander she had taken Flannery's measure. Was not afraid. Veronica explained diplomatically. 'Basically it is a mixture of potatoes, nettles and some herbs whose very existence are known only to Flannery. Wait until you taste his sauces ... divine.'

Flannery glanced sardonically at Veronica .... 'Why are you all Christian sweetness and tolerance this evening, Veronica? Why so expensive in your praise of the culinary arts of an indigent pervert?' Veronica failed to bat an eyelid. Nothing, it was apparent, was going to spoil her evening. But Elizabetha gasped. Looked at her .... 'I do not understand .... Pervert ...?' she pronounced the word as in French. 'Un grand pervert Madame ...' Flannery said with a slight bow towards Elizabetha. Who suddenly did understand. Flushed. And set about eating intently what remained of her soup.

They dined on trout with sauce and garnish by Flannery. Followed by roast duck of which there were three, again with sauce and garnish by Flannery — whose eyes assumed a glazed look whenever yet again anyone commented on the excellence of the dish. Dessert was homemade ice-cream by Veronica. A recipe of her mother's. Elizabetha laid down her dessertspoon. 'Excellent .... Sheer excellence .... You are to be congratulated Flannery ....' Flannery ground his teeth. Smiled grimly. Without asking permission he took out a crushed packet of cheap French cigarettes. Began to smoke.

'Do feel free to smoke if you care, Flannery. It is kind of Elizabetha not to object,' said Veronica, calmly. Elizabetha virtually squirmed with horror: 'Oh but I have no objection whatever .... If Veronica will permit I too will smoke ....'

'Excellent idea,' said Veronica who helped herself to one of her own cigarettes. Tonight she affected her cigarette holder. As did Elizabetha. But Elizabetha used hers with extreme elegance. Femininity. Veronica like a Chicago gangster. A corrupt upstate New York Irish politician.

'The drinks, damn it, Veronica. You don't think I've sweated like a pig for the privilege of eating my own swill ....'

Flannery's voice was savage. Veronica with studied gentility rang the servant's bell. The table was cleared unobtrusively by Nora and Mary, who then brought in trays with various bottles on them. Which they laid on the sideboard. Withdrew. Flannery groaned in delighted surprise ....

'Veronica .... Such plenitude .... Such extravagance .... From you, Veronica .... From *you* .... It's positively sinful ....' Very dashingly, unrequested, he moved about the table giving everyone a generous measure of their declared favourite.

'I'll stick to my usual white wine if you don't mind, Flannery ....' Veronica covered her glass with the top of her hand as though Flannery would use a wine glass for whiskey.

'That really is excessive of you, Veronica .... That white wine you drink is too foul even for swine. I always thought you drank that as a penance, Veronica .... As a penance, Veronica!

Veronica ignored him. 'I think it's all so jolly here I think perhaps, Elizabetha concurring of course, that we remain and have our drinks and coffee where we are. Such a beautiful evening .... Such a shame to separate the company.' Everyone agreed. Even Flannery.

'Forgive me for asking,' asked Alexander who had abstained from drink all evening. Was now drinking black coffee. 'But I think I taste or sense a strong French influence in your cuisine. Provincial rather than Parisian. Not a rich region. Poor soil. Small but delightful yields. Is it impolite to ask if this is so?'

'No. By God it is not Sir. Never had such a bloody intelligent comment about my cooking in all my life.' Flannery flushed with the success of his meal. Wine. And whiskey. Raised his glass in toast. 'Quite right Alexander, quite right.' He beamed at Alexander in broad good will. 'How about a dip in the river after all this. The moon will soon rise. I assure you it is perfectly safe. Bloody marvellous after a good meal ....' Adding judiciously. 'After the tums-tums have settled.'

Elizabetha: 'Tum-tums?' Veronica: 'Stomachs.' Elizabetha: 'So ....'

'Oh great,' exclaimed Peter. 'May I come Flannery?'

'Quite out of the question. You are up long after your normal bedtime as it is.' Veronica her old peremptory self. Tipping ash delicately into a silver ashtray. Angered by her refusal, Flannery stared at her in hatred. His eyes swelled. Like a pod about to burst seed. He bared his teeth. Ground them. His lips quivered. Dripped saliva. His hand clenched about his stubby whiskey glass tightened before their fantastic stare. Tightened even more as they watched. Veronica stiffened. Glanced guiltily at everyone. Sought to moderate her statement. 'Perhaps ....' Flannery rose to his feet. His entire body quivering, spraying spittle all before him as he spoke. Through gritted teeth ....

'Fuck you, Veronica .... Fuck you ....'

The veins on his temple enlarged were pumping visibly. Throbbed. Veronica closed her eyes as the waves of blasphemous hatred beat upon her like the waves of the sea in turmoil breaking upon a beach. She prayed silently. One could tell from her lips. Alexander stared ahead at the scene marvellously reflected in a gilt embellished mirror. Elizabetha examined the fingers of her right hand as if they had taken on an existence of their own for the first time and the fact intrigued her. Enthraled her. Her lips were tightly set. As were the lips of all others, Flannery excepted. His lips quivered. Shook. He spat. Ranted 'Can't .... Can't .... Can't ... you ....' Flannery stuttered. Speech failing him he slung the glass from him with all his strength. Which at any time was considerable. Now it was more so. Inhumanly strong. The glass shattered. Against the wall opposite. Shards splattered. Whizzed about.

'Let the poor bastard enjoy himself for once! Just for fucking once!! Before .... Before ....' Flannery rammed a fist to his mouth as if seeking to choke upon it.

Philippa rose. As though she was about to levitate before their very eyes. In the centre of her forehead was a gash ... neatly made. Such a wound as a gun held closely to the forehead, discharged, might make. Blood gushed from it in minute eruptions, evenly. All round the sides. For some seconds it was just like that. A crater. Very briefly. A flower. A crimson geranium. Then it trickled bright blood. Flannery glanced at her. Sobbed.

'Oh Jesus! Sweet Jesus. Sweet Birdy .... Do forgive me ....' Philippa approached. From behind. Laid her head on his shoulders. Clasped her arms about him. Midriff. Held him tightly. Tighter. Blood trickled onto his shoulder. It spread upon his blazer. A dark stain upon dark material. Yet somehow ... glistening.

'Silly goose Flannery ... there is nothing to forgive .... A tiny fragment of glass struck me a glancing blow. I shan't bleed to death. I don't fear death from blood. I only fear death from drowning. I swear.' She hugged him tightly, smiling strangely at her own grim humour. 'You've been so good ... so very good. There is nothing to distress yourself about. Veronica was simply being protective. Of course Peter may go. You all go. And have a swim in the beautiful fresh waters. Caress the river reeds. Touch the fresh green grass. All that is beautiful and good in nature. Bask in the moonlight. Delight in all that lives ....'

Flannery struggled for self control. 'Birdy ....' His face was awash with tears. 'Go now ....' Philippa kissed him. Like a chaste priest exchanging the kiss of peace in the ritual for Easter Sunday morning.

'My God .... Philippa .... You're bleeding ...? Oh Birdy ....'

'It is nothing Flannery. Don't be foolish. I do not fear blood or death from blood. I only dread death from water.'

She had said as much before. Her words were chilling then. Now they were extremely so. She made her statement with the innocent acceptance of the very pure. As if she had never known pain. All but Elizabetha and Alexander were not to know how pained she was at times. When things crushed her and watching they were unable to help. One almost hoped the burden would prove too much. That Birdy would break. Be free. Of pain. The pain of her periodic insanity. The times when she was forcibly restrained in a strait jacket in her room. Bridget, Veronica, Nora, Mary ... kept vigil. The ruffs, Timothy had come to know, were not sheerly austerely decorative and fetching .... They concealed wrists. Slashed. To the bone. One foul wound on her neck which had been inflicted with such destructive force it all but severed her life.

'I dread death only from drowning.' She. Philippa who suffered so. Said so. Calmly. Clasping her pale white hands together as if expressing a desire for tea. With. Or without sugar.

Flannery embraced her .... 'Jesus Birdy .... If I thought ....'

Philippa laid a forefinger on his lips. A consecrating figure enjoining silence on a priest of lower order. 'Hush. Go and have your swim. When you come back tell me all about it .... If you are not back and I am asleep, please let me sleep on undisturbed. I will come to you tomorrow .... With Peter ... and Timothy ... and you can tell me all .... But oh Flannery if there are beautiful trout or salmon swaying in the deeps .... Let them be. For my sake. They are so very, very beautiful. They are very dear to me.'

Bridget entered with a distinct lack of ceremony. Bearing a basin. A white towel draped over her arm. She took Philippa aside. 'Let me see my love. Let me see ....' Philippa, never very biddable, allowed herself to be led to within the radius of a candle. She sat on a chair. Bridget touched her gently. Smiled a sad secretive smile which Bridget invariably smiled when confronted by an object of her love. Miss Veronica. Bannion. The elevated host at Mass. The glorious monstrance during Benediction. Flannery at his most foul. And he, Timothy, when, in what had become a ritual, followed behind her, each Monday morning laden with fresh linen for all the beds, Bridget profuse in her thanks for his assistance. And feeling mean and small because such service which he had undertaken from a generous desire to help, had opened all the private rooms of Farrighy to him. He could trespass with impunity .... He realised. Veronica and Philippa had yielded access freely to him of their own. He knew it was at considerable cost to both. Was duly grateful. Because as a child. Not more than three or four .... When he thought those who loved him, loved one another as well as loving him. He helped his mother change the linen in their home. Relishing the sense of service. The smell of brittle sweet-smelling linen. He was a child. Innocent in as much as any child can be within the restrictive limits of their temperament. Character. While all the time his mother spewed hatred of his father. Her husband. All of which he could not comprehend. At all. But did. Later. Realising that each had sought to poison his mind against the other.

'Let's go if we're going for a fucking swim!' exclaimed Flannery. His voice was again savage. Meant not to hurt but to maim. If at all possible. He strode from the room. Jaw jutted. Teeth bared. Peter ran after him. Declining to take formal leave of Veronica. Alexander nodded towards the tray of drinks on the sideboard ....

'I think Veronica it might help ... if you would be so kind ...?'

'Please do,' said Veronica. As if of stone. Alexander approached Elizabetha. Kissed her on the forehead in a more than dutiful manner. He kissed Veronica also. She nodded. She nodded her gratitude. A beggar acknowledging given bread. He bowed .... Fractionally towards Philippa. And Bridget. Took a bottle of whiskey. Full. Paper seal unbroken.

'Please do not be concerned. If necessary we will stay with him all night. I will see that no harm comes to anyone.' He smiled. Unconscious of the arrogance of his words. Only it did not strike those he addressed as arrogance. But rather charming confidence. He left.

Bridget finished attendance upon Philippa. A piece of surgical padding was neatly taped with elastic plaster to Philippa's forehead. Like a mark denoting high caste. Philippa smiled in declared delight. Bridget moved about blowing out the candles on the table. She left one burning.

The darkness outside was dense. A silence such as is said to reign in the polar regions settled on the dining-room. They heard Peter shout loudly in joyous abandon. Tan barking furiously. Flannery sang remarkably well a sporting ballad of the utmost obscenity. Through the window fresh air entered. Circulated. It was fresh. Untainted. Very pleasing. Philippa without excusing herself left the room. Her long dress rustling. She passed from the room like an autumnal sigh. The sort of sigh one rarely hears — occurring only when all is still and hushed. Leaves falling by the hundreds with a barely perceptible sigh.

Bridget pulled a chair close to Veronica. Sat upon it. Uninvited. Pulled from her cardigan sleeve her small sticky brown bag of hard boiled sweets. Pulled one free of the congealed sticky mass. Popped it into her mouth. Shoved the bag back up the sleeve of her black cardigan. Took brown rosary beads from her apron pocket. Blessed herself. Devoutly kissed the small crucifix. Began her rosary of prayers. Her face pacific. Blissful. Almost blessed. As she prayed. And sucked with intense pleasure on the hard boiled sweet in her mouth unaware of what she was doing. Veronica extended a hand. Laid it on Bridget's lap. As she had laid her head on Bridget's lap when a child. The greatest reward possible from anyone .... That hard hot sweet which Bridget on memorably rare occasions took from her own mouth. Popped it into Veronica's mouth. Veronica relishing the conveyance of love. Elizabetha lapsed into silence. Her cigarette holder laid astride an ashtray. Fragrance rising with the smoke from it as unheeded it burned leaving a pale gold ash. Moths beat feverishly against the window panes. A few having gained entrance blundered about the one lighted candle. Curiously the air was laden with an air of silent suffering. Bridget smiled. Prayed. Waiting only the call to rise and continue her grateful servitude.

Tan barked. Yappishly. Hysterically. They were at Flannery's place. Soon would approach the slow flowing waters quite audible even when at a low level from the old Mill House. Commonly called 'Flannery's Place'. In the gathering, ever impacting silence undisturbed by the running dynamo or Tan's spirited barking Veronica imagined she could hear ... it ... the river. Bridget did hear it. Her sense of hearing was as acute as her powers of vision. Elizabetha ... because she could not yet differentiate between the sounds that reached her ears ... alone of all three, did not hear. Silently, bonds were being formed that would never be broken. All three were becoming inextricably enmeshed. While the river ran. Sweetly.

Musically. All three were moving towards a common consciousness of tragedy to come ....

While they sat in a still dankness. Pierced by the light of a single unflickering candle ... while it ran .... The river.

Flannery threw in the halfbroken door of greyed timber. Peeling green paint. With the fluency of a Master of Ceremonies at some Imperial Court. He ushered them inside. The stench was foul, a compound of cooking odours, stale urine ... sweat, turpentine, paint. Very dry geraniums. It struck them like a blast of heat as Peter, Timothy and Alexander entered. All three reacted instantaneously, in like manner. They remained rooted by their feet while their bodies from the hip upwards swayed backwards as if a galeforce wind was about to sweep them off their feet. Back outside the door. Peter was the quickest to recover.

'Oh Flannery .... What a fucking awful smell ....' He said it endearingly, affectionately. Stung, Flannery turned. Moving with immense speed, a facility one would not expect from one in his condition, he lashed out and struck Peter forcefully about the cheek. Peter staggered. Cried out. Flannery grabbed him. Shook him viciously like a terrier with a rat between it's teeth. Flannery roared ....

'I told you never .... Never ... to use language .... You hear me ...? Never use language like that .... I won't tolerate it ....' He was screaming, not shouting. His face flushed deepest red. His teeth again bared. Alexander intervened. 'I think perhaps ....'

Flannery stopped shaking Peter. Relinquished his hold of the boy, who was whimpering like a beaten pup. Tan, tense, alert, growled, crouched low, eyes intensely bright. Waiting to strike at Flannery. Flannery lashed out. Kicked him. The dog yelped with pain. Scampered about. Then once more crouched low. To defend Peter. If necessary ....

'Sweet unfucked mother of Christ!' Flannery exclaimed. Turned to the kitchen table on which rested the debris of many meals. Greasy plates. Some tumblers. Cracked plates. Little bottles of rancid pates; meats; butter. A jar of honey with drips which had hardened and crystallised stood uncovered. Above them from the rafters hung many flypapers with dead flies adhering to each one. Some green-blue. Black flecked with red. The delicate hues of decomposition.

'Sweet holy unfucked mother of Jesus *don't use language like that*!!' With a broad sweep of his arm Flannery swept the stinking litter off the table. Glass. Delft. Fell. Shattered. Tin plates and mugs struck the flagstoned floor with a great clatter making similar sounds with only the slightest variations in tone. One plate spun about. With mesmerising effect. Then it tumbled over. Lay flat. They heard it in the brief sense of stillness following. The river ....

Flannery grasped Peter by the arms. Pinning them to Peter's side. Crouched. Shook him again. Though with less violence. 'Look at me. For Christ sake look at me!! Can't you see what I am? Don't you see what I have become? Do you know what they think of me in town? Do you think I'm deaf to their filthy names? Their lousy, cheap remarks? Do you think I like that? You know how I loathe them without exception. Now tell me.' His voice softened.

'Tell me Peter? Do you want to become what I've become? My friends. The Lord Trawann and his filthy mob. Oates. His even filthier mob. Do you think I like them? Or that they like me? I know why they come Peter. You know why they come. They know why they come. Do you want all that for you, Peter?'

Peter. Hands still pinioned. Shook his head. He was crying quietly. 'Answer me Peter. I must have an answer!'

Peter shook his head. Muttered no. Flannery relinquished the boy's arms.

'But Flannery, I don't care what you are, I love you.' Flannery embraced him. 'Peter. Peter. I love you. Above all others, and above all things. I love you far more than I do myself. Don't weep. Good fellow. Good fellow. Don't weep ....'

Alexander pottered about. Searching. He came upon some cups on a shelf. They were all cracked or chipped. There were no tumblers to be found. He found some well chipped enamel mugs. Sniffed them. Grimaced with distaste. Set a kettle of water on the fire. Asked Timothy, to blow up the fire with a bellows. Feed the fire. Fan the flame. Boil the kettle. Timothy did so gladly. The foul air of the small kitchen was still too emotionally charged. Flannery he knew detested emotion in others. Such a display as he, Timothy, had just witnessed, Flannery would remember. That fact. Later he would take him to task over some petty irrelevant detail. Lacerate him verbally. Seek to crush him in revenge. Alexander he would not victimise. Flannery clearly liked Alexander. But Flannery detested him, Timothy. Would seek to demean him. To wound. He dreaded Flannery who aroused fear in him. Great but incomprehensible fear. The fire flamed high. He still spun the handle of the mechanical bellows. Stamped with the trade name of its manufacturers: 'Pierce & Sons, Wexford'. The kettle soon boiled. Alexander washed and cleaned the mugs thoroughly. Poured a generous measure of whiskey into one. Into another a lesser measure. Added water to both. Rooted about in Flannery's kitchen dresser. Its shelves laden with glass jars with glass stoppers. Holding what only Flannery knew. Alexander nodded in satisfaction. Flannery ruffled Peter's hair. Touched it in fleeting affection.

'Slip round, Peter. Tell Bridget or Nora or Mary. Flannery hungers for good bread. If there is no one there, take a loaf of brown bread. Bring it to me. I will explain its loss to Bridget.' Peter nodded gratefully. Restored once more to Flannery's favour. Ran off. Tan followed at his heels.

Alexander asking Timothy .... 'What would you like to drink ...?' Timothy squirmed with embarrassment.

'He only drinks Priest's Piss ... the stuff they hand out on Easter Saturday as so-called Holy Water ....' Flannery waxed hateful. 'Veronica and Timothy have much in common, amongst them the use of Priest's Piss, and consecrated bits of biscuits. Holy shit in other words.'

Stung. Tears of rage and impotent anger came to Timothy's eyes. He would have liked to strike Flannery. But he knew he was too much a coward to do so. He briefly considered flight. But flight would diminish him in Alexander's estimation. He did not want that.

'So Timothy, you are a teetotaller?' Alexander smiled broadly. 'There are I imagine worst things you could be. Make yourself some tea or coffee. There is no need to drink if you don't wish to do so.' Alexander looked at Flannery. Their eyes met. Interlocked. They tussled. Silently. Flannery yielded. Timothy set about making tea. Flannery sipped his drink slowly. He sat at the head of the table, feet stretched out before him. He glanced at Alexander.

'Do you know France well?

Alexander replies, 'No. Not very well. I know Northern France. But not authoritatively. I spent some summers there on cycling tours. On my own. I travelled extensively.

Flannery:

'Why?'

Alexander:

'I wished to see the battlefields of the war ....'

Alexander came and sat in a cane chair which looked on the point of collapse. He gazed intently at the fire. Only occasionally sipping from his glass. Flannery gazed at some point on the surface of the table. Sipping more frequently from his glass. Both unaware of what they were doing. They spoke thoughtfully. He, Timothy, realised that this was a necessary exchange of information, more than a simple social ritual. Flannery and Alexander were exploring common ground on which they might possibly extend. Establish the basis for what was likely to be a complex relationship. Flannery looked less bitter. Spoke less bitterly. Alexander slipped off his jacket and slung it aside on a kitchen chair. He undid his tie. Sighed, relaxed. He too was intent. His face too had softened. He too spoke more softly.

Flannery:

'Why did you wish to see the battlefields of France and Flanders? I presume you took in Flanders while you were jaunting around these scenes of mass carnage. Did you go to gloat?'

Alexander:

'I visited Flanders. Yes. Of course I did. There was no way I could avoid Flanders. Nor did I wish to do so. Nor did I go to gloat. I went simply to pay homage to countless thousands who died bravely. I respect bravery. I salute it as I do courage and valour in the face of adversity. Be that adversity armed conflict or simply the circumstances of one's life.'

Flannery (snorting):

'Courage. Bravery. Valour. Oh! Come on Alexander you know the poor bloody fools had no choice. They had to get up and over and into the thick of things or they'd have a very unceremonious bullet up the hole.'

Alexander:

'Yes. I allow for that. Nevertheless they did have an option. They could shoot themselves outright. Or impale themselves on their own bayonets. They could have calmly accepted what you term 'an unceremonious bullet up the hole.' Or perhaps more accurately execution at the hands of their comrade-in-arms. Or Superior Officer. Some did. Thousands possibly. Possibly far more than Army Officials on both sides will ever care to admit. But the millions. The millions went over the top and died. I salute them. I venerate them. I accept their gift of faith to me.'

Alexander glanced at Flannery. Flannery gazed at Alexander. Flannery's face surprised. Alexander had spoken as if intoning a Divine Litany. Normally his choice of words would have had Flannery snorting with derision or screaming in manic laughter. Flannery did not do so now. When he spoke, it was with respect.

Flannery:

'Your father ...?'

Alexander bit his lip. To stifle rising emotion ....

Alexander:

'Yes .... My father. A most honourable man who saw me once before he died. I was a child. A year old. I have no memories of him.'

Flannery:

'I'm sorry ....'

Alexander:

'And you ...?'

Flannery (laughed shortly):

'Hoards .... My uncles, my brothers — or step-brothers to be more accurate. All the first rate chaps I knew from school, socially, all the ones with any decency were killed off at the start of the Whole Big Show. They were amongst 'The First to Volunteer' — 'The Splendid Fools'. That sort of thing. All the second-rates such as I .... We all came into the game later. I volunteered of course quite early in the Show. I had spent some years arsing about France in the stupid delusion that not only was I an artist, I was a great artist! Took me some years to realise I wasn't even a minor artist. Took some swallowing at that late stage. But swallow it I did. Later I realised art was mostly cod. I ....'

Alexander:

'Cod ...?'

Flannery:

'Nonsense. Arsing about. One great gigantic fraud.'

Alexander:

'What of the great French artists — The Modern School for instance?'

Flannery:

'The biggest cod of all. Of course there were and are great artists but it took perception on the part of a few very astute critics to see how things were drifting. Any bloody fool can tell you the currents were running in your favour when you are safely through the harbour opening. Few if any can tell where you are destined for if you yourself have no idea. If you are out in thick fog in open waters without the remotest idea where you are going. The Modern School ... they're creatures of their masters and their masters are the dealers of Paris, London and New York. And they we both know are ....'

Alexander:

'Jews ....'

Flannery:

'Yes, the ubiquitous Jew. Make no mistake. Some know their business. Some make it their business to know their business.

Those are the money makers. They could not care less about art as an abstract reality than I could about the health of the Pope of Rome.'

Alexander:

'Picasso?'

Flannery:

'Superb draughtsmanship, composition, technique. All unquestionable. All he lacks is imagination. And integrity. Integrity is hard to come by in the field of art. I had precious little art in me, but I did have that. So I burned all my paintings.'

Alexander:

'A hard thing to do ....'

Flannery:

'Very hard indeed. I'd sooner roast myself than have to do that all over again.'

Alexander:

'But you still paint ...?'

Flannery (sharply):

'I paint. I prostitute myself for modest payment. I paint the portraits of what passes for Gentry in this part of the world. The Gentry .... Old and New. Astonishing as it might seem the Old Gentry have a great deal in common with the New.'

Alexander:

'Such as?'

Flannery:

Such as greed, avarice, ruthlessness. An insatiable desire for the wealth of the world. They also share a fear of death; no not like death. They fear the anonymity of death. The fact that they as people — their image — their likeness will all be reduced to filth and decay. In a short time no one will know what they looked like. No one will really care. Hence they flock to me and grease my grubby paw sometimes very generously indeed. I paint their portrait as required. I paint out the greed and meanness, their pettiness, their total lack of honour or fair-dealing. I paint bland uncaring faces. With mouths perhaps more generous than they really are. I loosen their tight savage mouths. Make them smile as stupidly as possible. I paint their eyes which are invariably like those of a piglet a little kindlier than they deserve. Usually they positively beam with pleasure and add a few quid for work well done. I have bestowed immortality upon them. Or so they think scarcely realising that the portraits of an older generation are sometimes used by younger generations as material for a bonfire. You don't know what immeasurable pleasure that thought affords me. It sustains me through all the vicissitudes of a rather difficult life.'

Alexander:

'But you still paint seriously. One can smell the paint, the turpentine, the dry virgin canvass.'

Peter enters with a loaf of brown bread. Stands by Flannery.

Flannery:

'What an observant little Hun you are! Yes, Alexander, I still paint. I paint rank obscene pictures which appeal to those who share my perversion. They are shipped to London and hence all over the world. They are extremely good. In some cases very fine indeed. They fetch quite high prices amongst collectors of such items. I of course am paid a pittance. One thing I can say, they are not without integrity; far greater integrity than that possessed by many a heralded and honoured painter, fifth-raters honoured as first-raters. Mine — mine are incomparable. That much I can safely say. And no, Alexander, you may not see them.'

Alexander:

'I wasn't about to ask to see them. I should very much like to see them but I have sufficient intelligence to know that viewing them is a matter entirely up to you. Perhaps in time you will change your mind.'

Flannery:

'No. I rarely change my mind.'

Alexander:

'So be it.'

Peter (Eyes, Mouth, Wide open):

'But how did you become a flier, Flannery?'

Flannery:

'How indeed. I pottered about designing propaganda posters pitiful enough to raise the blood of the thickest yokel in rural or industrial Britain. I, in a sense, piped, and like mice the fools followed. I sent them to their deaths. Countless thousands. Was thought a great deal of by my masters. From propaganda I got into camouflage of ships, planes. From camouflage into aeroplanes from aeroplanes into aerial reconnaissance. From there to a lunatic asylum which everyone charitably refers to as a Mental Hospital. I suffered from shell-shock for quite some time. In other words I was in every meaning of the word, be that meaning legal, medical or social, I was stark raving mad. Now I think we have both exposed our scars rather indecently to one another. I suggest we change the subject and our location. Peter, look to the table, then come and join us at the river, usual place.'

Peter nodded his head eagerly.

'Gosh Flannery that was really something, really something, really something wizard. What an interesting life you have led. Ours is all so the same, so boring, so predictable. Will you show me your paintings some day. The ones you smuggle out of the country?'

Flannery glanced at him affectionately.

'No, Peter. I won't. I want you to maintain some small respect for your poor mad Flannery.' Flannery indicated Timothy with a curt nod of the head: 'Are we taking that bollixless bastard with us?'

'Of course,' Alexander replied. 'Why ever not?'

Flannery spat and ground the spittle underfoot. Left the kitchen in long steady strides. Alexander touched Timothy gently on the head. Very much like an elder brother would touch a much younger brother of weaker character.

'You must learn to stand and fight, Timothy. I'll teach you to stand and fight. If nothing else I'll teach you that. It will be extremely painful. It will hurt. But you'll hold your own with any man and fight. Would you like that, Timothy?' His tone was soft. His large brown eyes saddened. He radiated

good-fellowship. Companionship. The things for which
Timothy hungered for most desperately.

'Yes, Alexander. I would like that very much.'

Alexander smiled. 'Good. Now come along for a bathe ....'
He saw Timothy waver. 'Don't worry I have bathing slips with
me ....'

Bathing slips. Timothy in common with all he knew had
always called them 'togs'. Veronica, Philippa, Flannery, 'slips'.
Just as he said 'swim' and they said 'bathe'. They were he
knew defining his position and relationship to them. There
were what Veronica quite frequently referred to as 'thin red
lines' defining areas upon which trespass was absolutely
forbidden. Those who did so knowingly were crushed with a
glance, with a tart retort, made to see the errors of their way. If
they persisted they were forbidden the house. Or ignored, cut
— in company. Such extremes were hardly ever necessary but
he had been made to see that they existed, and he too was not
to trespass. Veronica's statement that when he had finished his
education he would be taken by the scruff of the neck and
thrown out into the big bad world to fend for himself still
stood despite the close friendship that had come to exist
between them. Flannery was very little indulged by Veronica.
Certain liberties were allowed him but the matter of earning
his daily bread was entirely left to himself. He could presume
but he could not presume too much. Nor could Timothy. When
introductions were being made and Peter was present, Peter
was introduced as 'Master Peter'. Timothy as 'Timothy a
distant relative of ours'. Bannion had been friendly. Anxious to
be more so. Veronica intervened. Registered displeasure.
Bannion kept his distance. To his, Timothy's intense regret. He
was however allowed the unfettered friendship of Bridget. For
which he was grateful. They spent much time together. He
frequently visited her in her small house by the orchard. They
rarely spoke or discussed anything of consequence but each
enjoyed the other's presence. 'Slips' .... Alexander used the
word 'slips' as did Veronica. Philippa. And Flannery. Was
Alexander intent on defining and limiting whatever friendship

63

might develop? Timothy hoped not. He thought not.

Flannery moved with stealth across the wet-grassed fields with all the confidence of a nocturnal animal. The grass was spongy, fragrant beneath them. The moon was waning, still reflecting great light. Physical features were defined as if anew. Trees attracted more attention. One noticed the fullness and beauty of each one in a manner one would not have noticed in daylight. All cast long shadows. Which were grey. Lay like damp-felt on the ground around them. The hedgerows were high. Still, again Timothy saw them in a new light; with a fresher vision. Tan moved amongst them his yelps for once silenced. He bobbed and lobbed about with all the grace of a doe or a foal exulting. Glad of Alexander's presence, hungry for his affection and respect. Alexander obviously thought a great deal of 'respect'. Timothy wished to gain Alexander's respect. Retain it.

The approach to the river was over bad land. Ragwort grew in thick clumps or stood in isolation as did high thistles with an almost commanding presence. They too threw shadows which lay on the sparse yellow grass. They reached it ... the river .... Deep and dark it flowed between its wide banks. Further up it could be heard trickling over the shallows. The rivers was quite deep despite the temporary drought. Smelled freshly. Moonlight skimmed over its waters. Whole stretches gleamed like sunlight on a looking-glass.

Flannery stripped in a few deft movements. Stood by the banks. Plunged in hollering as his body struck the water. Alexander stripped with ease. Timothy shyly, shamefully, with a sense of sin as he did whenever he had to undress in the presence of anyone. Alexander threw him a slip. It seemed skimpy. Inadequate. But fitted perfectly well. Comfortably, to his surprise. Alexander's beauty struck him forcefully. It lacked the near perfect symmetry of Skipper's body. Alexander's body was slim, elongated. His arms and legs were proportionally longer in relation to the torso of the body. His skin was tanned. Lightly tanned. Altogether he was a figure of striking force and beauty. He was lithely muscular. As he moved or simply gestured one could see a marvellous interplay of muscle and sinew interacting. The impression was not just one of grace and beauty. It was also one of inherent strength. Remarkable for one so lithe and slim. He paused by the bank. To Timothy's amazement and pleasure, he very distinctly blessed himself before rising on his toes, extending his arms and diving all in graceful sequence. Alexander, he thought .... Alexander is a Catholic. He was deeply moved. Here he thought their minds could meet in a manner they never could with Flannery, Peter or Philippa. He hovered about on the bank too fearful to dive. Afraid to dive. Peter could dive with far more ability than Timothy who could swim a few yards at most.

'Of fuck it all you little shit. Dive. Jump. Do something. You've got a pair of balls haven't you?' Flannery at his most savage. As he forcefully cleft the still waters in superb over-hand ....

'Jump, Timothy. Jump. Don't worry. I'll look after you.' Alexander's voice was earnest. It was a command more than an exhortation. Hurriedly blessing himself. Holding the many religious medals which hung on a string about his neck Timothy ran. Jumped. Struck the cold water. Floundered. Went under. Flannery roared with delight.

'Drown you little shit. Drown!'

He surfaced. Cried. 'Alexander!' He felt Alexander turn him in the water, grasp him beneath the chin, draw him through the water. The strength and force which flowed from Alexander's body was intense. His touch was electric. Alexander was one of those whose blood was warmer than normal. As if from a far distance he heard Alexander coaxing him gently.

'Relax, Timothy. Relax. Please relax or you will bring us both down. My life as much as yours depends on you. On your trust in me. Relax. Just let me pull you through the waters and we'll both be perfectly safe .... I ... promise.'

Timothy opened his eyes. Relaxed fully. Confident now that

he would come to no danger. He felt them both cut cleanly through the river. Leaving a wake which flashed when caught by moonlight. Far above stars were visible. He smelled the water. The earth of the riverbanks. The damp grass. Alexander spoke to him. But what he said Timothy did not hear. He was fully taken by the moment. Mid-stream above the weir they paused. Alexander relinquished his grip. Timothy was immediately paralysed by fear. Floundered .... Went under. Alexander grasped him by the hair of his head. Pulled him up to the surface. Struck him very hard in the face. Flannery ran about the river's banks. Wild and naked. Shouting.

'Let the little shit drown. Let the little shit drown ....'

Peter appeared. Running. He watched events as avidly as did Flannery. But did not shout. Timothy opened his mouth to scream. Water gushed inside. He gasped for air. Alexander, his body rising from the water to lend his arm strength struck him again forcefully.

'Do exactly as I say, Timothy, exactly as I say. Understand?' Alexander's tone was one of command — command which would brook no refusal.

'Just lie in the water.' Alexander instructed. 'As if you were a log of wood. Float .... Don't *tell* yourself to float. Let yourself float. Man could swim before he ever walked. It's a natural state for man. So just float. I'll be here. Don't worry.'

Timothy closed his eyes. Pretended he was safe. Sound. On board a raft adrift on the waters. He breathed more gently. Feared less. Alexander whispered encouragement. Praise. Timothy did not now particularly care if he floundered. Drowned. It would be so if it were so ordained. Alexander began a slow count: 'One and two and three and four ....' Flannery took up the count in a mocking voice. Peter did likewise. Timothy no longer feared their scorn or contempt. He no longer feared death by drowning. He felt if he should fail he would fail honourably .... 'and twenty and twenty-one and twenty-two and twenty-three ....'

Alexander continued the count quietly. Emotionlessly. Flannery was silent. As was Peter. Alexander reached a count of fifty. Alexander stopped counting.

'That was excellent Timothy. Now I'm going to bring you in. Just allow me to grasp you by the chin as I did before.' Peter extended a hand to help Timothy climb the river bank. Flannery petulantly stood by. A white-bodied figure in the white light of the night. His groins black. Peter was excited.

'That was awfully good, Timothy. Awfully good.' For once Peter spoke to him with something approaching affection. Certainly he spoke with admiration. Alexander hoisted himself from the river, panting heavily. He laughed loudly. It was joyous celebratory laughter.

'Good, Timothy. Good.'

Alexander struck with the palm of his hand on Timothy's back. 'Right.' Alexander cried. 'We can't stay around like this all night. We need to get the blood circulating again. Strip Timothy. Then we'll run.'

Alexander stripped. Timothy stripped. Alexander tousled his hair playfully. 'Right. Start running for your life.'

Timothy did so. Alexander gave a bloodchilling roar. Began running about the field of thistles, ragwort, reeds. Flannery followed, and Peter. Both roaring like savages in pursuit of another human. Yelping Tan followed them. He, Timothy shouted. Listened to his own voice ringing through the night. He shouted without restraint. Followed the other figures running wild in the night. They ran. Yelled and ran and yelled and ran. He, Timothy felt that his will in some way had been subjected by Alexander. The thought pleased him, delighted him. He ran. And roared. And ran. And roared until all fell to the ground panting heavily, quite spent. Alexander spoke between gasps.

'Rub yourself hard with your own hands, like this.' He spread his thumb and forefinger wide forming a crude half circle. He washed down his limbs with them. Sluicing off the sweat and water. Between times he struck his thighs and arms and torso with palms of his hand. He hit hard. One could hear the slap of flesh on flesh. Timothy did likewise, and Peter. Flannery contented himself with a white handkerchief which he fetched from his blazer. Giving himself what could only have been the most cursory drying possible. They dressed. Everyone quite spent. Tired. Moved silently over the silent fields. Flannery, Alexander and Peter made for Flannery's place. Timothy excused himself, half ashamedly, intending to go directly to his room. Alexander raised a hand in farewell. Tired. Timothy turned happily. Entered the house. On the upper staircase stood a figure in darkness, aside from the slanting moonlight. He thought perhaps it was Philippa .... Wildly. Elizabetha. Then he recognised Veronica. She stepped forward, her hands thrust deeply into the pockets of her old cardigan. Her voice was soft. Concerned.

'Everything went well? .... Flannery?'

Timothy explained that everything had indeed gone well. Flannery he told her had regained his equilibrium. No longer wild, enraged. She nodded her head. Pleased. She inched forward. Moonlight struck her glasses. The lens. The gold rims. He imagined he saw the defect in her left eye. The cut across the pupil. How disfiguring it must have been to her as a young woman. A blemish. An attractive young girl. She was perturbed. That much he sensed. She wished to speak but could not ....

'Shall I call you for Mass in the morning?' It was merely a figure of speech. Bridget awoke him in the mornings. Helped him rise sleepily, hustling him outside where the horse harnessed to the trap pawed impatiently on the gravel. Veronica seated imperiously with her back held rigid. Hands itched to reach for a cigarette. Could not because she had made a practice never to smoke before taking communion. Waiting until Mass was over. She could take her first smoke of the morning in the front porch of the church. Her 'Robin Hood' hat with its pheasant's feather sticking out aggressively. (Dodging it while Veronica's head bobbed about as she spoke was something one learned to do.) Her tight kid gloves. Her magnolia scarf which he loved to see her wear. Her thick lisle stockings. Her heavy brogues of which she possessed a number of pairs all kept spanking clean. Bright. Objects of

Bridget's devotion — Bridget he had come to realise, had overly big hands which were ever restless. Needed to be kept occupied at all times. Bannion giving him a mocking glance. A friendly nod of the head. Bridget was devout. Bannion not so. Bridget was reverential. Bannion utterly irreverent. Bridget worshipped. Bannion scorned every movement at the central altar of the church during bad mornings of heavy rain or frost, compelled to seek the shelter of the church, he sat and sometimes nodded asleep in the back seat.

'Shall I call you for Mass in the morning ...?'

'Yes,' Timothy replied, 'Please do.'

It had become his custom since arriving at Farrighy to attend daily Mass in the village church of Carra. Village was too grand a word to describe the few cottages with roofs of reed. Straw thatch. All virtually ruinous. The parish served the needs of those scattered about the small farms which clung to the foothills fringing the southern half of the county. Timothy also received communion daily. Took a quick breakfast on return from church. Then set about cycling the ten miles to Gerards Cross where on most mornings Moss Twomey was waiting for him. Moss was old. Toothless. Grimed and greased. Paying no attention whatever to his personal hygiene. He was affable. Smiled. A foolish smile. But he was no fool. Rather a man with his own wisdom. His own high standards in the conduct of all his affairs. He invariably wore a few wild flowers, what some might term rank weeds, in the lapel of his coat. He knew their local names, their Irish names, their generic Latin names; their origins, their use in folklore medicines, references to them in the Gaelic poetry of centuries passed. Very simply. Delighted in being complimented on their beauty. Pleased to impart all that he knew about them. Timothy loved his company. Moss he knew liked him, would not tolerate the company of anyone he found to his dislike. Sometimes, in the winter, when the pressure to return to Farrighy was less acute than during the longer evenings of early spring and autumn, Timothy accompanied Moss to his home — a long low thatched cabin built over two centuries ago in the manner of the old Irish. Moss's daughter made them welcome. Waited generously on them. She was in her forties perhaps. Was once, undoubtedly, very beautiful. Her beauty had now faded. But her face retained a remarkable handsomeness. Her movements were graceful. So was her speech. At sometime in her life she must have been sought in marriage by many men, but she had not married. Had she rebuffed them in the hope of someone better? Or had they, for reasons only she could know, rejected her? Her black hair, still lustrous, was swept back. Tied in a riband at the nape of the neck, in the same manner that Philippa drew back her hair. But with Miss Twomey the arrangement of her hair did not impoverish further her good looks. Rather it enhanced her. Timothy thought of her as a Madonna. She went barefoot, always wore a shawl. Many of those Philippa and Flannery referred to in disdain as the 'peasantry' and whom Veronica more simply called the 'people' — particularly those from the lowlands and foothills — went barefoot in all seasons. Most possessed a good pair of brogues which they carried under their arms until pausing within sight of Carra village or Tibraddenstown they donned their socks and shoes. Only the older women wore shawls. The impoverished. Their shawls blue or subtle fawns and beiges, they huddled in what was their traditional dress. Though the tinker women held themselves aloft with disdaining grace. Loveliness.

She was referred to as Miss Sheila when Moss first introduced them. She was always 'Miss Twomey' to him. She wished it so. She wished it so for reasons of her own. He respected her wishes. Her voice was soft but strong. She spoke beautifully.

The interior of the cabin was meticulously clean but its floor was of impacted earth. It was perfectly warm and snug, appealing to one's primitive need for such protection. Its furniture was all of scrubbed deal. There was little of it. On the table, on the mantlepiece, stood jamjars. Both always held flowers of many kinds. Or simple small branches of ever-greens or berries, leafless stems. She disdained the multicolored paper flowers hawked by tinker women. Timothy considered the crepe flowers — orange, crimson, red, white, purple — had a beauty of their own. They were to be found in most of the 'people's' houses.

They took tea by the fire on bad wet evenings, Moss and his daughter and Timothy. Moss loved to discourse at length on anything that came to mind. Timothy liked the warm quarter of an hour by Moss's fireplace. The thick wedge of buttered griddle cake, the cup of scalding, well sweetened tea. Moss hadn't a tooth in his head. He heaped sugar into every mug of tea he drank. Miss Twomey rarely joined them by the fire. She engaged in innumerable small tasks. When she did, she sat gracefully, silent, bare feet entwined about the ankles, her restless hands nesting like just hatched birds seeking warmth. Reluctantly, Timothy would take his leave of them, knowing that he must go or Miss Twomey would not set about preparing their evening meal. Custom, he thought, dictated that they should not prepare a meal in his presence which they could not invite him to sit and eat with them.

Now being summer he no longer had to cycle to Gerard's Cross and journey with Moss to Tibraddenstown to the school he did not particularly like. Where he had made no close friends. Mostly Timothy thought due to his diffidence. He feared rejection. Never ventured.

'Shall I call you for Mass in the morning?'
'Yes,' he replied. 'Please do.'
Veronica wished him goodnight. And he her. He watched Veronica disappear along the long landing which led to her room which was all decked in white linen. Stark. Uncomfortable furniture. Her bed a simple iron cot of the kind common in poor country houses or workhouse wards. A prie-dieu which faced a figure of Christ crucified hung on a bare white wall. There were no other objects of piety. Bridget's room was a cavern of statues. And devotional pictures. And prints. And innumerable bunches of crepe paper flowers in jamcrocks. She burned a votive lamp before the central picture

of Christ exposing his heart so wounded by the world. The fact that Veronica who dreaded fire in Farrighy permitted her to do so had amazed him when he saw it.

Veronica's room he surmised was a fairly faithful reproduction of the cell in which she slept when as a young girl she had taken temporary vows in a convent in Belgium with a religious order named The Daughters of God. Young ladies entered the convent to undertake their schooling which was excellent and advanced. As much attention was devoted to deportment, graceful movement and the domestic arts as to educational excellence. The aim was to prepare the daughters of wealthy, influential parents to take their privileged position in society with confidence and yet bear testimony to God in their private life, private conduct. They were forbidden all contact with their families except under the most exceptional circumstances. Timothy had heard Veronica refer to this time as the happiest years of her life. Her life-long desire had been to return, become a professed member of The Daughters of God. She had never done so. Had he asked why not, he knew she would not only refuse to answer but take offence at being asked. In a tallboy Veronica had a whip. A ceremonial whip with knotted lashes sometimes used by those in religious communities to chastise. Mortify themselves. Timothy had yielded to temptation. Had snooped. Had been deeply shocked at what he had discovered. Deeply shamed by such conduct on his part towards those who trusted him. He never told anyone what he had seen. But Philippa knew and said so. She said so in company which included him, perhaps not realising that he alone of those present could verify what others dismissed as mere invention on Philippa's part. On the tallboy also stood a silver framed photograph of a young woman of prepossessing beauty. Her face could only be described as angelic. She was in her prime, eighteen or so. Inscribed on the back were the date 1898 and the words 'Jean-Marie DuPage. May she rest in peace'. Flowers often stood in a vase by the photograph. Veronica was a devout attender of what struck him as a shrine. Veronica clearly not only loved the young woman in the photograph. She venerated her. She was, he understood, the love of Veronica's life. He felt instinctively that here was the centre of the enigma of her very enigmatic life. He felt it would explain why she who loved privacy and aloneness as distinct from loneliness, accepted a life of loneliness and unremitting servitude to the needs of those about her.

They, Timothy and Veronica, conversed on the oddest occasions. Under the oddest circumstances. While travelling to Mass in the pony and trap. When at the beach at Blackstrand. Striding through the crowded streets of Tibraddenstown on a Saturday. Sitting beneath the trees of the mall beside the river. The glory of Tibraddenstown. Sometimes she stirred when they were alone by the fire in the library. She liked to linger on in the darkening room, seeking to prolong, the twilight which was a particular delight of hers. From time to time sighing deeply, she would begin to speak. Her voice low, without inflexion. She made no great disclosures. Revealed nothing of paramount importance. Yet Timothy realised that she was exposing what could commonly be called her soul to him. Intending that he fit the fragments together in the same manner in which she constructed the vast jigsaw puzzle on the circular table in the livingroom. 'King Louis at the Court of Versailles'. It took her considerable time to complete. He had only once seen it completed. There were vital segments missing, irretrievably lost, but it pleased Veronica to doggedly construct the puzzle as fully as she could. Having done so she demolished it. Set about reconstructing it once more. At some such time, Veronica had spoken of her life with The Daughters of God in Liege, Belgium, and of her love of those days, of those people who shared those days. Once she had mentioned the name Jean-Marie DuPage but he had not been alert to its use and aware of the existence of the photograph. On another occasion she had mentioned details of her past life and Timothy learned to scavenge and preserve them believing without any evidence whatever that they were of the utmost importance to Veronica and, in some quite incomprehensible way, to him. There was behind these casual confidences something of great importance to him.

It was not Bridget who woke him from early sleep but Alexander. Timothy had barely lain his head on the pillow, covered himself with a blanket and fallen to a deep happy sleep when Alexander urged him to awake. Shaking him less than gently by the shoulders.

'Wake up you sleepy-head. It is time to be up and about .... We have things to do. Important things ....' Alexander stripped the bed of its blankets and sheet. Left him shivering from the morning cold — and the belief that Alexander had taken leave of his senses. He glanced at his bedside clock.

'But Alexander it is six o'clock. Mass isn't until half-seven ....'

Alexander nodded agreement. 'Yes. That is so. But we're not going to Mass. We're going to the river.'

'To the river?' Timothy shouted in shock disbelief. 'What for ...?'

'To swim.' Alexander's voice was cooly pragmatic, lightly mocking. 'You don't think we are going to the river to fish, Timothy. Do you?'

Now it was as though he was the one who lost his reason. He stared at the window awash with rain.

'But Alexander .... It's pouring rain!' His voice was plaintive, pleading.

'No, Timothy it's not a question of pouring rain. It's more a matter of a deluge. A deluge, my friend,' he repeated with delight.

'Sweet Jesus!' Timothy exclaimed. 'What have I done to deserve this ...?' He had swung out of bed, feet planted on the cold linoleum of the room, experiencing rage and pleasure at one and the same time. Alexander struck him as being dressed like a boxer about to enter the boxing ring. To fight for his life.

'Oh this ....' Alexander was good-humouredly deprecating. 'This is my Physical Instruction outfit. I brought them with me. I also brought a second pair to rotate one with the other.' His brow darkened. 'The real problem is the shoes. I've only one pair and they are unlikely to fit you. I think it wisest that you wear a stout pair of brogues to begin with. We'll take careful measure of your feet and I'll see that my family forward a new pair as soon as possible. Until then stout shoes will have to do ....' He stared blankly at him. 'Up, Timothy. And dress. Up and dress ....'

Before he quite realised it Timothy had risen. Turned modestly away from Alexander, changed into a pair of boxer shorts and vest. He knew he looked unbearably funny. Alexander laughed, confirming his belief. He shook his head in amazement ....

'Timothy. Whatever graces of mind and spirit you might possess and I believe you possess both to some degree, you realise .... But .... Oh Timothy! You possess no grace of body ....' Coiled, Alexander fell upon the bed roaring with uncontrollable laughter. Timothy flushed with anger. Humiliation. Holding the small mirror before which he washed every morning. He did indeed look graceless. More — he looked a pitiful gosling, dazed, and just recently hatched. He laughed. Alexander shouted with laughter.

'I'm right, Timothy ... am I not ... I'm right ...? You look like an ugly duckling ....' Alexander's body was convulsed by further laughter. 'Oh Timothy ... God must love you very much. Else why did he create you ...?'

In a typical gesture of affection Alexander laid his right hand about the nape of Timothy's neck, pressed it affectionately. His laughter ceased. His face assumed a ponderous appearance as he sought to be serious. Alexander staggered to his feet. 'Your brogues are in the kitchen. I oiled them last night to waterproof them further. Come now. We've only a short time in which to exercise then we shall both accompany Veronica to morning Mass if she will consent to my coming. Move, Timothy. Move. You simply have no idea how terrible you look. If you run furiously there is a minute chance that whoever we meet will not recognise you at first glance!' Threatening to succumb to laughter once more, Alexander preceded him from the room at a trot. Along the corridor. Downstairs. In the kitchen they paused. Timothy donned socks. Brogues.

'Run, Timothy, run ....' Alexander commanded. 'If Veronica sees you she will never, never forgive you ....' he broke into laughter, leading Timothy from the house into rain which splattered everywhere with stinging ferocity. Timothy felt absurd, ridiculous. Ran as fast as he could to avoid meeting anyone lest he be the butt of their jokes. In the lower yard he ran right into Bannion with a sack of potatoes on his back. Bannion stared at him in disbelief, shed his load immediately, dashed after him, jeering. Deriding him with his unsurpassable capacity for verbal insult ....

'Right Timmo .... Right. Keep the eyes up. Keep the eyes up. Beecher's Brook is right ahead. Once over that the race is all yours .... Keep your head high man .... Keep looking straight ahead. Up man .... *Up* ....'

They reached the open fields by the river. Bannion slipped a foot forward. Timothy tumbled. Struck the ground. Believed every bone in his body was broken. Bannion fell by him.

'Oh Timmo .... Beecher's Brook got the better of you as it did of many a more decent man ....' Bannion roared with laughter. Timothy struck out in blind anger. Bannion expertly fended off every effort on Timothy's part to strike him.

'Pick yourself up, Timothy. Pick yourself up and run.' Alexander's voice rang loudly. Timothy feared Veronica, Philippa, most of all Flannery, would see. Delight in his humiliation.

'If you don't get up Timothy I'll make you.'

He stared at Alexander running in position some way ahead. Timothy scurried to his feet. Went forward oblivious of Bannion's scurrility. Laughter.

Drenched, they returned to the house. 'You see Timothy I have arranged a shower of sorts.' Alexander pointed to the pipes above the only bath in Farrighy House. Someone with a great distaste for taking baths had decreed that it be hidden in the bowels of house. Timothy had only used it once or twice. On each occasion he was fortunate to escape being scalded to death. Alternate bursts of scalding and freezing water erupted in great jets from both the taps. He had long refused to use the bathroom. Washed his body all over with a dampened sponge while standing naked on an old mackintosh in his bedroom. Alexander looked at him.

'It'll work perfectly I promise you,' Alexander exhorted in the characteristically superior manner which Timothy had started to loathe.

'But ....' continued Alexander, 'You will have to be very quick. We have only an instant in which to shower in cold. Then hot. Then cold again. You see this hammer? I have discovered that by tapping the pipes at certain points I can somewhat control the temperature of the water.'

Timothy stared stupidly at Alexander .... 'We .... We ....'

'Yes Timothy ....' Alexander said with infinite patience.

'We shower together ....'

Meekly, Timothy submitted. Naked he stood in the bath under a conjunction of pipes Alexander had engineered. Naked Alexander stood by him. Clasped a hammer tightly in his hand .... Struck the pipe once .... Chill waters gushed above their heads .... Flooded all over them. Alexander again struck a pipe. Hot, almost scalding water poured over them. Timothy gasped at the sudden change in temperature. Alexander struck one of the pipes he had already struck before but in a different position. Freezing water cascaded all over them. No longer able to tolerate the stinging jet Timothy escaped from it by stepping from the bath. Alexander turned. Twisted. A splendid animal. In what seemed his native climatic condition. Timothy stared at him. In love. Admiration. Unmistakable lust.

Later they attended Mass with Veronica. All three received communion. While all were intent in prayers of adoration of the Host just received, Timothy became aware that Alexander was tittering uncontrollably, much to the amazement of Veronica. He, Timothy, tittered also. Swiftly left his place in the pew and genuflected. Hastened from the church. His body shook in convulsive laughter. He wept with laughter. Did so in the trap on the way home. Alexander could not meet his eye. Nor could he meet Alexander's. Veronica stared coldly at them both. Refused to speak to them for three days.

PART THREE

An air of stillness pervaded the house. The windows of all rooms occupied were open. Fresh air entered but did little to mitigate the suffocating heat of the sun which had shone for the best part of the week. The land had a parched look about it. Grass was a pallid yellow rather than green. Leaves dead from drought tumbled in great numbers from trees. The level of the Awannbwee was causing some concern. The water tank which supplied the house was virtually empty. Water for all purposes had to be drawn from wells of which there were a number about the estate. One conveniently situated in the kitchen yard. Another beyond the lower haggard some distance away. Veronica had announced restrictions which had to be rigidly adhered to. Only a minimum of water could be used for all purposes.

Alexander and Timothy were both tanned. Looking the essence of good health. He, Timothy, was gathering strength. He lost some weight but his rather ridiculous body of which he was inordinately conscious, was now muscular. He felt stronger. Was progressing in his swimming. It no longer terrified him to swim in deep dark waters. The weir at Tibraddenstown which was Alexander's favourite bathing place held no terrors for him now. He could swim with all but the very best. Nudity no longer shocked him. Though he persisted in using a bathing slip when at the weir. He refused resolutely to take off the bunch of religious medals he wore about his neck. Feeling that to do so would be to concede something of importance. Others might, did deride him for wearing them. As they did about his practise of dipping his fingers in the water, blessing himself before entering. He had always done so. His father had taught him to do so. At the seaside. Howth, Dollymount .... More frequently at the Bullwall ....

He rarely thought of his parents now. Of O'Neill, once his best friend. His earlier life in Ard Na Greine ... a commonplace red-brick house in what was described by house agents as a respectable suburb, had receded to such an extent he had difficulty in remembering details of the house. His past existence in it. He prayed for his dead. Kept faith with them whom he had loathed. His loathing had turned to pity. Then, more significantly, sorrow. Veronica had taught him that. To be faithful to one's living. And one's dead. To bear testimony to them in all he did. His hatred had abated. He sought quietly to discover what was worthy about his parents. Why they had behaved so hatefully. To one and other. To him. Veronica not by indoctrination but simply by example had led him to the realisation of mortality. Mankind's imperfect state. He, Timothy, she had made aware of human frailty, and the humanity which must follow such a realisation.

He had come to love, respect her, the young girl in the photograph who had not smiled as freely as her young, laughing companions. She had indeed never failed him. He felt, very deeply, that she never would. Though it was Alexander and not she, Veronica, who had become the predominating influence in his life. Veronica was ever vigilant but Alexander dominated his life. In a manner which seemed not only good but very desirable.

He had unhesitatingly granted Alexander a primacy hitherto never granted to anyone. Alexander had become the love of his life. He thought not of profane love, rather of a companionship of souls. It was an innocent belief. It gave him, Timothy, great satisfaction. It filled a void that had seemed to exist from the very early years of his life. Philippa scowled to see him take pleasure in Alexander's presence.

Flannery was pleased. Immensely pleased. Like a man watching a playful kitten about to fall victim to some gluttonous animal.

Veronica who summoned him to her office to discuss his progress in the series of studies and exercises Alexander had set him, and which Alexander marked severely, said, with no apparent reason whatever 'It is good to know and to remember that those who love most are most wounded.' Her voice was sharp. Bitter. With experience. Otherwise she seemed to give their friendship her blessing.

Pleased by an immense amount of logs all three, Alexander, Bannion and he, Timothy were piling up for the winter, Alexander decreed that a little be done every day as an exercise. A discipline. By winter they should be well ahead in the need for logs.

Philippa was rarely seen. She worked on a series of parchments which Veronica who alone saw them, decreed to be exceptionally beautiful. Alexander, and Elizabetha who maintained a studied distance from everyone except Alexander, was also shown them. They were, as were all who were shown the parchment, astonished, scarcely believing that so odd a woman as Philippa could produce such work without stimulus of any kind. Without study or instruction of any kind.

She had declined to take him, Timothy, while she gathered leaves and berries, the bark of certain trees and bushes, roots of every kind which she refused to identify for anyone. Alexander she specifically requested to accompany her on such expeditions. They made a startling pair. Philippa, paler than ever. Alexander in summer shorts, loose wooden sandals, tanned and towheaded face and features contrasting with the brilliant white of his shirt. He never wore any colour other than white. It was thus he, Timothy, was to remember Alexander in the years ahead. Towhead. Tanned. The colour of honey or light amber. His firm white teeth which he exposed fully when smiling. His feet wedged into wooden-soled sandals. Held in position with two crossed, very short strands of thin ropes. Conversing with Philippa whom he respected deeply. Carrying a small shovel. A bucket to gather the roots Philippa needed for her inks. Dyes she blended in the utmost secrecy. Philippa a figure of Ophelian sadness, save that she, Philippa, wore deepest black. Not virginal white as had Ophelia. Her oiled hair glistening in the sun, entwined with beads. Flower heads. She rarely left her head unadorned. Conversing freely with Alexander — and he to her — in a manner Timothy had never seen her to do with anyone. Even Veronica was forbidden to accompany her on such trips in which hidden roots, lichens, berries, stones, crumbling mortar, were gathered; and in which lay the secrets which enabled her to create her astonishing inks. Covering the entire spectrum of colour. Beauteous hues of her own creation.

She, Philippa walking and conversing with Alexander. Alexander's arms full of branches. Wild flowers of all sorts while like a milk maid all in black Philippa carried the small bucket of roots. Alexander in his brilliant sun-reflecting shirt. Open at the neck. Modesty decreed that he left only two buttons undone because the growth of hair which centred upon the groin trailed beautifully up his muscular stomach, about his nipples and advanced to his throat. How at night temptations crowded in upon him, Timothy. Temptations which had to be denied. For to succumb was to be forever defiled. To suffer the loss of his immortal soul. Sin. And such beauty. So allied. So persistent.

Alexander in white. Philippa trailing her long black cloak even in such scorching heat. A figure from a gothic dream. Alexander came like a pilgrim to a blue and white clad figure of the Virgin Mary. Her holy countenance, her arms outstretched to receive the weary, the ill, the dying. Beneath her bare feet the ugly coiled serpent having in its mouth the apple of temptation. Coiled. Underfoot ... defeated. Above her head. Mary ... to give her one of her titles he particularly loved 'Star of the Sea'. A halo of twelve glimmering stars. He, Alexander. Mary's Chevalier. Mary Mother of God who valued above all else the attribute of purity. In the short nights

Timothy tossed .... Succumbed.

He, Timothy, sought to make atonement. During a Mission in Tibraddenstown Parish Church he had discussed in the confessional the nature and extent of his problem. The man had been humane. Told him that purity was above all treasurable to the heart of God, but warned him, quoting high medical authority that one who sinned as he did endangered their very manhood, their health. Physical and mental. He instructed Timothy to acquire a booklet which was on sale at the canvas covered stalls set up temporarily by those whose living it was to follow the 'Missions' from town to town. Timothy did so. Read it avidly. Discovered that Christ appearing in a vision to Saint Margaret Mary Alacoque had asked the faithful to keep vigil with Him for one hour once a month in the early hours of Friday morning. His day of crucifixion, to appease his Divine Heart for the sins of others, all of which opened anew the wounds of His Divine body. The anguish of his Divine Soul ....

The opening words to the Holy Hour when the Host was exposed once a month for adoration in the Monstrance on the altar of the village Church, and which he attended with Veronica. 'What .... Could you not watch one hour with Me?' A plea which had touched his heart since when he first heard it. A child of seven attending such devotions with his mother in Phibsborough Church in Dublin. Had struck Timothy very deeply, arousing in him compassion for the figure of the suffering Christ who had asked that question 'What .... Could you not watch one hour with Me?' Of his apostles who slept while Christ sweated blood as He prepared to become the ultimate sacrifice to the redemption of mankind. The booklet advised that those wishing to keep vigil keep to hand a picture of the Sacred Heart .... Some few flowers. A candle .... That the devotee arrange a simple altar in his bedroom if he slept alone, and rising in the early hours of a Friday morning once a month, pray before it for the redemption of all those immortal souls who might otherwise suffer ruination, perdition for eternity. He, Timothy, had made it his habit to keep such a vigil. The problem of anyone being unduly concerned by the shallow light of a single candle was easily explicable. His room lacked electricity. As did Alexander's. He depended upon an oil lamp for light. Sometimes he chose to read in bed. A candle on his bedside table providing sufficient light. Once Veronica had intruded after a cursory knock on the door. She entered his room while Timothy was kneeling on his bare knees on the hard linoleum floor. Keeping vigil. Before the shrine. The air of the room scented strongly with hot wax. The fresh scent of velvet roses. From Flannery's garden. 'I thought you might like ....' Veronica fell silent .... Stricken by so unexpected a sight. In her hands a large box of crystallised fruits made by friends of hers. Veronica loved such sweets, was far from being generous or open handed with them, carrying off each box of sweets to the security of her room, there to indulge herself while reading a western or detective story. Her preferred reading matter. Astonishment. Perplexity. Sadness. All registered fleetingly on her face. He scarcely noticed that she was in her nightgown with a warm dressing gown, with her feet wedged into what were readily seen to be men's slippers. 'I'm sorry ....' she had muttered. 'I'm so terribly sorry. Please forgive me I thought perhaps you had difficulty in sleeping and thought to give you some fruits.' She had fallen silent. Gazed steadily, sadly at him. 'Do please continue your devotions ....' Had withdrawn from his room. 'Do please continue your devotions.' But oh he thought, she had said it so sadly. He had continued his prayers. He continued to make his self-imposed observances. Veronica never even referred to the matter still less thought to discuss it with him.

He had continued his practise of prayer. In time it became a source of great consolation. Towards the end of the prescribed prayers he, Timothy, prayed earnestly for the living and the dead. For the sick, the poor, the hungry. For those afflicted in body and mind. For the faithful that they might remain confirmed in their faith. For the fallen that they might through grace rise again. He prayed for peace, for the salvation of all souls. Prayers completed, he quenched the candles. Replaced the picture of Christ back on its nail above the chest-of-drawers. Crept gratefully back into bed. Slept. He believing utterly. Absolutely. That what he had done was an act of worship pleasing, acceptable to God. He believed that the mind, if it could be called mind, of God was touched by such worship. In mysterious ways, appeased by it. All those on whose behalf he had prayed: the sick, the dying, the dead, would somehow be more mercifully dealt with because he, Timothy, chose to rise from his bed as an act of reparation for the excesses of sinful men everywhere. Some, sick in body and or mind would be healed. Know health. The wilful who indulged their desires of the flesh would know grace. Be reformed. The souls of the dead incarcerated in Limbo would fly to Heaven, the throne of the all merciful God. There to rejoice in the contemplation of the truth. Beauty of God. The ultimate reward for Fidelity, Repentance, Atonement. He, Timothy, kneeling on the floor of his room in a remote house in a remote county in the remote land of Ireland, would move the mind of God. He believed. Therefore he kept faith.

In the far distance the telephone rang. It rang with a persistence which brooked no ignorance. He resisted the temptation to run. Be first to it because though the phone was situated in the lower depths of the house near the bathroom someone was always nearer to it than one's self. One rushed only to hear someone lift the receiver and give the code 'Farrighy One'. He heard Veronica's voice thunder. Like everyone in the house while using the phone she felt compelled to shout though there was no need for it. Common sense would dictate that one speak softly. The softest of spoken words echoed throughout the entire house by some quirk or other of acoustics. Veronica exclaimed 'Mister Gleason. Yes. Yes. Oh Yes. Yes. Of course. Yes. Certainly. Yes of course yes.' Everyone listened enraged by Veronica's method of dealing with phone calls. She identified the caller. Lapsed into what she termed her lingophone which was a wry pun on the name of a firm teaching foreign language with the aid of gramophone records. She thought the pun exquisite. Failed to see why the enlightened did not share what she thought would be obvious to everyone of intelligence with a tincture of wit. As though chanting an obscure, very sacred chant. She chanted 'Yes' a few more times. Finally, abruptly, 'Goodbye'. Replaced the receiver on its hook. Minutes later she struck the gong shouting 'Boys, Boys, Boys' in the hope that someone would hear and respond. Timothy, dragging his feet about aimlessly in the upper reaches of the house tensed expectantly. Hopeful of some excitement he hurried downstairs.

Alexander who was, Timothy knew, seated at the small kitchen table he had retrieved from one of the outhouses jammed with junk of all kinds accumulated over years, was intent on his study. His room was small. Very spartan. A small wardrobe, a cot bed such as Timothy himself slept in. A small bedside table on which stood a small radio.

Alexander had climbed to the roof of the house. Had erected an aerial which enabled him to receive broadcasts from German stations. Last thing at night he listened to the late news bulletins from Germany. They often aroused him. Excitedly he would seek out Elizabetha. Inform her of the developments. Unconsciously lapse into German. He and Elizabetha conversed in German. But never in the presence of others. The back pocket of his shorts was jammed with pages from notebooks which had intricate calculations worked out on them. He was apt to pause in the middle of excited speech. His eyelids would flicker. His eyes shine in bright pleasure. He would whip out a notebook or one of the loose pages. Scribble furiously on it for some seconds. Excusing himself he would return the page to his pocket. Smile broadly. Excuse himself again. Take up the conversation at whatever point he had left off. Or interrupted the speech of another.

Unfailingly he spent a half-hour with his mother in her bedroom last thing at night before retiring. Both took very strong coffee. They conversed in German. Their conversation one assumed from their exchanges was lively. Intense. Sometimes he, Timothy who understood no German, believed he sensed discord in their speech.

Timothy also studied. But far less than Alexander. He would have liked nothing better than to share Alexander's room while they both studied. There were however what Veronica would call 'thin red lines'. Alexander did not tolerate trespass. He, Timothy, would have been content to sit. Watch Alexander at his work. Alexander would not have it so. But Timothy was prepared to accept what could not be altered. Delighting at the time Alexander would come to his study, still in his dressing-gown. Correct Timothy's papers. Examine his intently. Pressing him hard on his, Timothy's weaker points. Castigating his mathematics, algebra, geometry. Groaning with despair as he sought to unfold the world of mathematics as he Alexander knew it to be. 'Timothy. It is all so easy. Look ....'

Alexander would take Timothy's pencil from him. Scribble rapidly. Solve in seconds what had defeated him for hours. His English essays were marked excellent. Alexander would praise them. 'They are wonderful but really Timothy you are romantic. The world has little need of romantics.' He would laugh. He, Timothy, delighting in Alexander's laughter. At the same time imprinting on his mind the image of Alexander at any given time. As though his mind was a camera. Timothy, taking snapshots for future examination. Alexander he realised would not be long at Farrighy, a year or perhaps two. Elizabetha had said so. Elizabetha who rarely joined anyone for company. Preferring her own with a book or one of the innumerable German newspapers which arrived frequently from Berlin. Which she read studiously from cover to cover with great anxiety as if one day she expected to find herself confronted with the death-notice of a very close friend or relative. She ringed various articles and items with a red pencil. Some of which she gave Alexander insisting he carefully read these marked passages. Which Alexander did with great concentration, and he appeared perturbed at what he read. Inevitably they discussed the marked passages. In Elizabetha's room. Last thing at night.

Elizabetha reiterated. Alexander 'Stretched himself too far'.

But he was recuperating. Taking things easy. He was much more relaxed than when he had arrived. 'Was he not?' Timothy was asked the question. He replied. 'No.' Alexander did not look more relaxed than when he had arrived. Happier perhaps. But not more at ease. As for recouping; there seemed nothing wrong with Alexander. Not at all. As for rest. He was occupied from early morning. He and Alexander still took their morning swim, a series of exercises dictated by Alexander. Undertaken when ever the weather permitted.

Alexander never stopped. He was constantly active. A dynamo working at full power. Elizabetha smiled. 'Ah but you don't know what it is like to see Alexander work at full force.' She had smiled. Patronisingly. Prudence forbade arguing the point. He nodded assent. Left Elizabetha intent on the smaller items of one of her many German papers. Alexander would stay a year in Ireland. Perhaps two. He knew then what to expect. Alexander would leave just as he could expect to be finishing his secondary schooling. Would have to decide whether he wished to continue on to University. Choose a career which would not demand scholastic brilliance. Veronica had suggested the Civil Service, which would involve him passing a public examination. It would open up a dull but secure future. From time to time he day-dreamed that he might go to Germany. See Alexander there. Possibly stay some months. Or perhaps Alexander would visit Ireland again. Many times. He, Timothy knew it would not be so. Chose to believe that his friendship with Alexander would last for very many years. Perhaps a lifetime.

A cigarette hung from Veronica's lower lip. Her face was flushed. A little weathered though she detested direct sunlight. Always wore a small brimmed straw sunhat for protection. It afforded sufficient protection to satisfy Veronica. So she wore it. Neither Philippa or Veronica were ever to be found out in the strong sunlight of day. Elizabetha, in modest, but nevertheless fashionable summer clothing sought the sun avidly. Offering her body as if offering a sacrifice to the energising light of the sun.

Veronica twisted her left eye to protect it from the smoke of her cigarette. The entire matter could be resolved if she moved her cigarette even if only fractionally from where it clung to her lips. Peter came running. One could clearly define from his run that he was excited. Alexander was last to appear. He stayed on the upper landing calling. 'I can't come down. I'm not decently dressed.' Veronica snorted. She understood what he meant. Somehow she didn't quite approve.

'Quinn will be here first thing in the morning. You lot will be out in the bogs for some days. First you'll help Quinn harvest his turf. Then you harvest our supply. I can guarantee you will all sleep like logs and eat like hogs after your first day or two.'

Veronica was smiling broadly. She beamed, her eyes bright. 'How interesting,' said Alexander. 'This should be a real Irish experience ....' 'Oh yes,' retorted Veronica. 'Ask Timothy how much he enjoys the Irish experience of harvesting peat.' Alexander glanced enquiringly at him.

Timothy smiled wryly. He had helped harvest the turf the year before. To his delight he had Quinn praise not only his work but his willingness to work. Bannion, Quinn damned out of hand. Veronica, Timothy knew, had been very pleased. A little proud of his accomplishment. He had done a little to forward their quiet but steadily growing friendship.

He, Timothy mocked Alexander. 'Oh how you'll work Alexander! How you'll work. It'll all be very good for you. Mentally. Physically. It will improve your strength. Tone up the muscles. Loosen your sluggish blood! You'll be pleased with the results. That I promise.'

Alexander snorted. 'Ah so you sling my own words back at me, Timothy. Oh Timothy I'll have my revenge. That much I promise you.'

Chuckling, Alexander turned. Returned to his room. His studies.

Peter was speechless with pleasure. 'I may go, Veronica. I

may go?' He sounded as if half expecting Veronica to refuse his request. 'You may go Peter. You may go.' She tossed his rampant fair hair playfully. 'You may go.' And again he, Timothy, was struck by how sadly she said it. She turned and left them in the hallway. Peter grinned. Almost intimately.

'I must go and break the sad news to Flannery. Flannery simply loathes bogs and detests harvesting peat. He will be in rotten form for weeks.' He grinned again. Pleased at Flannery's coming enforced toil. Hurried off to tell him as much.

Flannery hadn't been seen for some days. Possibly not for as long as a week. He was painting. Furiously. As always when he did paint. His place was forbidden to all but Peter. Elizabetha had expressed the desire to see some of his work. Flannery had bluntly refused. Alexander he promised to show some work. When he had something 'good' to show. He wore a soft-brimmed white hat such as children might wear at the beach. He strode about his garden well tanned.

Pleased at the prospect of the days ahead, the presence of Alexander at all times, Timothy turned and mounted the staircase. On impulse he turned left at the upper landing. Made his way to Philippa's room. He didn't particularly expect that Philippa would allow him enter her room. Most times she refused to even answer his knock. With her acute hearing she recognised the knock of every individual in the house. She sometimes wouldn't reply. She would remain quiet like a mouse behind the skirting board. One heard nothing but one sensed with all one's being that the mouse was there as she, Philippa, was there.

He tapped gently on the door. Philippa called 'Come in Timothy.' Her tone was affable. Her response unusually quick, decisive. He entered. She stood beside her slanted table. A parchment stretched across its surface. Tightly stretched. Weighted. To keep it in position. The windows of the room were open. Sunlight fell almost directly on the parchment. On Philippa standing, pen poised in her hand. She wore a colourful dress of purple and green hues. She barely glanced at him as he entered and stood waiting.

'Do come in,' she said, 'and come and see what I have done.' She smiled, a free smile rather than the restrained one as was her manner. She looked healthy though pale. The tensions which furrowed her brow gave her a harrowed appearance. Was relaxed. The skin was not tight. Nor were her lips tight about her mouth. She was happy. Not ill. If only for a little while. He was glad. Experienced pleasure. He approached. Philippa stood back. Hand toying a little restlessly with the ruffed lace about her throat. He studied the drawing carefully. It was masterly. Beautifully executed.

It was, he saw at a glance a further version of the Irish legend which so obsessed her. The Children of Lir, fabled beings of a pagan era. They had transgressed and had been transposed into swans, condemned to swim the surfaces of lakes until such time as they would hear the bell of a Christian Church. For centuries they had suffered their fate until at last following the arrival of Saint Patrick in Ireland a church was built by the lake. The bell struck. They regained their human form. But their one-time beauty had gone. They were now old and haggard, aged and decrepit. Old. Unbearably ugly. And old. Defeated by their trials and tribulations. They died. Their spirits rose to heaven. Joyously they regained their early beauty as they passed through the portals of paradise. The bliss within. In Philippa's illustration they were at the very gates of heaven, shedding like outer skins their age and weariness. They were in the very act of entering paradise. A male figure. Splendid. Beautiful. Stood between them and the gates. He was radiant. Flames of light issuing from his entire body. His gold flaming wings. He held aloft a fiery sword which marked him as Michael the Archangel. The angel most loved by God. With one hand gestured them forward, his eyes bright with welcome. His face joyous. It was unmistakably one of Philippa's best illustrations. He said so. Congratulated her. The illustration was undeniably an idealised depiction of Alexander.

He glanced at Philippa. Her eyes met his. She knew he had recognised the likeness of the central figure to Alexander.

Their eyes met. Locked. Each staring frankly at each other. Philippa's eyes were defiant. Aggressive. Gradually lost their defiance. They registered ever deepening sadness and shortly were sorrowful. He was aware of her love of Alexander. Loving Alexander himself he recognised that love in another. He sought to say something, something which might lighten her intense suffering. Philippa was not unintelligent. She knew she did not at all possess the youth, the physical beauty which attracted the male. She had some distinct qualities, genius in her chosen field. But. She was not beautiful. Nor was she young. She could never hope to gain the love of those who attracted her and whom she loved. Philippa was very much a creature of passion. She loved passionately. She hated passionately. Generous in love. Venomous in hatred.

He became aware she was weeping. Looked elsewhere. Pretended not to hear her sobs. 'I'll fetch you a cold drink of milk from the buttery. An apple perhaps?' Philippa nodded consent.

He walked slowly down to the buttery. A cold stone room below ground level full of a long, wide trestle of stout seasoned timber on which rested heavy slabs of the blackest slate he had ever seen. Veronica had told him it had come from Wales when the house was being constructed two hundred years before. On these vast slabs some inches thick rested big earthenware basins. Many were chipped. Cracked. Which were once used to contain the milk from the many cows which had once cropped the rich grass of the lands about Farrighy. They were huge. Rather shallow. Deliberately so to enable the cream to be skimmed off with wooden laths. In a far corner stood three churns of an iron-work structure. Above them in the wall gaped a black hole. Through the hole in the wall had run a fan belt which was attached to the flywheel of the machine. Now completely seized up it had enabled the churns to be turned by steam from the boiler room beyond. It was simple. Ingenious. The invention of Thaddaeus. The almost mythical member of the Phipps who had acquired their lands.

Veronica had often spoken of Thaddaeus as though they

had been on speaking terms. Never mentioned how he, Thaddaeus, a Catholic had acquired some of the finest lands of Munster and held them in what was a jealously guarded Protestant preserve.

The machine he had designed and had constructed according to his designs was small, but run constantly could churn vast quantities of the finest butter for which there was a ready market in Limerick where the butter was purchased for shipment to London, particularly in times of war. He had, Veronica pointed out grimly, amassed a fortune both during the Crimean war and the preceding Napoleonic Wars. She said it was said of him that he wept bitterly at Napoleon's downfall. Firstly because Thaddaeus was a Republican by conviction, and secondly because the peace brought about by the defeat of Bonaparte had stopped his very valuable trading in bacon and butter to the British Armies.

Timothy loved the coolness of the room. Unlike the 'cold' room which boasted an early American form of the domestic refrigerator, the cold-room was used to preserve meats and fowl, at one time considerable amounts of both.

He gently skimmed the surface of one of the two basins still in use. He filled a cold earthenware mug with the milk. From the appleroom next door which was warm and dry he selected as delicious an apple as he could from the very diminished stock of the previous year's harvest. Somewhat wizened they had a distinctive flavour of their own which Veronica, Elizabetha, and he preferred to the early apple fruits.

Two very large bolts top and bottom were visible on the outside of the door to Philippa's room — the room could only be locked or bolted effectively from the outside. In her spasms of irrationality Philippa posed a threat to others as she did to herself. Timothy stood still. He knocked on the door but received no reply. After some time he left the mug of milk and the red apple on the floor outside her door. He thought he heard her cough dryly. Titter in the way which marked an onslaught of illness.

Silently he stole away. Avoided company all afternoon. He

took tea with Bridget in the kitchen. Declined to go for a swim with Alexander. Retired. Sullen. Ill-tempered. Anxious about the future. Alexander tapped lightly on his door as he slipped into a state of half-asleep, half-wakefulness. Invited, Alexander entered. Sat by his bed. Alexander was anxious. His brow furrowed. 'You're not ill, Timothy?' Assured he was not Alexander persisted. 'You're not disturbed by my joke about having my revenge on you for mocking me?' He, Timothy hastened to assure Alexander. 'Ah then. It is only a mood. The black mood of the Celt which is both a strength and a weakness to their race.' Alexander's tone lightened. He nodded his head solemnly, his eyes bright with affection. 'I am so glad. You see I wasn't joking about my revenge. I will still have my revenge. You never fear, Timothy. I'll have my revenge. You, Timothy mocked me, Alexander.' Alexander touched him, Timothy lightly on the shoulder a companionable tap. Raising his hand in farewell Alexander rose. Left the room, saying, 'Sleep well. We have to have our swim before we leave for the boglands.' Desolation overwhelmed Timothy. He was overcome by a sense of loss he almost cried out as he would to a sharp physical pain.

The evening light altered. A strange stillness had fallen over the house. There seemed nobody about. No door opened. Closed. No voice raised in good or sullen humour. Nothing but a sense of ever-impacting stillness which frightened him. Far, far more than as a child he feared the darkness. The darkening night air was tinged with a very pale green. It was quite visible. It lent an element of transparency to the darkness which would otherwise have been impenetrable. So noticeable that he thought it a glow. Slipped from his bed and looked out. Over the southern hills could be seen a light. Pale April green which he found inexplicable. Disconcerting in the extreme. He glimpsed two figures on the lawn behind the kitchen yard. Wide apart they nevertheless held hands. Arms stretched out. Entwined. He instantly knew them to be Elizabetha and Alexander. How skittish they are, he thought. How happy in one another's company. How like lovers. How unlike mother and son. He stared at them until it was too dark and cool for them to remain outside. They appeared in the light thrown out from the unshuttered windows of the house. They broke apart. Kissed lightly, again like lovers, parting, entered the house.

Timothy knelt for his night prayers. His mind wandered. He had to exert his will to complete the prayers, not let them slip into gibberish. Gratefully he went to bed. Slept. Dreamed.

A night of moonlight. Everything still. Quiet. He was before the house. The trees which lined the paths and half-circle before the house threw long grey shadows. He saw a rose bush full of sweet untainted whiteness. Pleasantly scented. He approached. Saw a figure by the bush. Realised it was a male. Unclothed. The young man was beautiful. His beauty of the kind one calls unearthly because one so infrequently witnesses such beauty. In the dream state, he, Timothy, realised that this youth was in some way Holy, Blessed. His eyes begged Timothy to approach. He, Timothy did. They met. Kissed. Very chastely. On the lips. He, Timothy extended a hand. Touched the boy about the chest. Nipples. Delighted in their warmth. The youth plucked a rose. Virginal white. Sweetly scented. Perfect in every detail. The youth offered him the rose. He took it. While doing so pricked a finger on a thorn. His finger bled. Stained the rose which in seconds was deeply red. Blood red. The youth looked infinitely saddened. Vanished from sight. He, Timothy, cried out in pain. Awoke. Aware that he had in fact cried out aloud, so great the pain of leaving so lovely a person. He felt overwhelmed. He knew his nature to be the kind which loved it's own kind. Not opposites. He was so marked. Clearly upon the brow. Far less mercifully than Cain had been marked. He would be thought of for as long as he lived as a man without honour. Someone, he knew, had sat in judgement upon him. Passed a sentence without hope of reprieve. He saw the bright candle which was his youthful hope. Quenched. Heard distantly the chant condemning him to perdition. He lapsed back into deep sleep. Alexander awoke him.

They broke the surface of the cool morning waters of the river. Both uncommonly reserved. He, Timothy, swam without pleasure. Failed to look Alexander in the face. As if somehow Timothy was soiled. They swam. Alexander urging him to swim further towards the part of the river where dangerous currents flowed. Where many a man had lost his life. He, Alexander, wanted him, Timothy, to be sufficiently competent to breast the most fearful currents. He, Timothy, tried. To the utmost of his ability. Alexander swimming by him willing to give him, Alexander's life for his, Timothy's safety. If at all necessary. He, Timothy, tried. Succeeded, though not altogether. 'Enough,' Alexander shouted. 'You are splendid my friend. I am proud of you.' The words were affectionate. Oddly they pierced Timothy's being more acutely than honed arrowheads.

They ran about shouting and hopping. Yelling like savages. About them were the mists of morning. The pale moon was co-existent with the risen sun. Both pale disks against a fair blue sky.

I will remember this morning forever. He, Timothy, thought. It might well be the memory which will present itself to my consciousness when I lie dying. I will remember that once I was as I am now. Naked, full of health and joy of life. A living link with the life all about me, grass, reeds, river, river sounds. The discourse of birds, the yelp of dogs confident with the advance of morning. The morning sunlight .... And Alexander. Of all that he would best remember and be thankful for was this communion with Alexander.

They dried themselves. Both were ravenous. Alexander quickly gathered reeds and rushes. Some yellow flowers for Philippa who was not at all well. Confined to her room. Ever watched by watchful eyes. Veronica's, Bridget's, Nora's or Mary's. Watchful. Dreading the coming crisis.

They ran home at a neatly timed pace. 'Last night,' said Alexander. 'Towards morning. Someone cried out in anguish. Great anguish. Did you by chance recognise who it was?' Timothy knew that Alexander was asking if it had been he,

Timothy, who cried out so. 'No,' he replied boldly, meeting Alexander's direct gaze, directly. Lied as he had not lied for many years, for falsehood, like obscenity, came difficult to him. 'No,' he repeated with a certitude which hurt him. 'I heard no one cry out.'

They sat with Peter and Flannery. Ate ravenously the bacon, eggs and pudding placed on their plates in a more generous helping than was usual. Flannery was dressed in a light white jacket which gave him the appearance of a dissipated plantation manager in one of the books of Somerset Maugham. He ate well, for once not disparaging the food of the English or Irish which to him were as stupid as each other in the matter of cuisine. Peter oddly, quietly, nibbled on a slice of buttered soda bread. His eyes seemed larger than usual. He was curiously subdued, squirming with suppressed excitement at an adventure outside Farrighy. Particularly if Flannery was to be in the company.

Bridget had not appeared. Nor had Veronica. Nora supervised the kitchen with a free hand. She made her presence felt. Proving that not only could she cook well but that she was also a competent manager. Bridget normally kept her in a subdued manner humbling the girl by derision at what she, Bridget, thought of as unnatural pride. But she realised that Nora would one day succeed her. Her humiliations were relatively mild though they drove Nora to spasms of white-faced anger. There was a defiant streak in the girl which had to be kept under control. Her high spirits needed just a little control and direction. Bridget was far too good a woman to seek to destroy her spirit. Now Nora enjoyed bossing Mary about, fussing over the men, chiding them for not eating more, warning they'd be so tired and hungry after a day's work in the bog they'd start 'ateing' one and other in the back of the turf lorries. Flannery she avoided. She was fond of him, Timothy. Shy of Alexander. Peter she knew would kick her as soon as look at her. He, Timothy became the object of her special concern. The sole object of the conversation.

Have the sense to wear a hat, make sure the lorry was

parked in such a way that it cast some shadow however slight. Slip his shirt off but only for short periods. You have the delicate skin God help you, and you're not as used to hard work as the others.

Flannery and Alexander relished her performance. As did Bannion. Bannion was almost walnut brown. His hair had been bleached white. He looked tanned and fit, but tired. He yawned frequently. Nora paid him some attention. 'How many different beds did you sleep in last night, Gur? Or maybe the girls simply lined up and you took them one at a time. Like a prize bull.' Bannion blushed. He blushed not merely on his face, the entire skin of face, neck and upper body coloured darkly. He glanced malevolently at Nora. Sat silent, far too shy to acknowledge whenever any of her jibes struck.

Quinn's lorry arrived. Quinn was persuaded with difficulty to take a mug of tea before moving off. He was a small weasel-like man, nicknamed 'the fox'. In admiration. Not derision. He was small. Thin. Sharp featured. The trousers of his rough serge suit was held close with a broad, brass studded strap which he used to maintain order amongst his quarrelsome sons, all nearly twice his size, dreaded in fight and yet themselves dreadful of the small man who was their father. He sported a sweat soiled ancient cap which he kept on at all times to hide his baldness about which he was uncommonly sensitive refusing to remove it even when in church in direct defiance of the parish priest who alternately tried to put the fear of God into the man or to beg unashamedly, as a singular mark of respect to God Almighty in whose house he was that he remove the cap. But Quinn knew it was a matter of pride between himself. And his priest. He told the unfortunate man — that he was always free to come down off the pulpit. Remove the cap from his head. Provided he was prepared to bear the consequences. The priest was not at all prepared to accept the consequences.

If some thought Quinn comical, they showed no signs of such in his presence. The small man carried a vicious whip and had been known to lash at anyone engaging his anger. His anger was savage. Direct. Rarely lasted long. He never bore a grudge. Always made his peace with his opponents sooner or later. He had a fine wife. A woman tall and queenly who towered above her diminutive husband. She was handsome. Undoubtedly she was once very beautiful. Why so able a woman should choose so crabbed a man who was many years older than her, was a mystery only the very foolish or the very idle tried to unravel. He adored his wife and their children of which they had ten. Six boys. Already bigger than he. More broad-shouldered. Taller. Four daughters all distinguished by their mother's beauty. Even temper. His daughters idolised him. He spoiled them. His sons feared him. They knew the true extent of his rages. How close to disaster they sometimes drove him. They were given to terrible quarrels over the slightest things. The father set one against the other in private or public, supervising the fight which he insisted be clean however fierce. An unrespectful or disobedient son he quelled with the use of his whip or the broad belt.

Veronica entered the kitchen. Quinn stood. In a gesture of rare courtesy. Took off his hat. 'A quiet house please God Mam.' A strange greeting, he, Timothy thought. 'For the moment, Mister Quinn. For the moment.' Veronica spoke sadly. Philippa was ill, cause of great but unmentioned concern for all. Quinn bowed jerkily. 'The help of God is nearer than the door, Mam.' He assured her. Replacing his cap. Resuming his seat.

Veronica: 'It is so, Mister Quinn. It is so. You will have your wife remember us in her prayers. She is always in mine, the good woman.' Quinn bowed his head while remaining seated.

He, Timothy, was not surprised at the courteous exchanges. It was as if two mandarins aware of the others rare qualities had chanced to meet. Observed the observances not from shallow practise but out of deep mutual respect. Veronica he knew respected Quinn as she did few men. Why he had never succeeded in having explained to him, but he, Timothy was by now so sensitive to the subtleties of Veronica's mind, he knew it was a respect hard won. Hard won. Dearly held. Veronica glanced at Bannion who was avoiding her gaze. Bannion was lighter and slimmer than he had been for many a long day. 'You really should work Bannion a little harder Mister Quinn. I think he is running to fat.' Quinn guffawed loudly. 'Well. By god he'll be like a whippet by the time I'm through with him.' Bannion blushed. Almost wept at the gross injustice of Veronica's comment. All laughed. At this outrage which was immediately apparent in his eyes. Veronica settled for a soft chuckle. 'Good-day Mister Quinn, and all of you. Please take care. Alexander in particular.' Quinn snatched off his hat. Rose. Bowed. Veronica took her leave of them.

They knew that she was returning to keep watch with Bridget over Philippa who was striding about her room in demented restlessness. She had been so for a week. Despite medication. Though physically weak. Exhausted. She continued to pace about. From time to time she laughed. Very loudly. More times she wept. Dragging her spent body about the room screaming at times for release from her torment. It was, all realised, too soon for the crisis of her illness. It would come. Ripen like the hateful fruit of some hateful tree. It would ripen and when ripened, would burst. Philippa would lose all reason. For how long no one could know. Nor did they speculate. Alexander had been to see her the previous evening. She had rallied sufficiently to speak a little with him. He promised as asked to bring back some alpine-like plants. Flowers from the bogs. Alexander had not spoken about Philippa's appearance. Or their meeting. He described her as 'greatly distressed.' Tight lipped. Turning aside. Refusing to speak further.

Quinn rose striking the table top with his crop. 'In the name of the Divine Lord of Mercy, will you stop guzzling yourselves and get out to the lorry before I whip you out to it.' His appearance was comical. His eyes bulging. Some foam flecked on his lips. He, Timothy, thought the speech amusing. Was again struck by Quinn's phraseology. The man never blasphemed. Would strike any man who would continue to blaspheme or profane once he had objected to it. Bannion however knew his man better than he, Timothy, did. Swigging the dregs of tea in his mug, he rose instantly. Was clambering over the side of the lorry before anyone quite realised it. The crop struck the table a second time. Alexander nodded acknowledgement. He, Timothy, stared at Quinn never having witnessed such conduct. Mouth agape he stared at he who was savagely grinding his black stumps of rotten teeth. Alexander caught Timothy by the quiff of his hair. 'Come,' he said, warningly. 'Come instantly.' He did so.

Flannery was already seated in the back of the lorry. A portable easel carefully positioned to minimise the jarring effect of the lorry in motion. Nearby a large portfolio. A tin can for water. His box of watercolours. Two of Quinn's sons were there. A year or two in the difference between their ages. Both so alike. Like all the male Quinns. He failed to remember their names. Could not distinguish one from another. Thought of them, as indeed he did of the girls, collectively rather than individually.

One son saw the faint glint of amusement in his, Timothy's eyes. Quinn's behaviour struck Timothy as somewhat amusing. The son muttered from the corner of his mouth 'Wipe that smile off your face or by Jesus he'll do it for you.' He, Timothy was shattered. The tone of the son's voice was unmistakeable. He, Timothy, respected the odd little man. Knowing him to have a wisdom of his own. A man who insisted on certain standards of behaviour. Which he insisted be respected in his presence. In his absence in so much as any conduct or conversation affected him. And his. The sort of man Timothy would have dismissed out of hand some years ago if he saw him striding along a Dublin street as a country yokel of low descent. Very low intelligence. The son who had spoken saw his distress. 'It's Miss Philippa has him upset,' he muttered by way of explanation.

Quinn emerged from the house. His jaw tightly set. Nora hurried after him. Splashing him with water from a bottle. Having drenched Quinn, who blessed himself quickly. Climbed to his seat at the driving wheel, she proceeded to drench all in the back of the lorry. 'Stupid whore,' Flannery shouted in outrage. 'I want none of your Pope's piss.' Muttering pious aspirations as was Bridget's custom, Nora used the bottle in such a manner that Flannery was struck by the last of the water remaining in the bottle with less than pious force. Right across his mouth. Flannery gasped at the outrage. Bounded to his feet. The lorry shot forward with a loud roar from the engine. Flannery was planted squatly on his backside, deprived of even elementary dignity. No one laughed. At least not outrightly. Enraged he shouted. Sat in the corner of the lorry. Refused to speak when spoken to.

Twilight crept across the rolling boglands. In the west the sun was setting. Its sunset colours a blaze of glorious colour. Like a monstrance, he, Timothy thought. Or like the vast nebulae which one might well expect to see surrounding the face of God himself if God chose to show Himself. Flannery, Alexander and Timothy were together. The others had gone with the last lorry-load of the day. Most of Quinn's sons were at Farrighy. They had already begun to stack the turf into what they called reeks. Already two such reeks had been made. Two sons were already thatching them with amazing skill. Farrighy would be assured of a good supply of peat for the winter. Nearby stood three reeks of peat. Last years harvest. They had been allowed to stand. Dry for a year. Hard as stone. The shrilled sods burned brightly. Warmly. Though perhaps too quickly. Used with wood and coal they imparted a pungent fragrance to the interior of Farrighy which was not particularly pleasant but which one got to like. Particularly in the winter months. Heavy as it was with the connotations of fireside warmth. Hot drinking chocolate. Strong tea brewed by Bridget and to which she and Timothy were both addicted. Much to Veronica's horror. Who invariably chided Bridget to no avail.

The harvesting of the turf was well advanced. One day more. They should complete the task for Farrighy. The turf for Quinn having been harvested some days before. They did eat like hogs and slept like logs as Veronica had tauntingly said they would. They were tired. Quinn was a hard taskmaster. It was a healthy animal tiredness. Their sleep deep. Restorative. They rose with groans to begin another day. Yet Timothy knew when the task was done. All the peat harvested. He would miss the comradeship of his fellow workers. The pleasure of undertaking a task which was challenging but could nevertheless be accomplished.

He worked as well if not better than others. Quinn very deliberately placed him amongst two of his sons who were less than industrious. Shamed by the pace of Timothy's work, they were forced to work in competition with him. Timothy was unaware of what was happening. His sons worked harder much to the delight of Quinn who loved to stand nearby. Taunt them for their slackness. Cutely enough Quinn had taken Alexander's measure. Placed him to work beside Bannion who was likewise shamed into working at a pace he would otherwise not have chosen.

Quinn grinned broadly. Ground the stumps of his teeth together. Cracked the whip in sheer perverse delight. The air was laden with muttered obscenities. So pitched in volume to ensure that they did not reach Quinn's ears.

Flannery disdained to undertake any work whatever. 'You've got two bloody niggers you've never had before. Work the bastards to death.' So saying he turned his back on Quinn. Strode about trying to seek an advantageous position to set up his easel. He was altogether lost in his task which was simply to capture the rolling boglands of infinite texture and variety. The scene was ever changing. Flannery worked with demonic swiftness completing in minutes what would have taken someone less skilled some hours to complete. Timothy was astonished by the certitude, the concentration with which Flannery worked! Oblivious of everyone. He worked on. Joining them only when the lorry laden high with turf left for Farrighy. For reasons of his own Quinn insisted on having his sons stack the reeks of turfs. Possibly because they were more skilled at such work.

The others happily waved farewell to the laden lorry. Sank

gratefully to the ground on a number of old army blankets scattered about. The blankets served as ground sheets. Later when night had fallen and they made the journey home, they would be cold even with blankets draped about them. A faint wind stirred. One would chance to see a ripple of movement low in the valley. Reeds. Bogcotton plants would quiver. Quake. Then like a tidal wave the faint breeze would gather strength. Move upwards in a series of movements somewhat like the advance waves of an incoming tide breaking on the beach. The sense of movement was startling, delightful. The coolness of the breeze broke upon them affording immediate relief from the relentless sunlight which beat down upon them for the greater part of the day.

All were tanned. Alexander, Flannery deeply so. Bannion even more so. Flannery lit a fire of kindling he scavenged from some of the lower hills. There the bilberry grew in profusion covering entire hills with low-lying shrublike plants. The berries of which were ripe. All had eaten them with pleasure relishing their tart, distinctive sweetness. They had eaten to excess. The berries soon lost their attraction for them. Timothy had been ill. Flannery had quoted a biblical passage to shame him. The wood of the old plants which were past bearing fruit was white. Scraggy. Reminding Timothy of an old woman's white hair billowing in a strong breeze. The wood burned quickly. Was sweetly scented. Noticeable even though they were surrounded by a variety of scents. Smells. All fresh. As if new to them.

Flannery brewed tea. Roasted some potatoes in the hot ash of the fire. Roasted chunks of raw meat he had the wit to pinch from the pantry, skewered along a sally stick which proved to be marvellous. Any reservations anyone might have had about the lack of hygiene, and Timothy had some, were quickly forgotten at the first taste of the roasted meat. Bannion produced apples from his jacket pocket. He shared them. They proved extremely tasteful. Flannery congratulated Bannion on his foresight. Bannion simply grinned. One could not know whether in satisfaction or derision. He and Flannery had little to say to each other at anytime. Timothy, with an audacity which surprised him, suggested that Flannery might care to capture the last blazing light of day as the sun set behind the distant hills now looming darkly against the sky. Flannery affected horror. 'Oh God no. You utter fool. Only the most terrible painters paint sunsets.' Flannery's tone was sharp. Contemptuous. Meant to crush. Timothy replied with equal sharpness. 'Turner I believe rather liked that sort of thing.' Flannery gasped like a landed trout. Alexander winked distinctly. Bannion yelped in outright delight at Flannery's comeuppance. 'You bear watching, serf.' Flannery commented grimly. 'If nothing else serfs must know their place.' Riled, he rose and strode off in disgust.

Alexander said softly: 'I do believe Timothy you're beginning to strike back. That's good. That's excellent.' Timothy was pleased. Smug at his retort to Flannery. But Flannery would strike harder. Bite deeper the next time round. To his astonishment Timothy almost looked forward to the exchange without dread. Flannery rejoined them. His easel and sketching stool all neatly folded into one bundle tied with canvas straps. Under his arm he carried a now bulging portfolio, which he carefully laid aside.

'Could I have the pleasure of seeing some of your work.' Alexander asked politely. Flannery glared at him. No one dared to ask if they could see his work. If one came as much as within twenty yards of where he was working one was told Fuck-Off with little ceremony. Only old Quinn had been spared that. On the few times he had approached. Stared at Flannery's work, he was heard to comment. 'Nice. Very nice.' Turned away leaving Flannery shattered. His face livid with rage. 'Yes. You may see my work.' Handed the portfolio to Alexander. 'May Timothy and Bannion also see them. I'm sure they would very much like to.' Flannery shrugged his shoulder dismissively. Stretched back on the ground, propped his head on an arm. Idly plucked a reed. Began to chew its stem. He affected nonchalance. Darted about sharply, seeking to see in Alexander's eye his response to the sketches.

Alexander's face was blank, utterly impassive. The very picture of detachment. Alexander glanced carefully at each sketch examining them patiently, thoroughly. He then passed each one, one by one, to Timothy. Timothy also affected indifference. Flannery never having afforded him the privilege to see any of his oil paintings or any other works. He was totally unexpectant. From his first glance at the first sketch, Timothy gaped in astonishment. Glanced swiftly at Flannery who in turn turned aside. Not before Timothy had seen the triumph. Pleasure in his eyes. The sketches were simple to a point of austerity. Each was basically a sketch in black paint with colours and hues added. The black was applied with absolute decision, executed in a very short while as he realised from having surreptitiously watched Flannery at work. The colours and hues were added in daubs. Often over-reaching the limitations of the basic sketch, they were added with what appeared abandonment, but the result was harmonious. Excellent. In some Flannery had sketched in a few figures standing. Staring ahead at the scene below which was of bogland which looked like a vast inland sea of greens and browns. Contained the high hills and mountains on all sides. Timothy instantly recognised Alexander as the most prominent. One or two were of Quinn and Bannion. There was none of him, Timothy. Seeing them he instantly wished to have one. Preferably of Alexander. He knew he could never ask for one. He knew none would be ever offered to him. He felt hatred and bitterness rise in him. He had never wittingly harmed or hurt Flannery. Nothing could account for Flannery's hatred of him. He, Timothy was a Catholic. A serf. A pleb. To be kept in his ordained, low state.

Blood. Timothy had come to realise the importance of blood. Blood not simply as the red fluid which was pumped through the complex system of veins and arteries, but blood signifying superiority of Race, Religion, Position. Flannery a bastard by law could claim kinship with Veronica's many Protestant relations. They readily accepted him into their ranks. Timothy while he could claim no blood relationship with Veronica or her people would never be accepted. They did not pretend to accept him. They never would. Flannery earlier in the week had referred to Alexander and he, Timothy as 'two extra niggers'. The choice of words had stunned Timothy. Alexander had merely smiled sardonically. Timothy had quailed. So foul a phrase. So lightly used. So intentionally wounding.

Alexander nodded his head appreciatively. 'Yes. They are excellent indeed. You are to be congratulated, Flannery.' Flannery grunted roughly. Was pleased. The pleasure was there to be seen in his eyes.

'What do you intend doing with these?' Alexander asked quietly. Flannery hesitated before replying. 'A few, two or three I will offer to a friend. Those remaining I will destroy.' As he spoke Flannery glanced at Timothy.

Timothy felt physically sickened at such calculated hatred, a loss of what he thought of as incomparably beautiful works; any one of which he would love to own.

Alexander gazed intently at a small black insect crawling up a blade of grass he had plucked. His voice was low. Even he, Timothy, was alerted. He had never heard Alexander speak so before. Flannery too was alerted. 'Would that friend by chance be Elizabetha?' The question seemed suspended visibly before them like inert matter suspended in a solution to demonstrate some principle. 'Yes,' Flannery replied shortly. 'Elizabetha.' Alexander stared hard at Flannery. His eyes malevolent in a manner Timothy would never had thought possible. Murder was in his cool, steady glance. He crushed the beetle crawling up the blade of grass he held in his hand. 'My mother will doubtless appreciate your kindness and fore-thought. I am sure she will select only the finest. She has unerring good taste in these matters.' Flannery nodded. 'Which is why I am offering them to her.' Alexander nodded. Commented no further. Rising he strode away into the gathering darkness. Clearly displeased. Greatly displeased.

Timothy rose. Went to the sack of bilberry kindling Flannery had gathered further up the hills. He set some in the

fire. They took light. He drew his blanket about him. Boiled a
kettle. Made strong tea. Silently handed everyone a mugful.
Alexander had not yet returned. All accepted. All sipped the
scalding sweet liquid gratefully. Their stomachs rumbled.
Audibly. All were scanning the desolate scene below hoping to
catch sight of the lorry lights which would signal Quinn's
return. There was little turf left. A half lorry or so. No more.
They would soon get it into the lorry. Be off to Farrighy.
Everyone was hungry. Cold. Wishing to leave the scene, the
real barbarity of which could only be experienced in heavy
mist. Or pouring rain. Or night.

The wind had risen. Low. Not very strong. It rustled
desolately through the heather. Bilberries. The tufted reeds.
The swaying bogcotton plants tipped with a bail of wool. It
struck Timothy as the keening of old women mourning. Now
it was soft, low, poignant. It might rise he feared as the keen of
old women did. Rise and rise to a demented pitch which
induced terror. Racial grief. Among all who heard.

He started. Thought 'no'. Then he started again. As did
Bannion and Flannery. 'That's it.' Bannion said gratefully.
'Jesus I could eat a fucking horse.' Each watched eagerly as the
lorry approached, its headlights sweeping across the desolate
landscape. Its throbbing engine disturbing the silence. The
silence of gathering night. Timothy realised that he was happy
that Quinn had come. He had thought irrationally that
something untoward might occur. He would be left to the dark
night in the bitter land about him. How easy it was to
remember grievance. Wrong. Hurts done if one was compelled
to live in such a lonesome place which would yield only the
barest necessities of life. Harsh servitude made more black and
bitter by the memory of the lush green lands from which the
English had driven his ancestors. Taken possession. Hatred
and a refusal to forget could prove the only motive for
existence. Now, he, Timothy told himself. Now you can
perhaps understand if only a little of the wild big boned
mountain men and their women who descended to
Tibraddenstown for the fairs trafficking in anything which

might yield a little extra money which would enable them to drink themselves into oblivion or to relive old wrongs. A fight or quarrel inherited from people. Long dead. Long dust. And perhaps also you can understand why the drunken lout or slut sitting in mire would sing heartbreakingly of a love lost. A son killed. Or a lament for the lovely green grass of the low plains.

Alexander had once commented to Flannery in what Timothy appreciated to be an important insight when he stated. 'You Irish ... Flannery. You salt your wounds to ensure they will never heal. Your black moods stem from black minds and the bile of black bitter memory. It moves me to say. May God have mercy on you all. You will always be so.' Flannery had snorted dismissively. Timothy had stared, and had been stung at such an appraisal of his, the Irish race. Now he realised Alexander had been correct. Timothy was glad that he would sleep in Farrighy tonight. Not in a mud cabin with a roof of rough reed thatch with a hole in the roof as a chimney. He was not, in so far as he could judge, a victim of his nation's history.

The lorry arrived. The engine throbbed for a few seconds. Died away. In the silence they heard a single forlorn bird sing. Sweetly. Briefly. How terrible the silence, he thought. How more oppressive. How much more wounding it is than the most horrendous of dins. Quinn tumbled a barrel from the back of the lorry. Spun it on its rim until it was close to the last load of turf awaiting removal. Standing upwind he threw a lighted match into the barrel. With an audible roar it leaped into flame. Red flame. Thick, black swirling smoke poured from it lighting the land about. It seemed to Timothy that the light from the barrel was the first light to break through the long darkness. Centuries long.

'Right,' Quinn shouted. 'The sooner you're home the sooner you eat.' But he pronounced eat as 'ate'. Timothy thought wryly he would only to happily both eat and 'ate'. They set to sling the sods of turf into the lorry. Alexander emerged from the darkness bare to the waist, his white shirt wrapped carefully into a bundle which he gently laid aside. He joined them at their task. Quinn stood close to watch. His teeth grinding together. His jaw thrust forward.

They worked steadily, eagerly. The barred sides were attached to the sides of the lorry. They were hardly necessary as there was less than a quarter load of turf. Suddenly they were done. All stood as if astonished by the fact that they had reduced great stacks of peat to a few worthless sods left lying about. Flannery produced hot tea. They drank and as he, Timothy had been doing for the last few days, smoked cigarettes. Avidly. Quinn approached with a whiskey bottle. Poured generous amounts into the mugs of those who would take it. Alexander did. Surprisingly. Less surprisingly, he, Timothy did not. They sank to their knees or haunches onto the wet spongy earth. Thankful the task was done. All experienced a sense of pride in their accomplishment.

Alexander turned to him, Timothy. 'Oh Alexander. How you'll like harvesting turf from an Irish bog. How excellent it'll be for you. How it'll improve the tone of your muscle. How it'll improve the circulation of your blood.' Alexander rose, circling about Timothy as he spoke, much like a dog having successfully cut off all the possible escape routes of his hard hunted quarry. Alexander was smiling with pleasure, but his eyes. He, Timothy saw to his sorrow, gleamed coldly with what struck him as outright hatred. It chilled him.

'I told you, Timothy. I would have my revenge. That time has come. I'm about to extract my revenge. Oh how you'll like it, Timothy. How good it'll be for you.' Alexander dropped his mug of tea. Was upon Timothy before he, Timothy, could realise it. Alexander scooped him up in his arms. Held him tightly. Alexander's strength was astonishing. His arms were like vices. His chest was a hard unyielding piece of metal. He, Alexander laughed. His, Timothy's blood ran cold. Alexander bore him to the edge of a small sump they knew to be shallow. He waded into the mire beneath. For one wild moment Timothy thought Alexander sought his death, and had dropped him into one of the deeper, far more dangerous sumps which were scattered about. Against which they had been warned, bearing spreads of pale green water plants with minute leaves and white flowers. The surface would at first glance appear to be solid. For an instant he, Timothy thought he would sink in the mire. Drown in its boggish mud. He screamed. In sheer terror. Alexander relented. Immediately. He waded through the mud.

'Timothy, I'm so sorry. I was mean and spiteful. Please forgive me.' Alexander lifted him from the mire. It took considerable effort to lift Timothy free of oozing mud. Alexander brought him to firm ground.

'Oh God Timothy. I had no idea. I simply thought to teach you a lesson. But only a little lesson.' Alexander's eyes were bright. Compassionate. To Timothy's relief the look of hatred had gone. Alexander smiled affectionately as he always seemed to do. Perhaps, Timothy thought. Perhaps it was all but a mistake on my part. He wished fervently it was so. But in his heart he knew it was not so. Alexander had shown a capacity for sheer hatred which Timothy had never experienced, even between his warring parents at their most vicious.

Alexander squatted by him. 'Timothy. You're all right, aren't you. There is nothing really wrong. You weren't physically hurt?' Assured he was not hurt. Alexander hurried away.

'Don't move I have some clothes for you.' Soon he returned bearing bundle of clothes. A beach towel, and a pair of shorts. 'Strip everything and wrap the towel about you.' Alexander instructed him, again hurrying off. Timothy did as instructed. Alexander returned with a dampened piece of towel with which he gently rubbed Timothy of the foul smelling mixture of mud, peat, rotting vegetation. 'You see Timothy how Germanic I am. I prepared my revenge carefully, down to the last detail. I've a complete change of clothes for you and towels to dry you. Thorough. Very unIrish.'Timothy changed into a pair of shorts and a shirt of Alexander's. He was about to rise when Alexander placed a hand on his shoulder restraining him. Squatting Alexander leaned towards him as if to whisper.

He whispered. 'I am sorry, Timothy. I did try to hurt you, Timothy. Of all people.' Leaning closer Alexander's lips brushed his. They lightly kissed. No one could have seen them do so. It was a brief action which stunned Timothy. Alexander smiled broadly. Bright, generous, affectionate as he had always been. He helped Timothy to his feet.

The others had clambered aboard the back of the lorry. Timothy joined them as did Alexander having retrieved the bundle he had laid aside so carefully some short while before which he, Timothy believed to contain orchids and other wild flowers for Philippa. Bannion glanced steadily at Timothy. It was a curious glance. Half pity. Part contempt and perhaps, a little sadness. He, Timothy flushed. Bowed his head as if ashamed. Bannion turned to look at the burning tar-barrel. Bannion had seen Timothy realised. A friendship had been broken. Respect lost. For ever. Timothy knew that it was not simply a passing mood of Bannion's but a binding judgement. Timothy was astonished how it hurt to have Bannion behave as he did.

Quinn climbed aboard the lorry. Coaxed the engine into roaring life. Jolted forward. Moved across the rough bogland to what was in reality no more that a rut, grandly called the 'road'. Behind them the burning tar in the barrel blazed brightly though not as bright as it first had. They watched it recede until it was a simple beacon in a sea of black inpenetratable night. Before they lost sight of it they all cheered uproariously. Timothy joining them surprised at the volume of his raucous cry. It was in some way the cry of the victor and the last defiant cry on the Irishry before leaving the forlorn land of their birth for the distant, alien cities of Boston and New York. In that respect it was a piteous cry. Cutting and cutting deeply into the very fibres of the mind. Flannery alone had not joined them in their roar. He sat huddled in a corner as if expecting to be whipped or beaten. 'Jesus help us. There's death abroad.' They thought him drunk. Simply disturbed but Timothy was to remember the comment.

Farrighy was a blaze of light. Even as they approached they heard the sound of music. Accordion, whistle, flute. The beat of hand and the sound of steps lightly tapping out the dance on the flagstones of Bridget's kitchen. They entered to be greeted by a great roar. Everyone slapped them on their backs. Shouted compliments to them. Bridget gently led them to a laden table. They sat. She took from the oven of the kitchen range a huge side of pork crisply cooked. It smelt so delicious Timothy felt he would have bartered his soul for some. Bridget carved them generous thick slices serving Timothy with some of the crisp outer slices knowing he loved crackling and burnt rather the rare meat. Nora followed serving roast potatoes. Mary followed in turn serving three vegetables. Sauce and other relishes were served by Bridget who moved slowly along the big table at the head of which sat Quinn. All his sons seated at the kitchen table which had been lengthened by the addition of a trestle table. Everyone waited. Declining with all their will-power to set upon the food on their plates. Bridget bowed her head. Singer and musicians fell silent. Bridget intoned grace before meals. 'Bless us Oh Lord and these thy gifts, which of they bounty we are about to receive, through Christ Our Lord, amen. Eat well. You all deserve it.' Like wolves they fell upon their food. Flannery who curiously had waited while Bridget said grace found himself without a knife and fork. Using his hands he slid meat into his mouth, head thrown back like a seal being fed fish. 'Oh, Christ Flannery. That is a bit much. Even by your standards,' said Timothy. Peter chuckled, plainly delighted at being included in the feasting.

Peter had paid a few visits to them wearing a sun hat he was absolutely forbidden to take off. He had loved working with them. Joining them for a mug of tea. Flannery allowed him a few cigarettes. Peter appeared to enjoy them. He seemingly was quite used to smoking though, Timothy had never seen him do so. Veronica, had she known would have been enraged. Now Peter laughed as did others at Flannery's barbarous manners. Timothy felt Peter was happy in a manner he had never known before. His eyes were innocently bright.

Tanned, he looked in excellent health.

Mary pestered everyone with more potatoes. Nora followed with the vegetables, Bridget with the meat. Everyone protested strongly they had quite sufficient and could eat no more. All three women unheedingly shouting good-humouredly. Quinn exclaimed 'Slap it on Mam, slap it on. A sparrow couldn't hop on what you've given me so far.'

The musicians struck up some music. Some young girls who were unknown to Timothy danced Irish dances gracefully, their bare feet tippy tapping on the bare, stone floor. Veronica entered, plainly shy at having to face such a large company. Quinn stood. Jerked his upper body in a bow. Sat, continued to eat.

Veronica, Timothy thought, was gauche. Uncertain. She smiled rather fixedly. Her hands thrust down deeply in the pockets of her cardigan. 'Eat up everyone,' she urged them. 'Don't stand on ceremony. God knows you've won the right to eat heartily.'

'Ate it is, Mam .... Sure a sparrow would expire on what we've had to eat so far.' Quinn winked at the company. Veronica registered horror. 'Why Mister Quinn have you not been given sufficient?' She was genuinely distressed at the very thought that her hospitality had been found wanting. Quinn saw as much. He rose and lifting his chair moved it to the left of the range. Nearby on wooden planking stood three barrels of porter. Nearby some half a dozen bottles of Irish whiskey. 'Codding I am, Mam. Pure codding. When was food or drink or anything else scarce in this house. God bless it. And all in it.'

'I show you something Mam you've never seen before. Strike up there Johnnie.' He urged the accordionist. 'Come hither Kate and keep me company.' Kate a girl of striking loveliness, one of Quinn's daughters, joined him shyly. The accordionist played a barndance. Old man and young girl together with fluid ease which was astonishing and which could scarcely be described. The wizened old man, his mouth clamped tightly, his jaw jutting, danced with all the lightness of a young man who knew himself to be perfect at the dance. Kate matched him step by step. Gleaming black hair which hung down her back lapping as she did so. Everyone took up the rhythm. Urged them on with cries of encouragement in Gaelic.

'Good .... Good .... Beautiful ...' Veronica relaxed. Smiled with pleasure, striking her hands in rhythm with the others. Alexander came through the doorway from the hall. Timothy was unaware that Alexander had even left. With him was Elizabetha, shy. Loathe to join the celebrations. Bannion fetched a chair for her. Alexander sat by her on the bare floor. The music and the dance finished. Quinn and Kate bowed to each other with all the lovely pleasantry of a couple at a court ball. There was thunderous applause. A roar. Calls for more, more. But Quinn laughingly declined. Took his seat by Veronica and lighting a stubby pipe, settled down to enjoy the evening as a contented spectator.

Encouraged by Quinn's performance, others now came forward. Danced and sang. Songs growing bolder as the stout and whiskey livened them up. Alexander and Elizabetha stepped forward. Alexander borrowed the accordion. Strapped it about his shoulders. Began what was unmistakably a Bavarian piece of music. Elizabetha began a peasant dance. She danced lightly. Gracefully. With an ease no one would expect her to have. Her shadow, heightened by the oil-lamps and candles brought forward to light the kitchen more fully, danced upon the whitewashed plaster walls. They concluded to rousing cheers and demands from everyone for a repeat performance. Laughingly they obliged. Timothy was struck by their dark shadows on the kitchen walls and floor. It's like a dance of death he thought though there was nothing funereal about either dance or music.

Oddly he also remembered seeing the vast painting in Veronica's office on the far side of the house. The painting Veronica dismissed as simply hideous beyond words but which never failed to move him. 'It's entitled 'Parting' — as you may have noticed by now,' Veronica had said dismissively. Timothy watching the gay uninhibited behaviour of the carousing company thought distinctly. 'There is ill about tonight. Death or damage will be done.' The laughter and banter all about belied his words but he knew what he felt would prove true.

Quinn called. 'A song Mary Joe McKeckney, a song.' The shout was taken up by all present. Clapping hands in unison with their voices. A redhaired girl, blazing hair piled high in big artificial curls about her head stepped forward. She was vulgarly dressed in what she considered the height of fashion. Her face was powdered and roughed. Her lips bright with crimson lipstick. Timothy had noticed her. She was with a tall thin fellow with gleaming black hair plastered backwards from the forehead to the back of the head. Timothy was struck by how much like Bobo's friend Skipper he looked. He sported a badly cut suit of cheap material. A bright, unsuitable tie. The girl had been staring frankly at Alexander all evening. Sexual desire plain upon her face and in her eyes. Much to the disgust and the rage of her escort. Both of them smoked incessantly. Pretending an elegance and air of worldliness which was patently false. Both worked in a factory in England. Were home on holiday. It was understood they would eventually marry. The girl stepped forward brazenly. There was nothing coy or shy about her. She boldly stepped into the centre of the kitchen coughing delicately into her bunched hand. A silence fell. Others had heard her sing before. Timothy realised that she would prove an incomparable singer. She sang in Irish. The Culann, possibly the most beautiful of all Irish songs. She sang beautifully. Poignantly. Saddeningly. Timothy thought how her voice would ring through the desolate wastelands where they had worked all week. She sang sweetly, with great grace. Voice and song in startling contrast to the vulgarity of her brash frock. Wedged shoes. Hair piled high in artificial curls.

My God, Timothy thought, she must be beautiful. Under all that hideous make-up was hidden a girl of simplicity and loveliness so careless of her beauty she aped the current fashion in her ignorance. She finished to cries of pleasure. Veronica applauded with more than a casual clap. Now she vigorously applauded. Joined in the chorus of demands for another song. The girl whispered to the accordionist who struck up the opening chords of 'The Spinning Wheel'. The girl began her song.

They heard a scream. A wild scream of demented agony. Horror struck. All felt silent. Peter staggered forward holding his hands to his head. 'My head. Oh Veronica my head.' He screamed, circling about the centre of the kitchen. He screamed again. Fell to the floor. Flannery hastened forward. 'Peter. Peter. Peter,' he shouted. Loudly smacking Peter on the face. Blood gushed from Peter's mouth. His right ear. Stricken. Veronica moved to the now still figure on the floor. She laid a hand on his wrist seeking his pulse. 'Poor fellow,' she said quietly. 'He's dead.' Her face frigid, an emotionless mask, she rose. Left the kitchen. Bridget shuffled forward. Kneeled. Blessed herself. Intoned the opening prayers of the rosary. With the exception of Flannery all others kneeled. Blessed themselves. Prayed. Bridget in Gaelic. The company in English. Their prayers like the gently lapping of calm waves breaking against a bulwark. Flannery, face aflood with tears, tried to kick the senseless body on the floor. Again. And again. A senseless gesture of grief. In the far distance Philippa screamed. The tenuous thread, Timothy, realised had broken. Philippa had once more lapsed into madness.

Even in death Master Peter was surrounded by the solid red lines of Veronica, and he, Timothy, was never to know who he, Master Peter, had really been. Whose child, from what woman? And never dared ask of what congenital disease he, Peter, died of. Nor why his death had been always suddenly expected. All this was shrouded in dark, Celtic twilight, surrounded by solid red lines. Forgotten to all, but Veronica's almost silent prayers.

PART FOUR

Flannery sat at the head of the table. In the chair usually occupied by Veronica which she refused to yield to anyone. Flannery was hugely pleased with himself. Smoking a cigarette of scented tobacco. Toying with his fingertips about the rim of a brandy-glass in which rested a handsome splash of brandy which sparkled brightly catching the light of the chandelier above the table. The prime source of light in the diningroom. Red candles unlit stood in the two candlesticks in position on the polished surface of the table. Flannery's fingers on the rim of the glass made music of a kind. The strange soulful music one might imagine blowing about the innumerable planets in the compacted darkness of outer space. But no, he, Timothy thought. No. Not at all like that. The music is more like what one hears when one holds one ear to a telegraph pole. Distinct, sad music.

All had dined handsomely. Flannery had cooked a freshwater salmon with perfect accompanying dishes. Everyone enjoyed their meal. Everyone said so. Pointedly. Flannery affected to disdain praise. But as all had learned, he snapped, rather like a vicious rat if anyone took his cooking for granted, failed to praise his efforts. Handsomely. He presented a picture of the ideal host at his most considerate. Alexander had chosen not to dine. Veronica was visiting friends. A rare departure for her. The position of host had therefore devolved upon Flannery. Who was relishing the role. His hair was no longer wild. It was neatly cut. Trimmed. Sleeked back fashionably with the liberal use of lavender scented brilliantine. He wore a light off-white jacket — white would have been, well, rather vulgar — of a light material Timothy could not identify. Flannery sported a red cravat of special magnificence. In the lapel of his jacket he wore a rose. A perfect red rose from one of his own much neglected bushes in his much neglected gardens. As he raised the brandy glass to his lips, gently agitating it as he did so, and sipped, as if from a chalice of consecrated wine, gold flushed at the cuffs of his sleeves. On the rings on the fingers of his right hand. Three rings in all. One bore an amethyst. One a cluster of minute diamonds. The other a brilliant solitaire. He appeared to drip gold like a potentate from the east. Like a potentate from the east he affected a nonchalance as if disdaining the baubles he wore. While in fact he relished flaunting such wealth. He laughed lightly at Elizabetha who wore many silver ornaments. Gold she had declared loudly not long after her arrival at Farrighy, and seated where she was now seated, gold did not become her. 'Silver' she declared with unpleasant certitude 'Silver suits me so. So much more than gold. Somehow, I don't quite know, I feel gold is vulgar unless worn by the right person in the correct manner.' What, he, Timothy thought. What does she think of Flannery now? Was he being vulgar. Or was he the right person wearing the gold correctly? Flannery laughed, or rather snorted. Elizabetha in her striking white evening dress twittered — as though both were schoolchildren sharing a smutty joke. Both were somewhat drunk. They had consumed a great deal of wine and port and brandy.

Timothy wished he was not with them. He had tried to excuse himself immediately after dinner but Flannery had behaved badly. Insisted that Timothy remain. They needed a foil, a fool. A witness to their drunken flirtation.

Flannery addressed him, Timothy, while glancing sidewise at Elizabetha. 'We don't see much of Veronica these days. Not that we miss the bitch. But sometimes, she amuses me. Like a childmonkey trying to stuff a banana up its arse. Not quite realising it is aiming towards the wrong aperture.' Elizabetha guffawed. Splurted wine she had been about to swallow. Some splashed on her dress. Staining it darkly. Anger flashed in her eyes. 'Look what you made me do,' she exclaimed, lips curling. Nostrils flaring.

'Never mind, Pet,' Flannery said mildly, smiling placatingly. 'It will come out in the wash as the master said to the maid.' Elizabetha shrieked in laughter. Dropped her lower jaw. Brayed like a donkey. Flannery winked at her. 'I was saying, we don't see much of Veronica these days. These days Veronica is much given to prayer and fasting, atonement for past sins. Real and imagined. She pines so for Philippa. That demented wretch under lock and key in St. Joseph's nursing home. That asylum. I for one am glad. At least one can sleep at night without having to hear her screams. Her obscenities. Her cries of torment. Kinder to shoot the poor bitch. Just above, and a little back from her right ear. Bang. Blood. Brains. Pulverised bone everywhere.'

Elizabetha laughed shrilly. Flannery glared at her. 'You find that funny? You stupid German.' Elizabetha paled. Stared at Flannery. She slid a hand across the smooth surface of the table top. 'Oh come Flannery, let's not quarrel. This is the adventure of a lifetime. Elizabetha in the land of the Celts. There is so much that stinks and is rotten. Everywhere I smell the stench of putrefying flesh. I, Elizabetha dare not walk alone. You Flannery are my escort. You must protect me. Let's not quarrel.' Her eyes were large. Luminous. She smiled but in her eyes was that chilling light Timothy had seen in Alexander's eyes when he had taken revenge for his, Timothy's mocking comments about Alexander's enthusiasm for so much physical exercise. 'How you will love it Alexander. Oh how it will improve your body. Send the blood racing through your veins.' Flannery, Timothy thought, this woman seeks your ruination. Will accomplish it. In time. As that realisation struck home, he, Timothy thought. Does Alexander harbour the same intent for me? Yes. He does. An interior voice replied and he,

Alexander will also achieve his end. Calmly, Timothy sat beneath the blazing chandelier contemplating his own destruction as if it were a matter of no importance. A clock chimed the half-hour. He, Timothy, thought. I seem to find myself listening to the slow passage of time as I did on my first night in Farrighy. Before I got to know and in some measure to love — Veronica and all here at Farrighy.

As Flannery had said Philippa was in a private asylum. They had kept her at Farrighy for as long as possible in the care of two strong, competent female nurses who alternated their hours of duty to see that Philippa was never left alone. Day or night. Dr. Bradshaw attended her. He advised rest. Enforced rest, heavy sedation and a strict diet. From time to time under his supervision Philippa was bound hand and foot in wet bandages.

She was left to lie on her bed, the bed protected by waterproof covering. A fire was lit in her bedroom fireplace. Built up to a steady heat. Kept at a certain temperature for sometime. The bandages dried. Constricting severely as they did so. Philippa wept in pain. Swore obscenely. Begged release. Veronica staring at a blank part of the wall. Lips and eyes lightly closed. Doctor Bradshaw watching with utter disinterest. A nod from him. The bandages were undone. Barely conscious Philippa was returned to her freshly made-up bed. An opiate was administered granting some relief from long agony. Veronica, Bridget, Nora and Mary. All took turns keeping vigil by Philippa's bed to ensure that not only strangers would keep watch. She suffered greatly. The opiates were not as effective as might be desired. Philippa was building up a resistance to them. She was fast approaching a stage where they would be effectively neutralised. Nothing would then stand between Philippa and raw, unending insanity. A state of unbroken pain. Stripped of all human dignity. Eventually the time came when Philippa's life was endangered. She was moved to St. Joseph's Home for supervised treatment available only in the hospital.

Veronica was shattered by Philippa's illness. She shed all

surplus flesh. Was now bow-back under the crushing burden she was forced to carry. Her clothes, particularly her cardigans hung from her now gaunt frame as if some sizes too big for her. Most distressing of all, the look in her eyes verged on despair. Timothy felt deeply for her in her sorrow. Prayed that she might be spared further pain. Sometimes at unguarded moments he succumbed to his emotions, wept for her, Veronica. Veronica the unsmiling figure in an old photograph. Though she did not smile as had all the others, one nevertheless realised instinctively that she was a young woman of great spirit. Courage. Now Philippa's illness was slowly, insidiously sapping her strength. Stalwart throughout the lives of all those who knew her as mistress of Farrighy, she was crumbling before them. Witnessing her decline, Timothy thought of the slow death of a splendid animal. Once lord and master of his wide dominion. The fall of a splendid tree in a forest of many less splendid trees. All felt for her in her troubles. Bridget in particular. Nora, Mary and he, Timothy. They united as if in a unique fellowship, sought in every way to mitigate Veronica's suffering.

Veronica, to Timothy's great regret turned not to him in her trial but to Alexander who became her closest companion. He was with her constantly or as constantly as anyone could possibly be. He neglected his own studies but still swam morning and evening in the river. That much Alexander allowed himself. Alexander brought Veronica her food because Bridget could not do so. Would not allow Nora or Mary to do so. He spent hours with Veronica listening to the low moans of Philippa tied to her bed by stout, restraining ropes. Later, after Philippa had been removed to the Home, he attended Veronica in her room where he read to her from the works of Theresa of Avila and the writings of other, lesser mystics. Timothy was intensely jealous of the favour shown Alexander. He felt embittered. To some extent betrayed. Sometimes he climbed one of the two backstairs in the house, now rarely used, commonly referred to as the 'servants' stairs'. He squatted on the step of the landing to Veronica's bedroom.

Squatted. Hardly bearing to breathe knowing that if he were caught there he could not hope to offer an acceptable excuse. Hating Alexander for being above him in Veronica's affections though he was well aware that the books were in French and he, Timothy, could not possibly read from them even if requested. His French was bad. He realised as much but illogically he persisted in his jealousy of Alexander. Curiously Alexander while speaking English perfectly, spoke French with a slight Germanic slur. Timothy listened to Alexander's mesmerising voice. It rose and fell like the hum of a bee in its flight from flower to flower. The upper half of the windows were lowered as was the custom during Summer or any spell of good weather. Veronica liked them so. The light white curtains wafted in the faintest of breezes like so many white prayer flags. If one concentrated one could hear their movement as they billowed gently. Timothy had come to like being there. At the step to the landing by Veronica's bedroom. He had come to hear Alexander read. Veronica would have some peace of mind. If only for a short while. Listening to Alexander's measured reading. Listening or rather half-listening to the muted sounds of activity in the house. Which were not considerable. And as twilight advanced, the sounds of the countryside at night. His jealousy abated somewhat. But it still hurt. Curiously, Timothy liked that hurt. Nurtured it. Fed it. Kept it alive. Would not forgive Veronica for choosing Alexander to read to her. That Irish opiate: The comfort of salted wounds.

Bridget rarely smiled since Philippa had been removed to the Home. Her splendid eyes were dimmed. Harrowed she crept about the house attending to what few duties she could attend to, fingering her rosary beads in the deep pocket of her white apron. She too had seemed to age considerably. Was not as active, as dutiful as she had been. She accompanied Veronica on her trips to the Home which was some miles outside the city. They travelled in a motorcar commonly referred to as a hackney. Such trips were a measure of Bridget's bravery because in common with many old Irish women, and men, she had a mortal dread of Homes of all kinds, particularly the workhouses where the old were often abandoned by their families. The word asylum aroused in her a fear worse than the fear of death. Committal to such an institution was for her a sentence to dreadful misery. A life devoid of dignity. Quite without hope. Alexander accompanied them. Timothy was never invited. It was some consolation to know that Alexander was never invited into the Home. He had to be content to sit with O'Leary the hackney man or go for a stroll for the duration of the visit. Heavily laden with fruit, flowers, whatever special delicacies she thought might especially appeal to Philippa, Veronica and Bridget entered the Home, to be fulsomely greeted by the nuns. Their warm welcome was never extended to Alexander nor O'Leary however bad the weather might be. Timothy relished that fact. Relished it meanly. Intensely.

'Yes,' Elizabetha said. 'I too think that'd be much more merciful. A quick bullet or perhaps a painless poison .... That'd be much more merciful. And practical.' She paused. Drank deeply from her brandy glass. 'Poison. A painless poison. That way there'd be no mess. An uncle of mine. He hanged himself. It was horrible. So ugly to see. And the fuss. One would think it was the end of the world. They should be poisoned I think. The incurably ill. Idiot children. Others. They should all be put down painlessly. It'd be more merciful.' Flannery somewhat sobered stared at her, open-mouthedly. Focusing his eyes with difficulty upon Elizabetha. 'You think that? You think that poor dear Birdy should be put down like a dog because it would be merciful and practical?' He stressed the 'practical' heavily. Elizabetha failed to detect the hard edge to Flannery's voice. The emphasis on the word 'practical'. She was altogether unaware that Flannery had set a trap. 'Yes,' she replied. 'Pain serves no purposes whatever. It's not a virtue to suffer pain gladly. That's stupid. Pain is so pointless. Besides being terrible for whoever. It's not a virtue to suffer pain gladly. That's stupid. Pain is so pointless. Besides being terrible for whoever has to suffer. It's so inconvenient for others. It would be merciful to eliminate them altogether.' The trap was sprung. Flannery: 'Do many in the "new" Germany think as you do?' 'Yes I think they do or at least very many do.' She shifted uncomfortably in her chair. 'Jesus help all,' Flannery exclaimed. 'What is to become of us? He had turned and spoken directly to him, Timothy. Without rancour. 'The woman is quite mad. They are all quite mad. Out of their living minds.' 'Oh no,' Elizabetha retorted. 'It is you French and British who are stupid. You allow yourselves to be manipulated by filthy vermin. Rats. Jews.' Elizabetha rose. Possibly to sweep in anger from the room. She was unsteady on her feet. Leaned heavily on the table for support. Flannery addressed her softly. 'I'd rather you didn't speak of any race or the followers of any religion in the sluttish manner you have. This obsession with the Jews. It's all mad bollocks. Sheer bloody bollocks and it's time you bloody Germans were told as much.' Elizabetha recoiled in horror. Almost toppled over as she attempted to assume outraged righteousness. 'How dare you speak to me like that you filthy degenerate. You pervert the young. Yet you dare to address me like that.' She mustered spittle in her mouth. Very carefully. Spat into Flannery's face.

The door opened. Alexander entered. 'I heard the essentials of your argument as I approached. You may not be aware of the fact but you've been shouting at each other like two drunken louts.' Elizabetha was pale with fear. 'No,' she protested. 'No.' Alexander ignored her protest. He appeared to be staring at a point just above his mother's head. He too was pale. Seething with anger. 'You've been drinking mother. To excess. You're a disgrace. A drunken slut shouting drunkenly I can accept. It's the nature of sluts to behave like that. On your part I find such behaviour unpardonable. You dishonour your husband, my father. You dishonour my father in me. You dishonour me. I suggest you go to your room. You've had quite enough to drink. You've spoken too much. A glass of warm water and a little honey will help you to sober up. When you reach your room ring for one of the servants. They'll bring it to you. A good night's sleep will do you good.' Elizabetha swayed. 'How dare you. How dare you address me in such a manner and before these people. You. You filthy hog. How dare you.' She struck Alexander in his face. Alexander recoiled. He turned slightly as if to leave. Spun quickly about. Struck Elizabetha across the face. Blood erupted from her nose. The corner of her mouth. Elizabetha sought to staunch its flow with her bunched fist. 'Please don't strike me, please Alexander. Don't. I beg you.' 'No Mother,' Alexander replied calmly. 'I won't strike you again. Go to your room. Immediately.' Elizabetha, her hand running with blood nodded assent. Staggered forward uncertainly. 'Help me Alexander. In God's name. I can't walk.' She wept. Alexander retorted 'You've behaved unpardonably. You deserve such public humiliation. You're quite capable of walking. Try. Try Mother. Try.' His tone was one of ringing command. Elizabetha stared wide-eyed at him. 'I can't walk Alexander. I've had too much wine.' 'Well why not say so Mother. In that case I'll help you to your room. Please take my arm.' Elizabetha hesitated. Took Alexander's arm. Staggered forward. 'Excellent Mother. Excellent. You see you can walk. Perfectly.' They proceeded to the door. Elizabetha haltingly. At the door they paused. Alexander turned to Flannery. 'Perhaps you could ring for some coffee. I should like some when I return.' 'Of course,' said Flannery. 'I'll ring for some immediately.' Alexander inclined his head. Smiled grimly. Opened the dining room door carefully. Ushered his mother through.

They heard Alexander acclaim his mother's efforts to walk. He enunciated each word clearly. As if to a dolt.

They heard Elizabetha, the cold disdainful Elizabetha, whine. Like a much whipped hound. Fearing a further whipping. They realised that this was not the first time she had been treated in such a manner. It had happened before. Possibly a number of times. Timothy rose, grateful that he could now leave. He felt if he were remain he would be violently sick. Flannery smiled at him. 'Don't go, Timothy. What you've seen is nothing but a prelude of what is to come.

I imagine whatever happens it will prove fascinating. I know you feel ill. You look distinctly ill. All the more reason why you should remain. I want you to see for yourself what your adored Alexander is capable of. You don't deny that you adore him? You can't. It's all too noticeable. Sometimes sickeningly so.' Flannery paused. Lighted a cigarette. Inhaled the perfumed smoke. 'You think Alexander is a man of honour. My friend, did it ever strike you that those who most speak of honour possess it to a lesser degree than others? Was what you have just witnessed the behaviour of a man of honour?' They heard Elizabetha cry out. Once. Twice. 'What a stout, brave fellow your friend is. See how he treats his women.' Odd, Timothy thought. Flannery said 'his women' rather than 'his mother'. Flannery was rarely inexact in his use of English. 'Care for a drink?' Flannery's voice was cordial. Timothy declined saying 'No thank you'. Flannery as of old, scowled in contempt. 'I fear drink,' Timothy blurted out. 'I fear drink in the same way I fear physical violence.'

'And women,' Flannery said quietly. Timothy replied equally quietly. 'Yes.' He regretted that he had confided so much in Flannery. Flannery reached for the brandy bottle. 'If you decline to drink I'm afraid I have no alternative but to help myself.' Which he did. Generously. He swirled the brandy about in the glass. Smelling it appreciatively. 'My God one can see why they call it the nectar of the gods. It's simply magnificent.' He sipped some. Laid aside his glass. Stared meditatively at the chandelier above. Then glanced at Timothy. Flannery's eyes were very blue tonight. Bluer than usual or so, he, Timothy thought. Light and shadow interacting on the pupil of the eye. Nothing more. Flannery spoke gently with some effort. 'What you said about being afraid. That took some doing. A certain bravery. I think Veronica who I don't particularly love does possess a certain wisdom of her own. She might well be right about you.' He took a handkerchief from the breast pocket of his coat. Red. Silk. As magnificent as the cravat he wore about his neck. 'You needn't stay for the second half of Alexander's performance. I won't think ill of you if you choose to leave but I'd like you to remain.' Timothy nodded. 'If you wish me to stay, then I'll stay.' Flannery nodded his head in turn. 'You know what is going to happen of course?' 'No. I don't,' Timothy replied. Flannery sighed. 'Our friend Alexander is going to beat the shit out of me. Oh I'll give him as good a run for his money as I possibly can, but make no mistake, young fellow, Alexander seeks blood and is determined to have it. Alexander is a killer. He has all the instincts of a killer. Moreover he is aware of the fact. He has weighed the whole matter up. He has rationalised his urge to kill. He hasn't killed yet. But he will. Given the proper circumstance. For God. For his country. For his beloved Fuhrer. He'll kill. Slaughter. Hundreds. Thousands.' Flannery paused. Sipped from his glass. 'And why not. Isn't slaughter on the field of battle thought glorious? What better way to achieve glory than by shedding the blood of others. It really is quite a simple matter. Slaughtering others. I ought to know. I slaughtered quite a few in my time.'

Flannery began to remove the rings from his fingers. With some difficulty despite the fact that he was lean. His fingers slender. He laid them aside on the table. Timothy experienced an overwhelming greed to possess the gold and diamonds on the table. He thought senselessly. I will grab them and run and run until they tire. No longer hunt me for what I have stolen. It was a revelation. He had thought himself devoid of any great desire for wealth. The trappings of wealth. Flannery took the cigarette case from his inside coat pocket. Removed the cigarettes. Stuffed them into his coat pocket. Laid the case beside the jewels. 'Now you see why men worship gold, Timothy. Not just because it is a rare metal but because it is so very, very beautiful.' Flannery invariably referred to him, Timothy, as a 'Catholic shit' ... and yet had thought fit to upbraid Elizabetha about her reference to the religious beliefs of others. 'Stupid of me to have worn them. They belong to Alexander's father. Why Elizabetha thought it necessary to bring them with her to Ireland is quite beyond me. But bring them she did. And for some very good reason. She thinks, does our cold Elizabetha, like a chess player. She thinks ten moves ahead. She persuaded me to wear them though I knew it'd be folly to do so. She has used me as a means of striking out at Alexander, perhaps she thought to provoke him. To humiliate him.' Flannery sighed. 'Whatever her intentions she miscalculated. Miscalculated badly. And I? I have been not only insensitive but incredibly stupid. I've offended Alexander. Not just Alexander alone. No. I've offended his father in him as he so quaintly says. There was a discreet knock on the door. Nora entered. 'I was just about to ring for you, Nora. Please let us have some coffee.' Nora nodded. 'Is there something,' Flannery asked as Nora lingered. 'Do you know when Miss Veronica will be back, Sir?' 'I'm afraid I don't. I shouldn't slip off to the crossroads at Carra. Miss Veronica will expect you to be here when she returns.' Nora nodded dejectedly. 'Very well, Sir.' Nora withdrew. Hardly had she done so than Alexander entered smiling pleasantly. He glanced briefly at the jewellery on the table. 'That was wise of you, Flannery. Very wise indeed.'

'Timothy I've been speaking to Veronica. I think she is being a bit self-indulgent about what I read for her. The mystics I imagine are not without value to a woman of her sensibilities and intelligence. She derives great consolation and relief from them. I am only too happy to help in whatever way I might. I suggested, mind you suggested — that perhaps a little light reading might help things considerably. I therefore suggested that she have something light read to her, a novel, perhaps some traveller's tale. Or perhaps some history or biography. She seemed at a loss for some time so I suggested that she choose a book which she had read in her childhood and which afforded her particular pleasure. She immediately mentioned Thackeray whose work, and I quote, she "adored" as a child. She said there was bound to be some of his work lying about somewhere. I took the liberty of suggesting that you, Timothy, might read to her each evening after I've read the more serious matter. She was enchanted and asked that you begin tomorrow night at about ten. That is the hour of day she finds most unbearable and would like to help pass it by having you read to her. Veronica must be weaned from her obsession with death and decay. She has been far too harrowed by such matters since Peter died. Forgive me if I have presumed by electing you to read for her but she was so happy at the idea I dared to do so. Am I forgiven?' 'Yes, Alexander,' Timothy said. 'You are forgiven,' but thought 'You have presumed Alexander, but then you have been above all presumptuous from the moment we met.' 'Thank you, Timothy. I knew I could count on your kindness above all else.' Alexander sat to the table as though sitting to a meal to which he had been looking forward for some time. A slight rap on the door. Seconds later Nora entered bearing a tray on which rested a pot of fresh coffee. She laid the tray by Flannery. 'Shall I serve, Sir,' she asked nervously. Nora as everyone knew was not quite as skilled at serving table as one might expect for one in her position. 'Thank you no, Nora. We'll serve ourselves. Thank you.' Nora withdrew.

Each poured his own coffee. Added or did not add, milk and sugar as he wished. Outside the night was still. Dark as already winter approached. The night air which drifted in from the partially opened windows was faintly moist. Damp. Which seemed so conductive to sound. Timothy thought so as he remembered first hearing the reverberations of the hunter's guns as they hunted on the lands around Farrighy. Veronica very sensibly let the hunting rights, and by agreement a generous allocation of game birds. He winced to hear the repeated discharge of the gun. Philippa was always distressed. Inconsolable at the slaughter of such beautiful birds. It had hurt him curiously the first time. Those first few shots. Stunned by the knowledge that a splendid bird had fallen to a hunter's gun. A curious innocent hurt like first seeing a star fall. Being told that it signified the release of a soul from purgatory. Assuring its entry into heaven. So his mother had told him. That first time he saw a star fall. And he felt chilled to the bone.

There are so many millions in purgatory. So very few stars fall. As each sipped their coffee in silence it seemed as though one could hear the leaves fall from distant trees in distant woodlands.

Alexander: 'I feel like having a cigarette this evening. Perhaps, Flannery, you could let me have one of yours?' Flannery took one from his coat pocket. 'Rather crushed I'm afraid,' he apologised as he handed it to Alexander. He handed Alexander his, Flannery's lighter to light the cigarette. Alexander did so. Inhaled. Coughed slightly. Handed Flannery back his lighter. 'You'll both have to forgive me. I don't usually smoke. I find it rather unpleasant.' He gazed at the jewellery on the table. The gold shone brightly. The brilliant diamonds sparkling as if emitting a bright energy of immense power. Alexander stared steadily at them. His face hard. Rigid. He all but snarled. Timothy realised that Alexander was struggling with Flannery. This was the psychological stage. The fight would come later. Both stages were of crucial importance. It would prepare the ground and the combatants for the engagement to come.

Alexander exhaled faintly green smoke. 'Quite pleasant,' he commented. One assumed he was speaking of the cigarette he was smoking but one could not be entirely sure. Alexander addressed him, Timothy, affably. 'I've excellent news for you, Timothy. Those missing components for Chugg have been located, believe it or not. In a remote village to the north of Buda-Phest. I took the precaution of enlisting the aid of the German Cultural Attache at the German Embassy in Buda-Phest. I realised we were looking for a very small needle in a very big haystack. It happened that the attache was a friend of my father. A comrade-in-arms from the last days of the Great War. How he ended up becoming Cultural Attache in the German Embassy in Buda-Phest is quite beyond me. He promised his assistance. I thought he was merely being polite but no. It seems he was quite sincere. He made widespread enquiries managed to track down information on the manufacturers of Chugg. Can you imagine, Timothy. We strip a motorcar engine down to the bone so to speak only to find that some vital pieces are worn out and are no longer of any use. But when we institute a search for those vital pieces they're not to be found.'

Bannion and Alexander had lovingly stripped the engine of Veronica's sleek, lovely, but utterly unpredictable motor car. They hoisted the engine free from the main body. Held it suspended on an improvised hoist which itself took considerable time to erect. Having done so they proceeded to strip the engine carefully tagging, laying aside all the component pieces. To their dismay they discovered that several wheels and cogs were worn out. Timothy could hardly distinguish between wheel and cog. Though he had eagerly agreed to help, he soon became bored, left the task to Bannion and Alexander. Both tanned by the continual spell of sunshine tanned further. Alexander's skin looked brown as a brown berry. Bannion tanned to such an extent that he looked like a rather pale Asian rather than an Irishman. Flannery had watched them at work in the early stages. 'You'll take the damned things to pieces with no great difficulty but how in the name of Christ are you going to put it together again?' Alexander had smiled condescendingly. 'Never fear Flannery. We'll succeed.' Veronica has assured them that her father who bought the car had wisely bought spare parts. Duplicates of the pieces most likely to deteriorate. A search was begun but proved fruitless until they discovered a crate stamped with the Trade Mark of the manufacturing firm. There were indeed spare parts in the case. Some carefully oiled. Others wound in waxed paper to preserve them indefinitely. Bannion and Alexander had howled with delight. Taunted Flannery for his lack of faith. Flannery had smiled enigmatically. Asked sagely. 'You've found spare parts but what on earth makes you think they're parts you require?' Alexander paled. Flannery triumphant. Passed quietly on his way whistling tunelessly. So it proved. The components they had come upon in the case were not those now required. Alexander was stupified. Bannion accepted things a little more philosophically.

Shrugging his shoulders he had faded silently from the scene like a ghost departing its parent body. Alexander was left to explain to Veronica who had only the vaguest idea of what they were up to what exactly had happened. Veronica not unnaturally had stormed against what she called 'insufferable arrogance.' They had, she said reduced her very elegant but sluggish car to a heap of inert bits. Pieces. She concluded by congratulating them on what she called their first rate stupidity. Bannion had beamed broadly at Veronica. He always beamed broadly when Veronica corrected him. Lost her temper with him. He smiled whatever was said. The indulgent smile of a mandarin witnessing an unseemly display of temper by one unschooled in her manners. His smile invariably reduced Veronica to speechless rage. 'Speak to him Bridget. Speak to him,' she would shout. 'Before I strangle the dolt.' Bridget would nod, signalling Bannion to steal quietly away. But while Bannion took the whole matter without concern it was altogether a different matter with Alexander. Alexander had been stung. Stung far deeper than anyone realised. What had been a simple matter of personal pride became a matter of German national pride. He wrote innumerable letters to manufacturers of cars in Hungary, Germany, France, the United States, even Albania in the hope that somewhere components rested in a remote garage or factory in a small packing case somewhat like the one they found in the outhouse at Farrighy. He received a few replies regretting that the firms concerned knew nothing whatever of the make of car. It was firmly established that the original manufacturing firm in Hungary had long ceased to exist. Chugg was custom-built specifically to the taste and requirements of its original owner. In the days before mass production of cars. The car, Veronica insisted, had cost the earth when the father had bought it years ago. It must therefore have cost its original owner a considerable sum of money in the days when as Veronica liked to say 'Money was money'. Alexander believed that the missing parts had most likely been made by hand, and were such magnificent examples of engineering skill they would somehow survive. They were to be found somewhere. He believed that someone — an engineer perhaps or even an unlettered peasant — had retained them because they were so beautifully wrought and could not bear to part with them. It was also possible that such a crate existed in the storerooms of some garage or dealer. Alexander hoped his letters would spur them on to make a search of their storerooms. The engine was placed on blocks in the old carriage house. Alexander oiled each part carefully. Veronica forbade not only any further discussion of the matter, it was strictly forbidden to even mention the car in casual conversation.

Alexander's hands had hardened. His nails once so trim, carefully attended, were now as broken and chipped as were Bannions. Timothy noticed as much as he now watched Alexander hold his coffee cup. Flannery looked directly at Alexander, faintly amused. 'Wouldn't it be wiser to wait and see what your friend the Cultural Attache sends you before you begin to crow too much like a cock. After all, you did have an unfortunate experience with Chugg not so very long ago.' Alexander grinned. 'I found the car manual in the crate together with the useless parts. It showed in great detail not only the engine in cross section but illustrated each and every component on the car and gave reference numbers for each part enabling me to cross-check. So you see Flannery. We have at long last traced our missing spares. I've discovered, after considerable effort the pot of gold at the end of the rainbow.' Alexander smiled. 'Does it please you, my friend Timothy that we have achieved our purpose? That we have kept our promise to Veronica that she can again drive in her beloved Chugg to do her shopping in Tibraddenstown?' Timothy said that it indeed pleased him. Suggested that Veronica might have more to worry about than Chugg. 'Yes,' Alexander agreed solemnly. 'Yes. You're quite right. I take a rather selfish pleasure in having traced the spares we needed. You'll have to forgive me. It's my German blood.' The word German was intoned naturally without emphasis or reflection of any kind.

Yet it hung heavily in the air. Alexander had used it with calculation.

Flannery grinned. Rather curled his lips. Scornfully. 'Are you Germans not apt to value the machine perhaps a little too much? Alexander stiffened perceptively. Flannery had chosen to make the first move. He, not Alexander, chose the field on which they would fight. Alexander could hardly refuse to dispute the matter. The psychological advantage had passed to Flannery. Alexander realised as much. Scowled bad temperedly. 'If you wish me to state my views regarding recent developments in German society I'll do so directly and without equivocation of any kind. Germany as a nation is reborn. Under National Socialism Germany has experienced a renaissance of both mind and body. God has been good to the people of Germany. He has given us Adolf Hitler as our Fuhrer. Our Leader. No longer will Germany or Germans be humiliated by the traitors who signed the documents of surrender to the allied forces of the last war. Traitors.' Alexander spat rather than spoke the word. 'Traitors who selfishly put their interest before those of the German nation. Traitors of the worst kind aided and abetted by their cohorts the international financiers. The ever perfidious Jews.'

'Perfidious Jews.' Alexander intoned in Latin the phrase as used in the Catholic rites of Good Friday. Timothy, once Catholic, flinched as if struck a blow about the heart realising for the first time the hatred those two words enshrined, marking as they did Jews as Christslayers. To be forever cursed among all men. Now Alexander, whom he loved above all others, had used the term in a loathsome fashion. 'Ah,' exclaimed Flannery triumphantly. 'We have arrived at the nub of the matter. The author of all Germany's illnesses. The Jew. The ever perfidious Jew.' Flannery raised his brandy glass in mock toast. 'Der Fuhrer. Adolf Hitler.' Alexander rose, wrenched the glass from Flannery's hand, smashed it forcefully against the mirror on the wall directly behind Flannery. The glass shattered. Some few shards flew. Timothy recalled seeing Flannery shatter a glass in the same way. Then a splinter had struck Philippa on the forehead. For a fraction of a second it budded like a rose. Quickly became a small red wound. Alexander was uncontainable. 'Yes,' he shouted. 'Adolf Hitler our beloved Fuhrer. Chosen of God.' He snatched a wine glass with a slight residue at the bottom. Held it aloft. 'Adolf Hitler.' He drained the glass. Replaced it on the table. In one clean sweep of his outstretched hand he swept the tableware off the table onto the floor. It clattered loudly.

But for heavy breathing, the room was silent. In the distance they heard the report of a shotgun. A poacher? An accidental discharge? He, Timothy felt aroused as never before. Sexually aroused to a pitch which demanded the spillage of seed. Lust, Timothy, thought. Blood lust. He, Timothy, who hated all violence and the shedding of blood. Was aroused. Fiercely. Pleasantly. Coupled with an intense desire to see, smell, possibly taste blood. Human blood. He, Timothy who once ... oh long ago it seemed, used to pray for all mankind and atoned for its sins, now wished to taste blood. See someone brought bloodily low. He thought of Veronica. 'I'm so terribly sorry. I thought perhaps you had difficulty in sleeping and thought to give you some fruits. Please continue with your devotions.' Veronica withdrew flushing with embarrassment having no doubt seen the lighted candles. The vase of flowers. The picture of Christ exposing His most wounded heart. And on the bedside table him, Timothy's copy of 'The Imitation of Christ' by Thomas A. Kempis from which he read nightly. His belief had been strong. His devotion most sincere yet now he, Timothy told himself. 'I no longer believe all that I then believed.' He knew now what he had known or more likely would not admit to himself that when Veronica had intruded while he was at prayer in the early hours of the morning he had experienced a sense of pride. He was elated because he realised Veronica would possibly think more highly of him for such unadmitted fidelity. Devotion. He had gloated on the incident like a hideous tick abloating on the blood from the underbody of the host animal. For so it had proved. Veronica became less guarded. Word unspoken had accepted him to a degree he would not have thought possible.

Now sexually aroused, rigid with tension he awaited a coming brawl to satisfy his desire to see blood spilled. He thought of excusing himself. Of leaving if he was not excused. Wait, an inner voice said. The best is yet to come. Be patient. Wait. Your desire will be fulfilled. He remained. Not without a sense of ignominy.

Flannery spoke quietly as if to an erring child. 'Do sit down Alexander. You look and sound utterly ridiculous.' Alexander nodded his head. Compiled. Sat down burying his head in his hands. 'Yes you're perfectly right. I'm behaving very stupidly and offensively. I ask you both for your forgiveness.' Flannery: shortly 'Granted'. Unsure that he should speak, he, Timothy remained silent. Alexander breathed through his nose like a runner preparing for a great spurt forward ... that extra endeavour. He grew noticeably calmer. Breathing under imposed control, he spoke with sharp precision.

'The state is analogous to a motor car. It's prime function to transport it's driver and passengers from one point to another at a reasonable speed and in relative safety.

Apart from oil and petroleum, all it requires is a driver capable of taking control. Should that person prove unsuitable or incapable then all who travel in her are endangered. The motorcar being the invention of humans and therefore imperfect, will not always function as smoothly as one might hope. Parts or components can be expected to wear out, to break down. Which is exactly what happened to Chugg. There are however other factors to be considered. The motorcar will not run as efficiently or as smoothly on inferior oil or petroleum — which frequently happens — the engine may choke-up entirely and be rendered useless. Which brings us to the Jews and a few other undesirables. The Jew. The silt in the petroleum.

'Continue Alexander. I've yielded the floor to you. I won't interrupt.'

Timothy sat still. Aware of an ever increasing air of unreality.

Alexander took a deep breath. 'The Jew. Let me tell you a few things, Flannery my friend. Somethings I know to be absolutely correct because I've seen them for myself. Others I know to be true because my source of information, I know, is unimpeachable. I've spoken to friends of my fathers. Comrade-in-arms of his who did not perish in the war or its aftermath. Whatever prejudice you have against them as Germans against whom you yourself have fought, you will I know accept my word that these are honourable men who would no more lie than they would dishonour themselves in battle or in the conduct of their affairs. They all had stories to tell. All different of course as their experiences were different. But all stated without hesitation that they, the men in the front line defending the German soil were betrayed. Stabbed in the back not by any rabble, not by hoards of Socialists or Communists but by respected men who essentially held the real power in Germany as elsewhere. The financiers most of whom were Jewish or had connection with Jews. They are the ones who stabbed the fighting men in the back. They are the ones who brought down the German Reich. Brought enemy soldiers into whole areas of Germany and allowed the occupying troops run rough-shod over the Germans of those regions. These people, Jew and non-Jew alike transferred vital funds abroad, deposited huge hoards of gold they had amassed through their control of the armaments factories and more vitally the food supply. They bled Germany and the Germans for all they could get. My friend, few Jews suffered as a result of Germany's defeat. They didn't suffer. No. They prospered. Like scavenging rats of the vilest kind they fed on the bodies of the dead. Having exhausted the bodies of the dead they turned to feast on the bodies of the living. I speak from experience. A family in Berlin in the district where we live were so debilitated by lack of food they couldn't seek help. They became weak. Too weak to shout for help. There were set upon by rats which began to devour them even before they were dead. Their cries were heard. The people had been already half-eaten. Think of it. In the very capital of Germany.

And Germany is above all a proud nation. A family of four children and a father and mother were eaten alive by rats. All over Germany people, men, women and children died of hunger or froze to death in the back streets and alleys of the cities. Not just from hunger and cold. Alcoholic poisoning. Suicides without number. My friend the lists are endless. The statistics are there. Compiled not by the National Socialists but by civil servants of the old regime who did their duty in a thorough manner and kept impartial records as they were by Law required to do. These people I emphasise strongly were not National Socialists. They were and are, men of impeccable background. Men of the utmost integrity. And Flannery, Flannery there are very few Jews on the list of those who perished. That fact is immediately obvious even to the most prejudiced of people. There are few Rosenthalls, Goldbergs, Steins, on those lists. Do you know what was the cheapest commodity in Germany following the collapse of the Reich? Simple my friend. Germans. Men, women and children of both sexes all available to those with American dollars or British Pounds sterling. You could buy virtually any German for a few worthless marks. For any purpose whatever. Brothels everywhere. Young girls and boys. Of seven and eight. All available to satisfy the lust of those paid for their services. There were no Jewish children available. No Jewish women in those brothels. Those compelled to sell their bodies to remain alive were German. German children and young women and yes, even young German boys and men sold themselves in a desperate effort to stave off starvation. Parents sold their children. Men their wives. Splendid young children, splendid young women and men prostituted themselves while the country of their birth lay beneath the booted feet of enemy soldiers and the finances of their country lay in the hand of Jewish financiers. You think perhaps I lie? How often have I lied to you, Flannery ... to Timothy ... to Veronica ... to Philippa ...? From your experience of me have I proved in any way untruthful? The evidence is there, Flannery. Go and examine if you wish to argue the morality of the Jewish question. You are honour bound to examine both sides of the question. You are morally bound to weigh the evidence of each side. Both sides, Flannery. Not just the merits of one side based on ignorance and distorted reports.' Alexander's voice was fierce. 'Now, Flannery, speak to me in defence of the Jews. Speak Flannery.'

Flannery shrugged his shoulders. 'I must admit I know only what is reported in the newspapers, and I don't pay those reports the attention I should perhaps pay them. I also admit I don't lie awake from sleep troubled by the so-called Jewish question but then neither do I wake from sleep troubled by the Moslem or Catholic or Hindu questions. I'd be lying if I were to admit that I am unduly worried about anyone other than myself. Mankind has not endeared itself to me. Nor have I endeared myself to mankind. So I can't pretend to any great concern. But I do think your argument is a bit simplistic .... If I may say so.'

Alexander moved in for the kill .... 'You know nothing by your own admission but what you learn from newspaper reports to which you don't pay a great deal of attention but you feel perfectly free to sit in judgement on the entire German nation because I happen to be German and you happen to dislike me. You must forgive me but I find that rather typically Irish if I may say so. But in all honesty the French and the British and the Americans and every other nation feels free to wax moral on the Jewish question at the expense of Germany and the Germans.' Alexander paused. Took a deep breath. Snorted. 'Hasn't it occurred to you that the English possessing as they do a vast Empire which covers the greater part of the globe has not thought fit to grant some unoccupied territory in a remote but fertile part of their Empire to the Jews? Think how simple it all is. If the other world powers wish to help the Jews of Germany why don't they resettle them in their countries? Well, Flannery, speak to me about the Jews of Germany. I assume you want to defend them?

Flannery shrugged his shoulders. 'I am hardly the one to speak. As I have said I knew very little about the matter.' Alexander was weeping. Breathing heavily. With difficulty. He drank what must have been cold coffee. Mopped his brow. Rose as if to leave his chair. Stretched forward and struck Flannery a stunning blow in the face. 'You filthy pervert. You pervert innocent children yet feel free to insult my country. My father. My blood.' He began to take off his jacket .... His necktie. Undid the jewelled links at the cuffs of his shirt, took off his collar, as if he were a priest disrobing after a High Mass of striking splendour. He looked steadily at Flannery lying back in his chair. 'We can make this a matter of death if you so like. Or shall we settle for an Irish brawl?' Flannery rose. 'An Irish brawl will suffice for the offence committed. I had thought to please your mother. Not to dishonour your father. I say this not in mitigation but as an explanation to which I think you are entitled.' Flannery removed his evening jacket. Undid his collar and tie. 'My shirt I'll remove in the backyard. I presume the fight will be in one of the outyards. To fight just outside might disturb Bridget.' Alexander nodded assent. Led the way from the room. Flannery followed, pale but determined. Timothy made no effort to follow. How, he thought ... can one love one so loathsome. He loved Alexander greatly. Perhaps beyond the point where love is lost. The loved one is a blinding rather than an illuminating light .... Yes ... he, Timothy, thought: I love him deeply but I do not like him. How could that be possible? This he thought is the hard edge of love. The point where love pierces. He was pierced. Transfixed by, love. An overwhelming sense of sorrow. Against the thuds of feet on the bare board of the main staircase, he heard a clock strike. What hour? he thought. The cursed hour of midnight when the sick yield up their lives, gratefully, in gently submission. The hour when those sick in mind feel most afflicted. Cry from the depths of their despair. Inanely he found himself praying. 'Have mercy on us O God. According to Thy great mercy.' Alexander shouting 'Come Timothy. Come and see how a German protects his honour.' He rose slowly and slowly followed Flannery and Alexander into a far yard.

~

Flannery lay on the partially grass-covered yard. The tilly lamp Bannion had placed on one of the surrounding walls at Alexander's request, or was it at Alexander's command? Hissed steadily. Its distinctly blue light lending a pale bloom to the entire scene. Nora stood by the gateway to the yard. She could not move though she wanted to. Her eyes were very full and white. Wide with horror. Disgust. Bannion stood nearby taking occasional puffs from a cigarette stub cupped carefully in his right hand. He was quite impassive. Taking a pull on the steadily diminishing cigarette, he inhaled deeply. Flicked the cigarette from his darkly stained hand. Turning abruptly left the yard. Later he would leave the house to visit his lady love of the moment. Bannion the great progenitor as Veronica tartly called him. The great broadcaster of seed. Little of which fell by the wayside. None of which was ever strangled by cockle. Bannion the great begetter. How, he Timothy wondered, how do they believe his lies? Blatant, patent lies? He, Timothy experienced sexual jealously. Inadequacy. Sheer envy overcame him. Bannion had glanced steadily at him, Timothy, before leaving the yard. He had avoided what he thought of as Bannion's accusing stare, could not meet his eyes. Why not? He, Timothy, had not offended. Yet from that glance he assumed that Bannion considered that Timothy had fallen unforgivably. Why should Bannion who fell so often. Always obtained forgiveness. Pass so harsh a judgement? It hurt him, Timothy, to have Bannion behave in such a manner.

At the pump in the corner of the yard which was on a low concrete surround with three shallow steps leading to the platform into which the pump was set, Alexander stood. A lean, lithe figure. He splashed the water he pumped all over his body with zest. He was feeling thoroughly pleased with himself. Flannery moaned. Moved. No one approached to help him. Nora and Timothy were simply incapable of movement. Timothy was appalled. Alexander had thrashed Flannery. Flannery had struck a few good blows but they had little effect on Alexander's hard, lean body. Alexander for his part had fought with an air of clinical detachment as if Flannery was nothing but a punchbag and he Alexander simply exercising himself. Inexpertly Flannery made to protect whatever part of his body which had been struck. No sooner had he done so than Alexander struck a blow on some other part of Flannery's body. Flannery moved to protect his chest. Alexander struck him in the face. Flannery moved to protect his face. Alexander struck a body blow. Flannery had virtually been pulped in a short while. Three times he had been beaten to the ground. Twice he refused to concede defeat, his face a mass of blood. The third time, struck a particularly hard blow. He had remained still. Unable to rise. He conceded. Alexander silently, turned away.

Alexander dressed carefully. Approached Nora. Speaking softly requested a basin of tepid water. A towel. A sponge. Some iodine. A facecloth. Some whiskey. Nora hurried to do as told. Alexander stood hands on hips, legs well splayed apart. The undoubted victor. Flannery at his feet. The undoubted vanquished. Alexander's face showed no glee. His eyes were not those of one who had just fought and won a fight. If anything they showed a certain sadness. Timothy remained at the outer periphery of light. He remembered Flannery. Speaking to him at the dinner table not long ago. In a civil manner, his voice not without a certain respect. 'That was a damned decent thing to do. It took courage.' Flannery had said, when Timothy had declared his fear of drink and women and of life generally. He, had thought, had hoped, it had meant the beginning of, not a friendship, they were too far apart for that ... but of a less hostile relationship. He hardened. His instinct was to hurry forward. Help as best he could ... but Flannery, Flannery he knew would never forgive such behaviour at such a time. If hatred it had to be, then hatred it would be. That, he, Timothy thought, is a denial of one of the most basic of Christian principles. A principle he had always sought to keep one way or the other. Now he consciously rejected the principle and with it the last remnants of his Catholic beliefs. He, Timothy, found himself thinking ... all is quiet .... No cock crows at all.

Suddenly he was aware of stealthy movement behind him. Out of the darkness two figures had come close to him. Had done so some time ago. Had seen everything. A large figure. A man. A very big man. A small figure. That of a child. Instinctively he realised it was Buck Oates, the most detested of what Veronica referred to as Flannery's menagerie. A towering figure, he stood, feet apart, effectively concealed by the darkness. Oates spoke hoarsely to him, Timothy. 'Flannery put up a good fight. Aye. A good fight to any man's reckoning. No one can deny that. But Flannery should have been cute enough not to have tackled with your man there in the first place.' Oates moved into the full light of the Tilly lamp. He was tall, at least six foot six. Broad shouldered. With a tight compact body which suggested great strength. He was known to be fearless. A man who liked a fight. Who fought dirty. He had once killed a man in a brawl. He stood trial for manslaughter. Had been acquitted on a legal technicality. He had however served several prison sentences, one of three years duration. Only the drunk or very foolish became involved in Oates or his affairs. The figure with him was that of a small barefooted tinker girl aged perhaps twelve. He, Timothy could not distinguish any of her features. She remained beyond the light of the Tilly lamp. He thought of her as having a proud bearing.

Oates approached Alexander, his face cleft in a broad friendly grin which one knew instinctively to be far from friendly. 'A great fight, Master. A great fight altogether. The best I've seen for many a long year. You were great, Master. Great entirely.' Oates took a hipflask from the back pocket of his jacket. Uncorked it. Took a long swig. 'Oh God. Great stuff ... great stuff.' He offered the flask to Alexander who contemptuously refused. 'Don't say a fine fellow the likes of you doesn't take a swig.' Oates succeeded in asking the question which seemed civil enough as offensively as possible. Alexander shook his head. Turned aside. Nora came through the yard carefully carrying a small basin of water. A white towel draped over one arm. Tucked under her right arm a bottle of whiskey. Oates took the bottle from her. Uncorked it and took a long hard drink. Alexander kneeled. Began to wipe Flannery's bloodied face with a cloth dipped in water. He did so with great attention. Gentleness. 'Can I lend a hand, Master,' Oates asked. 'I know a thing or two about this sort of thing.'

Alexander spoke coldly as possibly. 'With us it is a matter of honour to attend to the fallen.'

Oates smiled. 'Is that so Master? Well this is Ireland and here a whipped man is taken care of by his friends. Are you a friend of Flannery's, Master?' Alexander stared at Oates. Oates stared at him. Oates was smiling broadly in what is often described as devilish good humour. The sly weapon of the habitual betrayer, Oates' eyes however were not smiling. He, Alexander, shrugged his shoulders. 'It's a matter of indifference to me what you do in Ireland. I only sought to respect our German code.' Swiftly Alexander turned. Strode from the yard.

Frightened. Nora tried to follow. Oates however called her. 'Like the good girl that you are Nora go and bring another bottle of whiskey. Two if you can lay hands on them. While you're at it bring me a fine leg of beef, red raw and running.' Nora tried to refuse. She stood still, her mouth agape as she tried to breathe the moist night air. Oates spoke sharply to her. 'Go girl and do what I say at once.' Nora fled as quickly as she could. He, Timothy wondered at Nora's fear. Obviously she was very afraid of Oates. By nature spirited and defensive, her acquiescence to Oates' order surprised him. Nora must have good cause for fear. Otherwise she would hardly hasten to obey. The Tilly lamp hissed softly. Moths gathered about it seeking to gain the flame. Oates belched loudly once or twice. patted his fat protruding belly with satisfaction and wiped his lips with the sleeve of his coat. 'Here young fellow. Take this and mind you don't drop it.' He handed the bottle of whiskey to Timothy. Oates stooped. Bundled up Flannery who moaned softly. Carrying Flannery in his arms with perfect ease, Oates turned towards Flannery's place calling back to Timothy.

'Come on man. Follow me.' Timothy obeyed reluctantly. The young girl he could now see better than before, smiled. She had a very pale face. Large dark eyes. A small mouth. She smiled with madonna-like simplicity. Innocence personified. The dreadful thought crossed Timothy's mind. 'She is far from being innocent. She has been corrupted beyond redemption.' Even as Timothy thought so, he knew it to be so. Oates had been the destroyer. To some extent, Flannery. How or why he couldn't even imagine. Carrying the bottle, Timothy followed Oates. The girl in turn followed him. She moved gently in her bare-feet making no sound whatever. In a way Timothy could not express, he feared her. Oates passed through the mass of filth which was Flannery's kitchen. Went upstairs. Laid Flannery on his small iron cot in his bedroom which was perfectly clean. Timothy had followed for no good reason. He stood watching, his arms crossed. One hand gripping tightly the stem of the whiskey bottle. Oates stripped Flannery with little ceremony. From time to time Flannery gained consciousness. Moaned. Swore broadly. Lapsed back again into unconsciousness ....

Oates turned furiously towards him, Timothy, who feared he was about to be struck. 'Go down you shooneen and boil a pot of water. Make yourself useful. Leave that bloody bottle there before you go.' Timothy did as ordered. The young girl was sitting in a chair by the kitchen table. She glanced slyly at him clutching something tightly in her hand. She smiled a smile he found disturbing. There was something mean, very cunning in it. It was totally at odds with her youthfulness. Beauty. She was, he realised very beautiful. Not in the conventional manner. Her cheek bones were high. Prominent. Her hair was straight. Long, hanging behind from her head where it was held by clasps, to waist level. Her eyes were large, lovely. Set deeply in the face. Her mouth was small. Her lips rather thin. Her one bad feature. She was, Timothy realised, devious and sly, capable of calculated destruction. She would, he thought, inflict great pain without being unduly troubled. She might possibly relish doing so. He resented having to boil a kettle of water at Oates' instruction rather like a servant while she, the young girl, sat her bare feet swinging an inch or two above the flagged floor of the kitchen, her right hand grasping something which had appealed to her. Which plainly she had stolen. Her face was solemn. Deceptively innocent. The kettle boiled slowly. He waited impatiently, anxious only to escape. Oates shouted down demanding the water. He shouted back telling him to wait until the kettle boiled. When it had done so. He poured some into a basin. Brought it up to Oates in Flannery's room. Oates tested it with his finger. It was scalding hot. Oates swore loudly. 'God damn you to hell man. Why didn't you tell me it was hot?' Oates grabbed the whiskey bottle. Uncorked it, took a long drink then poured what remained into the basin. 'A cloth, man. I need a cloth.' In a chest of drawers Timothy found some white linen handkerchiefs which smelled strongly of mint. Bridget attentive as always had undoubtedly placed some leaves among the clean linen. Timothy brought two handkerchiefs to Oates who smelt them suspiciously like a mongrel smelling suspect food. He immersed the handkerchiefs in the water. With what appeared as infinite gentleness for so big a man he began to swab Flannery's bruised and bloody face. Flannery moaned. Swore once or twice. Oates spoke to him as one might to a sick child. 'Ah Flannery you got the trouncing of your life. There was a time there and I thought he was going to beat you to death. He was too young. Too strong. You should have been aware of that. I'm surprised. A cute boyo like you.' Flannery moaned, whimpered like a mongrel in uneasy sleep. 'God he beat you. By the living Jesus he did.' Flannery's eyes flickered. He opened his eyes. Tried to rise. Failed to do so. Fell back to the bed mutteringly fiercely. Oates: 'Ah you're not fit to put a foot under you, Flannery. And you won't for many a day. But I'll look after you and have you fighting fit once more.' Oates spoke with a degree of sincerity and attachment, Timothy found amazing. Flannery nodded his head slightly. Oates helped him take a drink of whiskey from the bottle. Flannery gasped. Then spoke. Very distinctly. 'Get that little bastard out of here.' Timothy froze. Left the room. Joined the girl down in the kitchen. She was feeding the fire some kindling. There was a furtive tapping on the window pane. He went outside to see who it was. Not without fear. It was Nora with some bandages. Another bottle of whiskey. What appeared like a leg of meat. Oates appeared behind them in the doorway. 'Who is it?' he demanded. Then recognised Nora. 'Ah it's yourself, girl, and a very good girl you are. No two ways about it.' Oates took the bottle of whiskey Nora had brought, scrutinised the meat. He approved begrudgingly. 'T'isn't the best but then t'isn't the worst. T'will do.' Oates reached inside to a pocket in his waistcoat. Took out a silver coin which he pressed upon Nora who taking it fled into the darkness. Oates laughed loudly. Called after her. 'I'll straddle you yet you virgin bitch.' He clapped a thigh with the broad of his hand. 'Virgin how are you,' he said. 'I'd sooner search for a silver apple. I'd have a better chance of finding it.' Oates took the meat side. Stuck it through a hook over the open fire. Left it to cook. 'Here you,' he said to him Timothy. 'Keep your eye on that and don't let it burn.' Timothy refused to move. Refused to take a seat by the fire and watch the meat. Oates gazed at him in amazement. 'Are you defying me, you shooneen.' Timothy turned. Left the house. 'Run maneen ... run. The banshee is about tonight.' Oates roared with laughter. The girl laughed also, a high laugh. Timothy hurried. Ran to the house. Flushed he stopped to draw breath. Why had he run, he asked himself. Because he told himself he feared a twelve year old with all the apparent grace and presence of a madonna.

Lights blazed in the house. Yet the house was quiet. As if deserted. Electric light shone in the kitchen. A few rooms upstairs. Oil lamps burned in the passage way. In the servants quarters high up in the house. He made some tea in the kitchen then moved quietly to his room. The lamp on the main staircase was burning brightly, its wick well trimmed. The flame perfectly straight. He changed into his pyjamas. In bed, he reflected briefly. Why is the house so quiet? Lapsed gratefully into deep sleep. Sometime during the night he dreamed of a horse he could see pounding the gravelled area directly in front of the house. It churned up the small loose stones, stones lower down which received no direct sunlight. Were therefore slightly grey and damp. It snorted in outrage. Whinnying loudly leaped upwards. Charged swiftly through the night of stars.

To his dismay he woke late. The kitchen was deserted. No effort had been made to provide breakfast. He thought ill-temperedly. 'I'll have to prepare my own.' Nora entered weeping into a small white handkerchief. Bridget, she told him had died during the night. In her sleep. Timothy's heart missed a beat. He felt weakened. Deeply shocked. Unaware of what he was doing he took a towel from the linen cupboard. Left for the river. Its waters were still. Crystal clear. He refused to consider Bridget's death. Instead he concentrated on his every move paying great care to everything about him. The fields in the dispersing morning mist. The high rushes. Reeds. Thistles. Some draped with dew studded cobwebs. He heard the bell of Tibraddenstown Catholic church ring for morning mass. The bells had for him all the imagined sweetness, clarity, of some great cathedral's bells. Morning was in his nostrils. A pleasant compound of freshwater, trod upon grass, faintly, farmyard smells. He undressed. Dived cleanly into the river. He shuddered pleasantly at the stinging cold. He had failed to notice the year was so advanced. He sported about now capable of forgetting how sharp and biting the water was. Alexander appeared on the riverbank. He called out a greeting. Timothy refused to reply. Alexander stripped, stood poised on the bank a figure of astonishing beauty. Timothy, gasped. Floundered a little as Alexander dived. They swam about in perfect unison. Executed a series of complicated movements. As though trained to do so ... cleaving the fresh waters cleanly .... Then, spent, they climbed onto the river bank. They dressed in silence. As they dressed, Timothy felt emotion assert itself. Waves of desolation swept over him as he realised that Bridget was no longer alive. Had ceased to breathe. Would speak nor move no more. In a short time he was weeping freely. Half-dressed he fell to his knees abandoning himself to his grief. Alexander continued to dress. Having done so he stood for some time watching the figure at his feet. Silently withdrew. Bridget: 'My mother was born fresh out of a ditch near Castlebar in the county Mayo. When she was dying, she said. 'Someone is making beautiful music.' Wasn't that the strange thing to say. A beautiful strange thing to say and she only an ignorant woman?' What music, he Timothy reflected. What music had his beautiful Bridget heard as she died while sleeping peacefully. He remained on the riverbank for a considerable time. Grieved bitterly, unseen.

Later in the day Elizabetha and Alexander left to spend some weeks touring the country. They went first to the southwest of Kerry. Later they would travel up the western coastline and continued to follow the coast in as much. Timothy experienced little regret at Alexander's departure. He was far too overcome by Bridget's death. Veronica mourned deeply but calmly. All Farrighy mourned Bridget's passing. Many hundreds attended her funeral Mass. Later her burial at Ratheoin where the Phipps had ancient right of burial in the ruins of the Abbey. Veronica was moved by so large an attendance. Their presence comforted her. Their prayers sustained her. How old and tired. How old and tired and defeated she had become, he thought as he watched her swathed in black by the neatly excavated grave. One more such blow as she had sustained at the death of Bridget might bring her low. Never to rise again. What then? He thought. What then?

Later he, Timothy, considered Bridget. His 'Mary of the Gaels'. She did little that was wrong. Much that was good. He believed that somehow goodness itself had been diminished by her death.

PART FIVE

'Do tell Timothy my very dear friend. Does not our saintly
Alexander never cast a lustful eye at anything which arouses
his baser appetites? Male? Female? Neuter? Or is he one of
those tiresome fellows who as they say in the bible 'lie with
animals? Surely not? Surely he is like us all, subject to the
assertions of the flesh however fleetingly is he not when all is
said and done simply spittle and dust as we all are?' Bobo eyes
agleam like a sly animal about to kill, slyly touched Timothy
on the bare forearm. Timothy winced unintentionally. Bobo
noticed immediately. Stiffened. Bared his teeth in hatred. Hid
his hatred. Smiled beautifully. 'Surely his blood is aroused
from time to time. Surely he feels the passion of the erect penis,
the tight scrotum? He is hardly fated for a life of abstinence. I
mean that would be such a waste. Do tell, dear Timothy. Oh
dear Timothy, do tell.' Timothy stared at Bobo in ill-concealed
revulsion. Stared at him steadily. 'There is nothing to tell,' he
said tightly. 'I know nothing about Alexander's private affairs.'
Bobo coughed lightly in a balled handkerchief which was
heavily scented. 'So then dear Timothy he does not lie with
you, however much you would like him to?' Bobo tittered.
Meanly. Then Timothy struck out at the bare-toothed Bobo,
striking him solidly on the nose. Skipper leaped to his feet. In
a second he had Timothy by the throat ... flat against the wall.
Was about to strike. Flannery entered with a few heads of
lettuce from the garden. Some shallots. 'Call off your bully

boy, Bobo.' 'Call him off instantly or I'll see he is taken care of once and for all.' Bobo coloured ... not white not black ... not red. But yellow. The sickening yellow of someone just recently dead. He stuttered. Spoke through the crimson stained handkerchief.

'Ah I see you refer to your friend Oates .... Your friend or perhaps I should say your ....'

'I should bloody well say nothing if I were you Bobo. You may not like the consequences.'

Bobo nodded at Skipper who released Timothy. Skipper stared at him smiling enigmatically. Timothy flushed. Looked away. Disgusted with himself. While pinning him to the wall Skipper had wedged his thigh between Timothy's to render him incapable of using his feet in self defence. Skipper had done so gently not roughly. Though his look was one of outrage his eyes were appealing, almost beseeching. Skipper's breath was fresh. Apple-fresh. Not at all foul as Timothy expected it would be. Briefly as Skipper held him fast to the wall, Timothy had wished that Skipper would kiss him with all the ravenous lust he had kissed the young lad in Flannery's place while, hidden by the bushes, Timothy watched. Love him as he had loved that callow fellow and had then soundly beaten. Timothy had realised all this in a moment. In a rare insight his mind revealed what had hitherto lay hidden in the depths of his unconsciousness. Skipper realised as much. Smiled. Shrugged his shoulders dismissively. Strode to the fire. Kicked the embers lying there with the tip of a calfskin boot.

'When the hell do we get to hell out of this kiphouse,' he demanded of Bobo rather than simply asking. 'In time Skip, in time, we must be above all patient. Relief will come.' 'It fucking well better,' Skipper snarled staring at Bobo with hatred. 'It'll come Skipper. Be patient. It'll come. Every dog had his day,' he said, turning to him Timothy. 'Timothy has had his. I shan't forget lightly.' Flannery snatched the handkerchief from Bobo's hand. 'For shit sake stop acting the martyr. It's only bloody blood. Have you never bled before.' Flannery washed the handkerchief under the kitchen tap.

Drenched. Squeezed it roughly. Shook it out. Held it to Bobo's nose and mouth. 'Don't worry,' he said savagely. 'You won't die. At least not yet.' Bobo winced at the reference to death. Timothy and Skipper saw clearly that Flannery relished Bobo's humiliation. 'So kind, Flannery,' Bobo squeaked. 'So very kind, Flannery, and Timothy, dear Timothy, do forgive me. It was insensitive of me to press you on matters of the heart. Thoughtless. Even cruel. Yes. Thoughtless and cruel of me.' Bobo raised a plump hand to his bloated lips. Kissed his finger tips then gently touched him, Timothy, on the right cheek. 'There I grant you absolution in this my kiss of peace. As The Master saith. My peace I give unto you. My peace I leave unto you. Am I forgiven dear Timothy? Do please say I am.' Bobo beamed benignly but hatred lurked in his eyes. Timothy nodded assent. It was, Timothy realised a stupid charade, one played with Bobo and which Bobo insisted others play with him. He distinctly lacked an air of reality. His emotions were subject to rapid and radical change veering from almost divine sense of pity to a demonic hatred coupled to a desire to crush all who angered him. Bobo was, Timothy realised, a child-man of stunted emotional and arrested sexual development. Would most likely, as was the case with all aberrants, destroy himself. He would pull the pillars of the temple down about himself and on the heads of those who happened to be with him at that given moment.

Bobo examined his handkerchief. 'There. The blood has stopped flowing. It's past. It's done. All is forgiven.' He beamed again. Everyone recognised the utter falsity of his words. Laying a hand on Timothy's shoulder he drew him aside. 'I do adore your friend Alexander. He is beautiful in every respect. Not classically beautiful in the ancient Roman or Greek way. Baroque rather than Renaissance. When he smiles he is like Adonis come again. When he is sad his eyes are sadder than those of Saint John of the Cross, and Timothy, dear Timothy the eyes of Saint John of the Cross are harrowingly beautiful. I think my own eyes sometimes reflect such sad beauty. Don't you think so dear Timothy. Don't you think so?'

He, Timothy did not think so. Refrained from saying so. Bobo touched him lightly on the arm. Tittered like a scullery maid being pinched on the arse by the stableboy. 'How shall I be expected to keep my hands off him I simply can't imagine.' Bobo giggled, touched Timothy on the arm again with his very small stubby fingers which reminded Timothy of wriggling white worms. His fingers for once were not adorned with rings. One could see on the fingers bands of red flesh where tight rings had once been. He was in a suit of pearl-grey. His tiny feet, small even for a small person, were wedged into slipper-like shoes. On each shoe was a bright silver buckle in the shape of a rose and leaves. He wore a purple cravat. About him hung a miasma of delicate perfume. It was not confined to any particular part of his body. Ears, throat, the wrists. When he moved the sweet scent moved with him.

Bobo tittered again. Squealing in delight. 'Oh what a sense of the tactile I have, Timothy. When I'm confronted by beauty, be it physical or material, I simply must touch it. I simply have to communicate with the person portrayed or sculpted and at the same time be one with the divine creature who created such beauty. Now I must leave you, dear Timothy. I have to go into the garden and compose myself for an introduction to your friend. My blood is simply racing through my veins. My heart is simply pulsating at an astonishing rate. I fear I might well die before we meet.' Bobo touched Timothy on the arm in farewell. Languidly drifted from the kitchen to the garden in all it's riotous splendour. He, Timothy, was grateful.

Flannery sat at the table eating a thick wedge of bread heavily buttered. Nearby stood a mug of tea. Everywhere lay empty champagne bottles together with bottles which had once contained rare port and brandy. Some liqueur bottles of a very fine quality lay everywhere. Bobo, The Lord Trawann, had been with Flannery for ten days. Veronica was indisposed, unable to investigate Flannery's place and rout Bobo whom she hated as heartily as Bobo hated her. Her indisposition was due largely to fatigue. The constant worry about Philippa's health. She had exerted herself too much. Had been compelled to take to her bed. Rest for some time. Elizabetha cared for her. Elizabetha also visited Philippa with Alexander as her companion. Timothy had been invited to accompany them. Refused. Faced with the fact that he had no great liking for Philippa. Did not wish to visit her. Bobo had taken advantage of Veronica's absence, chirping merrily. 'While the cat's away the mice can play.' He announced to all that he intended to indulge himself beyond his wildest dreams. Indulge in a bacchanalia which would be all the sweeter by the nearby presence of Veronica reduced to a state of impotent rage.

He and Skipper ensconced themselves in one of the bedrooms of Flannery's place. If Bobo were to be believed Bobo's relationship with Skipper was what Bobo termed 'spiritual' rather than carnal. Sacred rather than profane. Skipper, a lout of Celtic good-looks, was dark-headed. Had dark eyes. Was physically impressive. Exuded an air of masculinity which wasn't quite as convincing as it might be. Oddly other men sensed as much immediately upon meeting him. The result was usually a fist fight from which Skipper's opponents were the losers. Skipper left their faces a mass of bleeding flesh. Once aroused he was vicious. Those who tangled with him never did so again. Nor did any of their acquaintances. He had been a Guardsman but had been drummed out for conduct unbecoming. Had spent some years at sea as an Able Bodied Seaman. Dressed now in vastly expensive clothes he delightedly watched Bobo debauch himself without restraint. Great quantities of the most expensive foods, meats, cheeses and drinks were delivered to Flannery's place. Oates appeared, hauling with him some tinker children. Was especially made welcome by Flannery. Skipper procured some youths who were prepared to indulge Bobo's particular sexual preference.

Timothy kept clear of Flannery's place. Alexander was not with him. Alexander had undertaken a cycling tour of the south east coast. Timothy had not been asked to accompany Alexander, much to his dismay. With Veronica bedridden there was little to keep him busy. Bannion rarely spoke to him. Never invited him to accompany him into town or to swim at the weir at Tibraddenstown. Timothy fretted in the days of sunshine. The short nights when it was hot. Oppressive. They already had two storms of astounding ferocity which strangely excited Timothy. He was quite without fear. Liked to stand in the drenching downpour. Watch. As lightening seared jaggedly through the charged skies above. There was an element of the defiance in what he did. It was as though he was defying a God he, Timothy no longer believed in to strike him dead in vengeance.

He refused Bobo's kind invitation to swim with them in the river. Flannery who bloated easily in excess, waxed all the more destructive and venomous. Timothy had no wish to be with him nor did he wish to be with Skipper who would also be there. The sound of harsh brutal laughter had continued unabated. Then to everyone's astonishment when carousing was at its height, Veronica appeared with a shotgun which she levelled at Bobo as if aiming for a point on the forehead just above the bridge of his nose. Bobo screamed in terror. Ran into Flannery's place. Upstairs to the bedroom. Hid there under the bed until as dawn lightly infiltrated the room he calmed down. Allowed himself to be pulled from his hiding place. He heard Veronica's ultimatum to quit the place within twelve hours or be shot to blazes. Screaming loudly he threw every bit of clothing and what belongings were his into suitcases. Had Skipper pile them onto Flannery's Ford. Now heavily laden the cars stood prepared. Bobo had somewhat calmed down though he kept one eye open for the possible dreadful approach of Veronica. Timothy rarely envied anyone their possessions but he envied Bobo's glorious Rolls Royce. Its dark green body with wickerwork incorporated into the back carriage was to him astonishingly sleek. Lovely. Its interior was lined with pale green satin or silk. Now slightly fading. The leatherwork was also in green. Though it might well be described as excessive, Timothy found it magnificent. Behind stood the battered crock which was Flannery's own car piled high with suitcases of all kinds and sizes. It looked like the baggage car of motorised caravan about to cross the Ghobi desert. Alexander's small suitcase with a few necessities was piled upon the car as was his, Timothy's. Bobo had extended to them all an invitation to visit Castle Trawann which was situated some miles down the western coast not far from the city. Timothy had consented to go only on the understanding that Alexander would accompany them.

A Gothic pile, it was notorious for it's ugliness. General bad taste. Like Bobo's exalted title it came to him upon the death of a distant relative who had been killed in France during the Great War. The unfortunate young man had, like thousands upon thousands, met his death on Flanders fields. Making possible for a very poor Bobo a life of erratic luxury alternating with periods of destitution when Bobo over-drew on the interest of his invested capital which by the terms of the will he could not touch.

He was impoverished from early youth when his father deserted his mother because he refused to keep her in a manner to which she was accustomed. His mother professed to understand Bobo's 'sensitivity'. His need for the likes of Skipper. She, like Bobo, embarked upon a life of the utmost luxury, travelling widely. Coupling with every young man she could entice into her bed. She had died a very unpleasant death at the hands of one of her lovers in a squalid hotel in one of the squalid quarters of Cairo. Bobo had mourned but not greatly. And not for long. Maintaining that his mother had died in Athens in an aura of sanctity attended by the Daughters of Mary, a religious order of the Greek Orthodox Church. Soon after Bobo met Skipper who had appointed himself Bobo's keeper. For a price. Skipper provided undoubted security. Was utterly discreet when it came to pandering to Bobo's sexual needs.

Alexander arrived full of apologies, dressed simply in shorts, shirt, rope sandals. He had with him a bicycle which he proceeded to tie into position high up on Skipper's already laden motor. He carried a camera along over his shoulder. A knapsack which contained some green apples which he decreed was the only thing to be relied on to quench a summer thirst. Timothy experienced a sharp pang on seeing Alexander bring his bicycle. He would obviously go cycling about the countryside taking what he termed photographs of social significance.

These photographs turned out to be photographs of people living in filthy mudcabins in the mountainous region to the south and photographs of the coastal settlements of fishermen living in extreme squalor. Timothy was angered by these photographs. The photographs of men, women and children in rags. Irrationally he felt angry with Alexander for taking the photographs rather than angered at the appalling conditions many of his fellow countrypeople were compelled to live under. He was particularly angered by snapshots of barefooted boys and girls dressed only in torn rags. By the photographs of women of the western villages carrying great quantities of seaweed on their backs. He expressed his anger to Alexander. Alexander had explained as if to a child. 'These people Timothy live in terrible conditions. That is evil ... a social illness which must be treated as such. Before a cure can be affected one must diagnose the illness and provide those who'll have to cope with the problem with as much evidence as possible.' Timothy wasn't mollified. 'But Timothy, I've taken hundreds of photographs of Ireland during my travels with Elizabetha ... I've taken many on short trips. I've taken them myself. You have seen them. They're perfectly beautiful. Ireland is a very beautiful country. You yourself have admitted those photographs I've taken show Ireland in all it's varying beauty. As for the photographs of social significance, they show a noble people reduced to destitution by history and the force of circumstances. You haven't looked properly at the people in those photographs. They possess a dignity which is immediate and striking. They are above all proud despite their terrible living conditions. I'm shocked that you should feel I wanted to detract from such people by photographing them in less than favourable circumstances. I've come to love Ireland,'

Alexander said. 'I've come to love its people. Surely you accept my word when I tell you I've no ulterior motive in taking these photographs? Conditions will change. These scenes of poverty will fade but I'll have a photograph of them strictly for record purposes. Surely you take my word in this matter?' Injured, Alexander had gazed at him. Timothy nodded his acceptance of Alexander's explanation. Alexander had continued. 'I intend making a collection. I'll enlarge and have them mounted in a special album. It'll be unique. Sometime perhaps I may be able to show it to you.'

Alexander approached Bobo smiling nervously. He could not meet Alexander's eyes directly. His failure to do so saddened Timothy. Bereft of all bombast Bobo extended a pudgy hand to be shook by Alexander. Alexander smiled. 'I've heard a great deal about you. Flannery speaks highly of you. It's a pleasure to meet you at last.' They shook hands warmly. Alexander bowed very slightly. 'Thank you,' said Bobo deeply moved. 'You're as Timothy always said. A very kind person. Very kind.' He turned aside to hide his tears. Flannery roared. 'If this fucking caravan doesn't move soon I'll change my mind and bloody leave you without your luggage. So move. Fucking move. Quickly.' 'Oh,' squealed Bobo. 'We are to be pitied. Flannery is not at all in a good humour. We had better hurry or we'll be left take care of our own belongings.' All piled into Bobo's Rolls Royce. Skipper cranked it. Gently the engine purred into life. They moved off, Tan coming to mark their departure by dancing wildly about the car. Barking loudly. From the front steps a grim faced Veronica watched them depart. By her side Elizabetha waved a white handkerchief in farewell.

Waves broke gently on the shore almost as if apologetic for breaking the silence of night. Moist air tinged with salt circulated everywhere though there wasn't even the slightest breeze. Behind Timothy stood the Gothic mess which was Castle Trawann. Brightly lit it was hideous even in the twilight hour which was kind to most things. He moved towards it. He entered the hall. He was again struck by the all pervasive smell of dampness. Mice. Stale urine. Cooking smells. He wandered about mindlessly from room to room on the ground floor. Everything about the place was cheap. Paint. Wallpaper. Hanging. Cheap, very cheap furniture. The entire place looked as if it had been furnished by foraging about the second-hand furniture stores of the city. He thought 'how suburban' and then realised immediately what he had thought: How suburban ... what have I become. I'm suburban. All my standards and taste are unmistakably suburban.' He thought mockingly 'Do I belong to the gentry? No ... I'm getting above myself.' Trespassing as Flannery would say, over those thin red lines which so strongly delineate not simply the land possessed by one class but also its standards and mores. 'You are,' Timothy thought, 'exceeding yourself. Exceeding yourself to the point of excess.' He, Timothy, did not belong to Alexander's world. He was what Flannery would snarl: one of the lower orders though born into a reasonably respectable family house in a relatively respectable part of Dublin. Nevertheless he was one of that huge mass of humanity which by Veronica's definition were termed 'The Commons'.

He was bored. Unaccountably edgy. The night stillness he thought unusual. Close. Oppressive, it was exceptionally humid. The stay at Castle Trawann had proved of little interest. Bobo had at first taken to his bed where he languished. Skipper fed him fresh fruit, light meals with a deftness which could only come from a great deal of practice. Bobo sneezed a few times. Promptly considered himself in imminent danger of death. He instructed Skipper to summon Father Paul Murray S.J. from the city nearby, whom he liked to think was his confessor. It was Bobo's most earnest wish that he should be received into the Catholic Church, but only under the most dramatic circumstances. He was therefore intent on a death-bed conversion. He wished to die intoning the Nicene Creed. Skipper, long used to Bobo's innumerable death-bed scenes, squeezed the juice of a few lemons, added sugar, hot water and ordered Bobo to drink. Bobo screamed dementedly, accusing Skipper of trying to poison him. Skipper very sensibly pointed out it was not in his better interest to poison Bobo. To do so would mean he would have to stand trial for murder. Bobo's death would in any case deprive him of what was after all a life of relative ease. Skipper bared his teeth. Told Bobo he had five seconds to drink it or he, Skipper would pour the concoction down his throat. Skipper began to count. Bobo moaned pitifully, drank the lemon and water and then pulling the sheets up about his head he informed everyone of his intention of dying quietly.

Flannery painted. Not a great deal. Not very well. Certainly not to his own satisfaction. The luxuries he had anticipated in the quantities he had been used to on previous visits to the castle were not forthcoming. What there was he wolfed hungrily like a starving hound. He paid scant attention to the needs, desires of others. Flannery undertook to cook but to everyone's puzzlement the fare proved less interesting than that provided by a third rate hotel in a small country provincial town. Food was slung as if they were nothing but swine gathered about a trough squealing for food. Bobo dared not look at Flannery. Flannery glared at Bobo as if intent on slaughtering him at some later date. Silence rather than wild abandonment was very much the order of the day. Alexander slung some apples, cheese and hardtack biscuits into his knapsack. Camera slung over his shoulder he cycled out early in the morning on his photographic expedition. Timothy had hoped Alexander would invite him to accompany him on his trips. It would be a simple matter to hire a bicycle for the day from one of the cycle shops in the nearby village. Alexander had not invited him. Timothy was too proud to ask. He accordingly suffered. Bobo and Skipper, and inexplicably Flannery, had left the Castle early in the morning, though whether together or individually, Timothy did not know. Now he found himself lord of the unlordly pile which was the seat of the Lords Trawann. He had chaffed all day. Longed for the early return of Alexander, something he knew to be impossible. Alexander returned each night tired. Worn out from a day's cycling. He ate whatever food was available. Retired early after a swim. Was altogether unaware of what had happened during his absence. Wasn't particularly concerned. Timothy chaffed at being alone. He bitterly regretted having come. The day dragged and he longed to return to Farrighy. He could if necessary hire a bicycle. Cycle back to Farrighy. Have Bannion return the bicycle at his convenience. He did not do so. He remained. Expectant of things to come. Though what they might be he had no way of knowing. There was he knew an element of danger in remaining at the castle. A vague, nebulous sense of danger. He resolved to see it through whatever it might be. It was late. The evening was closing in. There remained an hour or more of daylight. He decided to swim. He fetched a towel from his bedroom and a pair of swimming togs.

The ill-kept garden with its many wild shrubs which bore fragrant flowers when in season was heavily scented with the smell of scented blossoms he failed to recognise. Still less name. Their scent was almost overwhelming. Everywhere. Shrub. Bush. Plant. Remained upright. Unmoving. He thought how odd. It is as if they are preparing to witness an event or series of events. Which they had witnessed before. The sea was beyond the castle walls. Beyond the walls lay the sand dunes. Beyond them ... the sea. The beach was of curiously white sand. Crescent shaped it followed the curving inlet. It was virtually inaccessible to all but those who had entry from the private grounds of the castle. It was as Bobo smirkily said, his very own beach. Most locals avoided the beach because by tradition men swam there naked. This created a sense of notoriety which kept women and children away. Visitors who chanced upon the beach, usually while out boating and who were tempted to land perhaps to picnic, were very pertly told they were trespassing. Would be prosecuted. Usually moved off swiftly though reluctantly. Those who refused to be intimidated, and pointed out that the beach lay outside the castle walls shifted rather quickly when Bobo appeared dressed in a splendid dressing gown of orange and black and red ... ran, screaming and slinging crab apples from a child's sandbucket. He presented so lunatic a figure that most people thought it prudent to withdraw, usually loudly advised to do so by lady-companions if they had any ... or by the mother of the family if it were a family picnic. Adding to his appearance was the fact that crab apples slung with great dexterity could prove quite painful on impact upon the body. Bobo's self-appeasing excuse was that if ever challenged in a court of law he could plead dementia in mitigation of any charges brought against him. Bobo also believed that he could under oath insist that he was pressing what he termed very sweet crab apples upon the trespassers. The stratagem rarely failed. Bobo was not only lord of his demesne but of the stretch of white sands which gave Bobo his title of Trawann and the castle its name.

Water now broke gently on the edge of the clear white sands. Apart from the sounds of the lapping waters, a heavy silence prevailed. In the distance huge cloud formations marshalled themselves as if for attack on some predetermined target. Softly distant thunder rolled mutely like mourning beats on a muffled drum. Timothy surveyed the scene. There was no one to be seen. Nothing sufficiently extraordinary to attract attention. He stripped. Dipped his hand in the seawater. Blessed himself. He no longer believed but nevertheless observed some of the old usages. From a lingering sense of fear, perhaps, or possibly for the pleasure of an old custom, itself of no great account. Fleetingly he wondered if his father who had taught him to always bless himself with water whenever about to swim in the sea, in a lake, or in a river — really did believe in God. And his mother also. Did they believe in Hell and Purgatory and all the other doctrines embodied in Catholic belief? Did they, pragmatic adults both of decided intelligence really believe that when they died, as died they had, that they would be judged by God immediately and consigned to Heaven, Hell or Purgatory for violation of ten commandments, not very well conceived? Did they foresee Heaven or Hell as their car struck another with such impact that his mother was thrown through the windscreen of the car. Killed instantly. His father. Did he implore divine mercy as he was impaled on the steering wheel column which transfixed his body. Did choirs of angels and saints and martyrs welcome them with hymns of joy and bear them joyfully into the presence of the enthroned God, the God of, above all else, mercy?

Standing still the cold waters stinging about his thighs, he wondered at the bitterness with which he asked himself those questions. He did not now believe it was so. No throngs of angels, Saints, martyrs, welcomed his parents into paradise anymore than they did any of life's teeming millions. He felt briefly a bitter sense of loss, because in a very childish way he believed that his parents, faults forgotten, and such good people as Bridget, should be rewarded for their simple goodness. Now he believed, they came from darkness and into darkness would lapse as did all living beings. This was now the major canon of his present state of belief. It involved deprivation. Heightened the transience of life to a frightened pitch. It was a fact of life. As such it would have to be borne as would all human sorrows. Death. Dark death was the price of bright white life. 'Amen,' he whispered almost audibly.

Threw himself forward into the cold, grey-green waters. The cold struck him forcefully causing him to gasp, all but cry out. He struck out firmly without fear of any kind. Alexander whom he missed very much whose absence was largely the cause of his ill-humour, Alexander who had taught him to strike back when struck, Alexander who had all unwittingly caused him, Timothy, the believer to become Timothy the non-believer. How could that be, Timothy thought. They had hardly discussed religion for more than five minutes. Alexander continued to believe. He, Timothy did not. He knew the exact moment when he ceased to believe. In Church for Mass with Veronica. Alexander, Bannion. He had taken communion as had Veronica. Timothy adored the received Host. Then listening to a rather long, bad sermon, he thought: This house is an empty house. God is not present amongst the gathered faithful. Nor was he present specifically in the transmuted Host. What the priest was saying about the divine providence and mercy of God was altogether without foundation. Sitting there. Thinking as he had been thinking. Sunlight streaming through the tinted glass of the windows, glittering on the silver trimmings of the priest's green robes, on the white marble and white cloth of the High Altar, the brass of the candlesticks. The unwavering flames of the lighted candles. On the faithful. Those sitting in silence all about him. Whom he considered good. Worthy people. Capable of fidelity of the noblest form. Treachery of the worst kind. Capable of mercy. Malice also. He thought they were not a sinful people: their sins he, Timothy thought, are not great. They merited Heaven if indeed Heaven did exist. They did not merit Hell if Hell existed. This is an empty church. There is nothing in it. With what was almost an idle, passing thought, all belief fell from him. He now no longer prayed at night or in the morning. He attended church with Veronica and Alexander largely because he lacked the moral courage to proclaim his non-belief. He thought also not to distress Veronica whom he loved. Had already suffered greatly.

The air was tinged with a strange green light which struck the moving waters obliquely. He felt air and sky and sea were one and he swam in the central core of life. He felt a sense of joy he had only experienced very rarely in the past. It was joy in simply being, of being alive, of having one's being, of breathing, of moving. He knew he would not have a happy life, but he, Timothy would in time to come experience from time to time great but fleeting, joy. He would have to be content with that. That was to be his lot in life. He turned from the shallows by the beach. Struck out in the deeper waters. He cleaved through the choppy waters with pleasure. Joy. Something he did not possess in any great part but something

Alexander and Bannion had in abundance. He swam about for some time, again noticing how green the light was. How green the waters he swam in. Exhilarated he regained the shore. Dried himself carefully with his towel. Then lay down on the towel. He was breathing with difficulty. His heart beating rapidly. He still felt the blood course swiftly through his veins. He felt spent. Exhausted, yet he was not despondent as he had been. He gathered his breath. Lay gently panting for some time then dressed slowly. Thunder crashed to the south. A faint flash of lightening low on the horizon showed briefly. So briefly that he wondered if it really was lightening. The air was denser, the light greener. Land and sea were hushed as if for a coming assault. He decided that he would retire early for the night. Read one of Turgeniev's novels, copies of which he had seen in what passed for the library at Castle Trawann. Turgeniev's works like most works of the nineteenth century Russian writers appealed greatly to him, thanks to the good influence of Brother McNally at Saint Patrick's, Tibraddenstown. They were a joy which never failed. Suddenly he was aware of a sweet, companionable smell. The smell of tobacco of the kind Skipper invariably smoked. He glanced about. Skipper was on his haunches smoking a cigarette. 'I've been watching you,' Skipper said. 'You swim quite well.' Skipper's voice was low, soft, above all friendly as Timothy had never known before. It was as if they were intimate friends of long standing. He, Timothy refused to speak. He felt he could not do so. Some instinct forbade speech of any kind. Timothy knew that if Skipper set upon him, he, Timothy would take Skipper's life. If necessary by sinking his teeth into Skipper's throat. He, Timothy, felt quite calm. Perfectly at ease.

'You're not afraid of me anymore. Are you?'

'No,' Timothy replied.

Skipper was silent. Smoked his cigarette slowly. Exhaling faintly green-grey smoke. 'That's good. You see there never was anything to be afraid of.' To the south there was a brilliant flash of lightning, followed after some seconds by thunder. 'A storm,' Skipper said nodding to the southern horizon. 'A bad storm,' he said, 'shortly heading towards us.' Skipper smiled. Flicked his cigarette from him. Like a comet it spun through the darkening air trailing briefly a shower of sparks. It fell to the sand where it's lighted tip continued to shine dimly pink. It was now quite dark. Above them were piled dark threatening clouds. To the south they could see the storm like a modern battle in progress. Skipper stood. Held himself erect looking him, Timothy directly in the eye. Skipper slipped off his shirt. Quickly stripped. Stood naked. He Timothy could plainly see the light of Skipper's eyes. There was no malice. No sly hint of further possible seduction. There was, Timothy saw, an almost infinite sadness and inexpressible pity. Naked, Skipper stood stock still. His body was remarkably white. The evening light and the flashes of lightening struck it to good effect. His beauty, struck him, Timothy, like a hammer-blow in the chest. 'My God. He is as beautiful as the risen Christ must have been as seen by those of the race that had crucified Him. Entombed Him. The women bearing oils. Scented herbs. Tributary flowers of the rarest kind.' He Timothy longed to fall at his feet. To confess all failings. All pain. All misery. He felt the figure of divine beauty. Had but to touch. And all would be righted. All love requited. All sins absolved. All sorrows healed. He Timothy bowed his head. Wept. 'I'll come to you later,' Skipper said quietly. Gathering his clothes he disappeared among the sand dunes. Lightning lit the scene with all the bright clarity of day. Thunder crashed overhead. Rain began to fall. In large single droplets at first. Then heavily. Steadily. Timothy stood still lacerated by the stinging rain. Lightning continued to flash. Thunder continued. Loud. Frighteningly loud. Timothy felt as though bereft by the death of a loved one. He stood by the roaring sea. Now high. Furious. The storm he calculated absently was directly overhead. Far out to sea lightning struck the water. It danced. Coursed towards the shore in strong jagged flashes. Turning he moved towards the castle. Made for his room. Changed his clothing. Shrieks of fear announced the presence of Bobo, The

Lord David Trawann.

Timothy entered the kitchen. At the range Skipper was frying food. Bobo, attired in his dressing gown of three brash colours squealed with delight on seeing him. 'Do come dear Timothy. Do come my dear friend and hold my hand. I'm petrified with terror of this ghastly storm. It's as if the hoards of Heaven and the hounds of Hell are locked in deadly combat for our immortal souls. Do hold my hand dear Timothy. Do hold my hand.' Skipper glanced at Timothy. 'Like some food? I'm preparing it. I advise you to eat all you can. There's none left.' He glared at Bobo who squealed. 'Oh Skipper you really are tiresome. It's only a matter of time.' Skipper kicked a nearby bucket of coal. 'Time my fucking foot. It's a matter of life and death. What do we eat in the future? Raw turnips and potatoes?' 'Oh no Skipper no. Things will be adjusted in time. All it takes is a little patience.' Skipper bared his teeth. 'Time is something I haven't got, my fat little friend. I'm addicted to food if you haven't realised as much before.' Bobo squirmed. Wriggled like a mongrel bitch inviting a mount. 'Bobsiewobbsiey will have to sing for his supper or be content with bare bones.' He squealed with pleasure. 'Oh Skipper isn't it delightful. I'll shave my head, don saffron robes of the lovely flowing kind and beg with my bowl like a mendicant.' Bobo turned to Timothy. 'Broke, dear Timothy. Dear Timothy. Broke. I haven't as much as one brass farthing. Whatever will I do? Am I not pitiful? Am I not pitiful beyond bearing?' Bobo tittered. Bunched his hands together, wedged them between his thighs; squealed. Squirmed in sexual excitement. 'Put out the plates,' Skipper said to no one in particular. Bobo tittered as the lightning flashed. Thunder crashed. 'Dear Timothy, God loves you very specially. Pray intercede for me in my hour of need.'

Since no one made any effort to lay out plates, Timothy did so. By the plates he laid knives and forks. A bottle of all but congealed relish, some salt. Mustard. He sought fresh bread but found only a hard stale loaf. 'It's only hard,' Skipper said. 'Think of it as toast.' Timothy cut some slices. Laid them on a plate. Frugal living wasn't apparently something new for Skipper, and oddly he thought, 'I've never seen Skipper glut himself on luxury foods unlike Flannery who devoured them like a starved pig.' Lightning flashed. There was a loud clap of thunder. Outside a felled tree struck the ground with great impact. Skipper glanced out a window. As did Timothy. A beautiful chestnut in the centre of a field was neatly cleft, the greater part having fallen to the ground, part of the trunk still upstanding. Its dipped leaves streaming rain. 'By God,' Skipper muttered in amazement. 'That was close.' Bobo peeked timorously at the stricken tree. Paled. And as lightning again flashed, dived under the table screeching in what both Timothy and Skipper realised for the first time was actual fear. 'Lord help us all,' he squeaked. His voice an octave higher. 'Oh Lord, oh Lord have mercy upon us.'

Skipper snorted in contempt. Tipped a few fried sausages from the frying pan onto the plates on the table. 'Relish this,' he said. 'There's no more from where this comes from. Poor Bobo. Skipper will have to hoist his sail and go and sing for his supper somewhere else.'

'Skipper,' Bobo exclaimed, appalled. 'You can't mean that?'

'I do mean it. I leave first thing in the morning. At the crack of dawn.' Bobo erupted in tears. 'But you can't Skipper. You can't,' he cried plaintively. 'I can. And I will,' retorted Skipper reaching under the table with a plate of sausages and buttered slices of bread. 'No dibs Bobo. No fun. No Skipper. Simple as pie. Eat that for Christ sake and stop snivelling like a pup.' Thunder again clashed. Lightning again flashed. A bare second or so between them. 'It's right overhead,' Bobo screamed. Shot from under the table. Dashed through the doorway. They heard his progress through the house as door after door was slammed in his search for a secure hiding place. 'That's him gone arse and elbow,' Skipper said lightly. 'We won't hear much of him for the rest of the night.' Timothy said nothing. There was nothing to say. The storm abated moving further north. Only the rain remained torrential. Direct. Beating a tattoo off everything it struck.

In the early hours of the morning Skipper came to his bed. Naked as he had been on the beach. Timothy abandoned himself to what he had so long denied himself. The terror and beauty of loving another. He relished the warmth of Skipper's body. Its hardness which denoted strength. Like all who are weak, he Timothy worshipped strength. Skipper's mouth was fresh. His breath sweet. They coupled. He, Timothy bit his lip to prevent himself from crying out in pain. Skipper whispered to him tenderly in tones of a very tender lover. Later he kissed him, Timothy, repeatedly. Declaring his love. He, Timothy felt happy. As if after a long and arduous journey, he had at last arrived at his desired destination. Skipper embraced him. So joined. They slept.

Someone struck him, Timothy, across the face with stunning force. Skipper dragged him from the bed. He, Skipper was fully dressed. Clean. Impeccable. As if about to depart. He struck Timothy again with the full force of an open hand. Beating him repeatedly on either side of the face causing his, Timothy's face, to swing one way, then another. Skipper, lips parted, was grinding his teeth. His eyes bright with aroused sexuality. He continued to strike out at him, Timothy, without pause. Then he began to pound his, Timothy's body, with a clenched fist. Timothy was screaming in agony. Blood gushed from his, Timothy's nose, mouth. Skipper paused, breathing deeply. Timothy heard Bobo squeal delightedly. He realised what was to come. Stretching forward he made a wild grab at Skipper's face. He, Timothy, managed to gain a hold. He sunk his fingers deeply into the flesh. Skipper cried out in pain. Struck him, Timothy, a blow in the kidneys which practically knocked him unconscious. He felt the brutal thrust as Skipper penetrated. Sought to restrain him, Skipper, by tightening the muscles about the anus. Skipper struck out again to the lower body. Weakened. He Timothy could no longer resist. There was little tenderness now with Skipper who appeared to use his penis as a means of wounding deeply. Deeply degrading. Skipper climaxed. Exhaled with a slow deep breath. 'Now my friend. You're well and truly fucked.' He withdrew. Slung

Timothy across the bed. Skipper laughed lightly. 'A good fuck is what you wanted. A good fuck was what you got. You'll never get as good again.' Skipper cleaned himself. Adjusted his trousers. Slicked back the strands of hair back across the skull where, well oiled, they lay. He snorted. Turned. Left the room.

Bobo approached, his voice sweetly venomous. 'Oh thank you dear Timothy for such exquisite emissions.' He fondled his thighs. The satin trousers stained about the crotch. 'Do let me be the first to herald your first fuck attendant upon the loss of your virginity. You will always remember in total clarity every detail of your despoilment. It will, with your first reception of communion, be as one of the most memorable occasions in your life. You will hunger unimaginably for its like with a hunger greater than you'll ever feel for food or drink. Your life will be a continuous search for such a fuck. Need I say you won't find it. You are outcast, dear Timothy. A sodomite. An animal society in general considered less worthy than any hoofed animal. You are as of now a man without honour. Your fellow men will never admit that personal honour and your sexual state can co-exist. And alas dear Timothy, quite without reason you value honour. What price honour now? You are outraged. Humiliated. Despoiled. Once your state becomes known. And known it shall be, if not now, later — you will seek to escape the inescapable: your true nature. You will flee to the ends of the earth to escape your destiny. To elude the hungers of the flesh. You will never elude them. Those howling hounds of sexual desire. You enjoyed the act dear Timothy with every fibre of your being. And why not? It is what your soul seeks. Not only did you enjoy the sexual act you enjoyed the following brutality even more. More than you will ever admit. You will now rejoice in all that is sordid and low. For that is sodom's nature. Sodom is no bright towering citadel but an incredibly foul, stenching place. How you'll love it! How you'll relish it! Timothy, dear Timothy consider this carefully. It is arguable that a soul that never knows sin can never divine grace. Think dear Timothy what great graces may accrue to your from your ordained state of ignominy. Now dear Timothy, Timothy of whom Veronica thinks so highly, let me be the first to spit on you. It is I assure you the chrism which will confirm you in your unholy state. You will in time welcome it more than you will welcome the oils of the last rites.'

Bobo carefully mustered spittle. Spat forcefully at him. Timothy. He, Timothy, flinched. Bobo squeaked delightedly. 'You are of the brotherhood forever. In it you'll live and in it you'll die.' Bobo raised his hands. Aped the priestly benediction, chanting gibberish meant to parody the latin of the rite. Withdrew.

Soon there was nothing to be heard but the soft roll of the now calm sea. In the far distance a dog barked. A passing motor roared, its engines running at full force. Timothy rose. Went to a mirror on the chest of drawers. Saw Bobo's filthy spittle on his forehead. Chin. Wiped it off disgustedly using the towel he had used after bathing the previous evening. He saw to his disgust that his body was soiled. As were the sheets. Involuntarily he bowed his head. Vomited. In acute misery he pulled the sheets from the bed. Wrapped himself in the blankets. Lay on the floor in the utmost misery. He felt inexhaustibly tired. Hoped for a sleep from which he would never waken.

It was late afternoon when he woke. Strong sunlight filled the room. For a moment he responded to the sunshine and to the relief of the storm's passage. His face pained. It was, he knew, bruised and swollen. He could hardly see through his left eye which was partially closed. His mouth hurt. His lip was, he suspected, split. Would therefore take a long time to heal. His misery had largely abated. He thought clearly, was not at all confused. He rose. Went to the bathroom. Ran some hot water for a bath. While it was running he examined his bruised bloodied face. He gently wiped away the blood. Dabbed at the painfully swollen patches around the eyes. About the mouth. He found some iodine. Unwisely applied it too liberally. It stung. Painfully. He realised it was stupid of him to apply it to cuts. Abrasions, which were so raw. Open. He eased himself into the bath, on the waters of which he had scattered some scented crystals, one of the many womanly things Bobo enjoyed. They were heavily scented. Overpowering at first but as they diluted and melted the scent became lighter, more subtle. Pleasant. Yet as the fragrance rose all about him he imagined he could still smell it strongly: the smell of his own shit. It soon passed. He yielded himself up to the sensual pleasure of lying in hot fragrant water. He was calm. Curiously calm. He resolutely refused to think of Skipper. What had passed between them. He even succeeded in quelling the mocking voice of Bobo which had seemed to echo on and on in his mind. In his room he carefully chose some clean underwear from amongst the small supply of items he had brought with him for his stay at Castle Trawann.

He chose a crisp white shirt which he loved to wear but rarely did so because he was afraid of being accused of copying Alexander who wore such shirts to excellent effect. He changed his slacks for a fresh pair. Was altogether pleased with his appearance as seen in a mirror. He, Timothy looked what his mother used grimly call presentable. Just right for an 'occasion'. He then searched for food. Discovered some stale bread without mould of any kind. In the kitchen he succeeded in rekindling the fire. There were three sausages in the meatsafe in the pantry. Some meat. Badly recapped jars of luxury pastes all of which looked extremely poisonous. He went outside to the garden. Pulled some fresh lettuces. Peas. Runnerbeans. He boiled the peas and beans. Eventually created a not very appetising meal. He found a recorked bottle with some wine still left in it. The wine was bitterly sour, nevertheless he drank some as he ate his ill assorted meal. Curiously his sense of taste was sharpened. He relished each piece of food as if discovering for the first time their particular taste. His personal taste in food was for the ordinary and commonplace, the unimaginative taste of the lower middle class. From time to time he listened to the silence of the deserted house.

A silence unbroken by the soft murmur of the sea in the distance, settled like a fall of snow. Lay everywhere. It was ever increasing. Ever impacting. Settling layer upon layer upon layer. He had found some of Skipper's cigarettes. He smoked. The tobacco was almost too strong for him. Nevertheless he persisted. He alternated sips of wine with long draughts of the heavy scented cigarette. He listened to the sea, now contained. Seductively murmurous. He was, he realised, listening for the sounds of Alexander's return, though he knew Alexander would not come. He went to a window. The sea was visible just beyond the castle wall. it was calm and still. Barely moving. Only the faint foam at the very edges of the water hinted at any movement whatever. How pleasant he thought it would be to walk barefooted. Impress one's footprints in the virginal white of the as yet untrodden white sands.

Strangely Timothy remembered O'Neill, his old friend in Dublin. He, Timothy, rarely thought of his home or his parents, though echoes of their bitter quarrels still rang in his memory, rising to consciousness unexpectedly. He no longer prayed for them. The dead. He remembered how fervently he had once prayed. For the sick. The dying. The living and the dead. O'Neill with his head of jet black hair. His coarse Dublin features. His bright blue eyes. O'Neill, the old Irish Irelander. Old battles, engagements still moved his blood. As they once must have moved the blood of those who had participated in them. Long. Long ago. He still felt the bitter sense of defeat. The outrage of the slaughter of the defeated Gael with their startling nobility of mind. Body. Their dark ancient ways. The litany of the defeated was still very loud. Real. To O'Neill. Coloured his every perception. He was tied hand and foot by the emotional bonds which had shackled the Gaels for centuries. In some respects always would. O'Neill the hater of all things English who so loved the English poets, venerating them as he did the old Gaelic poets of Munster, seeing nothing whatever wrong in such a contradiction. O'Neill the tenement dweller at prayer before a shrine in some Dublin church.

O'Neill was, above all other things, devout. Attended daily Mass before cycling down to the Bull Wall for a swim before school all through the year, and who insisted that no matter where they were going in the evening, be it a film, a concert or a swim — they first visit a church for prayer. O'Neill pale. Full of ancient wrongs and hatred at prayer before the cross with the carcass of Christ slung across it, seemed to possess at such times all the grace, nobility, of the Gaelic dispossessed. O'Neill, Timothy reflected was what Veronica would term 'decent'. Veronica was sparing in use of the term. He, Timothy even more so.

About him on the pale wheaten boards of the bedroom floor were scattered what in the dying light looked curiously like crushed, white blossoms where he had stamped out each cigarette nub with a savagery he had been unaware of. He laid aside his empty glass. Listening for Alexander who he knew would not come. He turned aside on the blanket spread upon the floor. Slept. The wine had been heady for him. He Timothy had drank more than he had imagined. He awakened some hours later. The room lay in almost total darkness. In the background the sea now beat fully against the sands. He rose slowly. Slowly made his way downstairs.

It was a night of stars. The night air was faintly moist auguring rain or drizzle to come. He turned towards the beach. Gained it. Stood, a silent figure, gazing at the smooth waters of the untroubled sea. Light sparkled on its surface. Its movement was almost imperceptible. It rarely looked so beautiful, he thought as he slowly walked southwards down the beach. His feet sank slowly on what were untouched sands. He left a deep imprint with each step he took. He reached the point where a large outcrop of rocks barred entry to the beach at that point. He skirted the rocks slowly shouldering them and walked up the sandy slopes which lead to the top. He gained the summit. Below the sea beat faintly on the rocks. Ahead lay a vast body of water. Its surface swept by the beams of a lighthouse situated on a headland further down the coastline. He made his way to the edge of the precipice. He stood for sometime overwhelmed by a desire to fling himself forward. He remembered Skipper. His brutal assault. He remembered Bobo his vicious taunts. What lay ahead of him but misery, he thought, and pressed forward. He virtually teetered on the brink. For one moment he felt himself being impelled forward then realising where he was he took a step backward. Stumbled. Fell. Lay on the sandy slopes glad not to have fallen prey to the impulse to destroy himself.

A figure stepped forward. Alexander addressed him, Timothy, gently. 'That was a wise decision my friend. Very wise indeed.' Timothy's teeth clattered. His body shook convulsively. He was overwhelmed at what he had contemplated a few moments before. Alexander squatted by him. 'That's excellent, Timothy. Now you know what real fear and courage are like. You now know courage in a way no other man could teach or tell you.' He, Timothy stuttered, still cold from fear. 'Would you have left me to jump,' he asked with difficulty. 'Yes,' Alexander replied, 'I would have left you to jump. It had to be your decision. It is your life. Only you could decide.' He paused. 'I think you made the right decision,' he repeated, 'well done, my friend.' 'How did you know I was here?' he, Timothy asked. 'I saw you leave the castle. I knew immediately something was wrong. I realised sometime ago that a crisis was developing. I sensed that it had finally come and so I followed you, deliberately keeping out of sight. Now Timothy I want you to meet a friend of mine.'

A figure stepped forward from the night shadows. He, Timothy thought it was Skipper or Bobo. He suffered a blinding sense of terror. He found himself confronted by a young and beautiful girl. She was lithe and lean with hanging black hair. The light of the lighthouse swept her. She was very beautiful, Timothy realised.

'This is Sarah. Say hello to her — but Timothy, she likes to be called Sally. I refuse to do so and insist that everyone address her as Sarah. It sounds more beautiful. More apt.' Suddenly Timothy was weeping. Sarah kneeled by him.

Fondled him in her arms. 'Go ahead Timothy,' she said softly, 'cry all you have to. It must have been dreadful for you but Alexander was right. It had to be your decision. Don't mind crying.' She was, Timothy who had never been in a young woman's embrace, discovered, both soft and lovely but somewhere in there among all her undoubted femininity was a core of steel. Strength. Courage. Brave endeavour. And profound pity. All were encompassed by the form of the lovely Sarah in whose arms he, Timothy, was weeping hysterically. 'I'll see to some food,' said Alexander slipping away. Sarah continued to stroke Timothy's head and gently kissed his forehead from time to time. She spoke softly, so softly, Timothy would never be sure that he had heard her. He gained some self-control. He felt ashamed at what he considered weakness.

Sarah produced a packet of cigarettes from a bag which lay on the ground beside her. 'Perhaps a smoke will help.' He nodded numbly. She lit one. 'Everyone cries, Timothy. I've been known to cry myself sometimes.' She turned aside and watched the beam from the lighthouse periodically sweep the dark silent waters. Above the night was perfect with stars. She motioned to Timothy to come and sit by her. He did so now much recovered, though somewhat ashamed. 'Let's be mean,' she said lightly, 'and let Alexander prepare something to eat for us all.' She tried to engage Timothy in conversation. He was silent. Embarrassed by the entire incident. Silence settled between them. They smoked their cigarettes. Discarded the nubs. Alexander hailed them from below. 'You had better come in,' he shouted, 'or I'll eat everything in sight. I'm ravenous.' Alexander had found a practically empty room. He had lighted a fire with driftwood which sparked. Blazed. He had laid out a tablecloth. Scattered some cushions to sit upon. Here and there lighted candles burned brightly in the most unlikely of holders. On a tablecloth he had laid some food. Cheeses. Cold meat pies. Salad. Tomato. Sliced cold ham. Together with some fruit. It was by any standards a splendid meal.

'There really wasn't very much for sale in the village. We will have to be satisfied with what we have.' They both sat on some cushions. Sarah slipped away with apologies. She returned shortly in a white dress which was simple. Becoming. 'Ah,' said Alexander. 'I thought you wouldn't be able to resist showing off yourself to best effect now that I have some opposition.' Sarah sat. All were hungry. All ate well. Having eaten they took coffee by the fire. Sarah and Alexander made several efforts to involve Timothy in conversation. He was far too exhausted to enter into conversation even of the lightest kind. Presently he excused himself. Alexander rose. 'I think perhaps I should look at your eye. It's rather badly swollen. And your lower lip is split slightly. May I take a look at them. I've some antiseptics with me. I carry them in case of emergency.' Timothy nodded. Too tired to refuse, longing only to get to bed and sleep. Alexander attended him well. 'Your friend Skipper knows a thing or two when it comes to beating someone up.' Timothy recalled how savagely Alexander had beaten Flannery. He felt like making some sharp retort but decided against doing so. It would antagonise Alexander. He, Timothy, longed to sleep. Alexander was soon through, having first bathed then applied an ointment to Timothy's bruised flesh. He protected his, Timothy's lower lip, with cotton-wool dipped in a liquid of some kind and a strip of plaster. He was a most competent and gentle medic. Timothy was grateful. 'Get as much sleep as you can.' Timothy tottered. Almost fell forward. 'Here let me help you.' Alexander slipped a hand behind his back. Half lifted. Half dragged him to the bedroom. Gratefully Timothy fell forward. Alexander covered him with a blanket. Soon he, Timothy, was fast asleep.

Several times during the night he felt himself fall from the clifftop to the sea below. Terrorised he screamed. Woke. Conscious of the fact that he was in Sarah's arms. She held him tightly whispering softly to quell his fears. He tried to express his gratitude. He, Timothy, slept. And woke. Clutching tightly the warm body of the young girl. He was at a loss to understand how she came to be there. Was grateful. Intensely so.

Alexander rapped on the door. 'Make yourselves decent,' he called out. 'I've brought breakfast.' He opened the door. Edged it wide open with his knee. Entered bearing a tray laden for breakfast. He laid the tray by the bed. 'I think we had better see what we're doing.' He pulled the curtains. Strong white light streamed through the window into the room. Alexander prised open the lower window. Fresh air, slightly salted, entered. Circulated in the laden atmosphere of the room. 'I think we'll eat on the floor. It's better than trying to balance a tray on the bed. There is no need to dress. Just grab a sheet and wrap it round you if you are cold. I hope you are both hungry. I'm starving and I've fried rather a lot.' Alexander approached the bed. Kissed Sarah directly. Fondled her black hair which sparkled in the sunlight. 'She is beautiful is she not, Timothy? A dark haired beauty. You had a splendid guardian last night, Timothy. Don't you think she is kind?' He, Timothy, to his shame could not look directly at Alexander. Not in his eyes. Alexander took, his, Timothy's chin in his hand. He forced Timothy to raise his head. 'Look at me directly,' he said. 'You have no need to feel ashamed. It's I who failed. Not you my friend.' Timothy looked at Alexander directly. 'That's better,' Alexander exclaimed. 'That's much better.' But it was not better.

He, Timothy, remembered leaving Flannery's place early in the morning some months before. The grass was soft. Wet beneath their feet. Birds were singing as daylight gradually broke. Flannery had been there. Oates seated comfortably by the fire drinking heavily. With him was a rough of twenty or so. He was a striking young man who all too readily smiled. He, Timothy, sensed the young man's nature. So did Alexander. Both had stiffened. Treated the young fellow coldly. Pointedly excluding him from the conversation. Refusing to occupy the chair he had vacated. Offered to them as they had entered. They stayed only a short while. Why, he wondered had Alexander and Timothy been calling on Flannery so early in the morning? He could not remember.

They left. Alexander's face had been grim. Lips held tightly together. 'In Germany,' he muttered fiercely .... 'In Germany men like that shoot themselves. Or are shot.' Now both bathed in the morning sunlight, he Timothy remembered bitterly. His body still ached after his, Timothy's, beating. He slipped from the bed wrapping a sheet lightly about him. Sarah rose. Stretched languidly like a beautiful animal. Padded to the window where she stood gazing at the scene outside. 'My God Timothy but she is really a beauty is she not?' Timothy agreed she was. Alexander rose. Going to her he enfolded her from behind, fondling her breasts. Her smooth, tight stomach. The mound between her thighs. Nuzzling his fair head in her long black hair which was one of her finest features. 'Alexander,' she exclaimed. 'You are a man of lust.' 'But you like me for my lust. Is that not so?' Alexander asked lightly. 'Yes,' she replied. 'I do.' 'Come and eat before the food is cold.' Sarah padded quickly from the room. 'I'm bursting. I must pee.' All three laughed. Alexander piled food on a plate. 'I should eat, Timothy before it goes cold. Sarah won't mind our bad manners.'

Alexander bit into a sausage. 'My God this is delicious. We haven't eaten any solid food for about two days. We've existed on apples and cheese and love-making. Eat up Timothy, all's well again. All's well.' Sarah entered the room. Took a position by them on the floor. Timothy thought she showed a splendid spirit. Alexander and he wolfed bacon and eggs. Sarah peeled an apple with infinite care. Having peeled it, ate frugally like a penitent eating a penitential meal. She shook her head, the lustre of her long black hair brilliantly enhanced by the strong light of morning. 'Thank you Timothy. For not rejecting me.' He, Timothy met her glance directly. 'It's I who ought to be grateful. And I am. Very much.' She flushed, pleased by his, Timothy's gratitude. She and Alexander had met some days ago. Most likely were lovers from their first night together. Now Sarah was to leave. She had to return to England shortly. Later in the day after a morning on the beach, they parted in the city. It was plain Alexander felt their parting deeply. She,

Sarah had been the only woman Alexander had showed any interest in since arriving in Ireland. He declined to comment on the parting. Was silent. Morose. He, Timothy felt the pain of parting also. Sarah was his only experience of a woman. It had pleased him. Had moved him.

On reaching Farrighy later that night in the late dusk they found the place ablaze with light. Veronica greeted them joyously. She was full of spirit. Seemed to have recaptured all her old strength. Energy. Both of which were considerable. Birdy, she told them, was returning home. The most virulent period of her illness was over. She had made some small progress and would, everyone fervently wished, continue to do so. It was hoped that shortly she would resume her old life. Once again decorate scrolls. Vellums. Which she did with the utmost mastery. His, Timothy's heart sank. As he suspected did Alexander's. Philippa was a spent being, like a lifeless mass passing through endless space. Dull. Without light or life. She had settled into silence. A silence he, Timothy believed would now never be broken. Death would have been a more merciful fate .... A more desirable destiny. Living she was quite without interest in anything. It was impossible to know if she felt or experienced anything. Or who and where she was. Birdy. Sweet Birdy. Was bereft of all consciousness .... Dignity.

PART SIX

The leaves had fallen from the trees on the riverside Mall in Tibraddenstown. The river bed here was shallow. The waters splashed pleasantly over stones and shingle. Now there were trout to be seen feeding in the shallows having rashly forsaken the safer, deeper waters upstream. To see them thrash about in the shallows was one of the great summer treats which aroused much attention. No one quite knew why they behaved as they did. White bellied. Speckled with brown and crimson spots. Thrashing wildly about catching the fading sunlight they seemed like the fabled silverfish of folklore. Only the very unsporting, unprincipled, possibly also the hungry, caught or sought to catch them while they sported with such delight.

Veronica was in a tight beltless coat with a fox-fur collar. Fox-fur about the sleeves. She walked slowly in the gathering dusk with Timothy. Elizabetha followed. Behind her came Philippa linking arms with Bannion. She wore her black trailing cloak, its cowl thrown back resting on the broad of her back. Her movements were lethargic. Erratic, as if she was lame in one leg. She carried a cloth bag which was already bulging. Her throat jerked forward from time to time rather like that of an ungainly seabird attempting to feast on too large a fish. Her eyes for the most part dull. Lifeless. Lit up somewhat every time she spotted a piece of coloured paper on the pavement. The discarded wrappers of the most expensive sweets in most cases. She would slip her arm from Bannion's. Pick up the piece of paper from the gutter or the pavement. Bannion held her firmly. Sometimes having to tighten his grip or Philippa would dash out onto the street to pick up a piece of paper regardless of the traffic. Sometimes the gold foil which was used as wrapping for a particular chocolate bar was cushed underfoot. Lay on the pavement. Or in the gutter. Philippa prized these pieces above all others. Her second preference was for a scarlet or ruby transparent wrapping such as Timothy remembered as a child carefully smoothing the paper and then closing one eye to gaze at the world through the paper at a world made richly red. Or amber.

Elizabetha followed them without interest. She was elegantly dressed in a fur-trimmed coat. The fur pieces looked expensive. One knew them to be more expensive than any Veronica possessed. Elizabetha looked pale. Strained. Spoke little. If addressed replied shortly, discouraging further conversation. Compulsory conscription had been introduced in Germany for all males over eighteen years of age. The news had thrilled Alexander who had left for Germany immediately to enlist for his term of conscription. Enrolment before legally necessary would be viewed favourably by the authorities. Military. And Civic. It would indicate eagerness. A desire for self-sacrifice for the needs of Germany. Which were to transcend all other needs. It would demonstrate more tellingly what was everywhere being hailed as most commendable: The New German Spirit. The desire to serve the German state. Alexander reacted strongly to the announcement. He was aflame with zeal. Insisted that he return to Germany. Elizabetha had begged him to remain. They would, she said, be soon returning to Germany. In the meantime Alexander needed to recuperate further. To gather his strength and energy in order to pursue his studies. Elizabetha pointing out that as a scientist he could serve German far better than he could ever hope to do in the rank and file of the army. He refused to listen to her. Had gone to Germany as soon as was possible. It soon became evident from letters received from him that he was finding it no easy matter to enlist. His health was not sufficiently good. His education as a scientist was proving the greatest obstacle of all. The German authorities shared Elizabetha's view that he could serve Germany best by completing his studies. Then offer his services to the state which would decide where and how he might best serve it. Alexander resisted. Insisting that to be a better scientist he must know the people he would serve in his science. The authorities were not particularly impressed by his argument. Alexander decided upon influence. Enlisting the many friends of his father, some of whom had risen to positions of power in the New Germany. Alexander's letters became less frequent than before. Something Elizabetha viewed with pleasure. Obviously, with or without influence, Alexander was not progressing as well as he had hoped. Had he been accepted for military service he would have been immediately inducted into the ranks. Would be well into his basic training. She hoped the obstacles encountered by Alexander would prove insurmountable. She was decidedly unhappy. She lapsed from time to time into a nether state of mind neither sleeping or waking. Her emotional and mental faculties less than distinct. From time to time she sighed deeply as if heavily put-upon. She gazed about her, her eyes without liveliness. She sighed deeply from time to time unaware that she was doing so.

Veronica was smoking heavily. She inhaled deeply. Smoked far more cigarettes than usual. Her restless hands also showed her inner turmoil. Anxiety. She had hoped that Philippa would return to illuminating her manuscripts which in the past had afforded her much pleasure. Considerably helped her self-esteem. But it had not proved to be the case. Philippa was a spent body. Dull, lethargic, without inner light. She showed no interest when shown her most splendid parchments. The rows upon rows of glass-topped bottles which contained her various inks, which she made with great difficulty, aroused no interest in her. Here she had been if not happy — and it was questionable if she had ever been really happy — she had been at least industrious. Executed works of originality. Beauty. She turned aside from her manuscripts as might a lover from her loved one's grave. One knew instinctively it was to be forever. Her, Philippa's mouth was constantly, inordinately dry. Her speech impaired. She rarely spoke a coherent sentence. Signalling her wants by gross pantomime gestures. Expressing distress. Discomfort. By a series of animal-like grunts. Unpleasantly made. Her only enjoyment lay in colour. She was enchanted by it. All its hues. Gradations which enchanted her to an extraordinary degree. She would lift a hand to the sky at sunset. To capture the many splendid colours. At night she would reach for the stars. She sought to dip her hands in the bright pool of colours created by light. Filtering through the stained glass windows of a church. Spreading coloured pools on the flag-stoned floor. Her eyes took on a curious light. The eyes of a pleased, idiot child. Veronica wept to see her so and he, Timothy, like all others, found it most affecting. More affecting than he cared to show. Veronica encouraged Philippa's delight in colour believing it might in time lead to an interest in more commonplace matters. She calmly watched Philippa stroke the material of a dress Elizabetha or some caller might be wearing or the glitter of gold or silver should they be wearing jewellery. Philippa might pull a thread. Remove some fluff from the dress she admired. Place it with the other stuff.

Those who understood, Bannion included, who were sympathetic to a degree one would not have expected, brought her scraps of brocade or rich silks. Satins which gave her particular pleasure. She would whine with pleasure. Seated by the fireside would stroke them lovingly for hours on end. Elizabetha showing remarkable perception, thought to ask the proprietors of draper shops. Clothing shops in Tibraddenstown let her have some of their commercial samples of their finest materials. Dressmakers of which there were a few in town also obliged with the result that Elizabetha had quite an amount of stuffs of various kinds which she doled out carefully to Philippa. The richest. The brightest. The most beautiful she saved for the periods when Philippa lapsed into a state of acute emotional pain. Wept bitterly for hours on end. Her weeping interjected with low animal-like groans. A rapid jerking of the neck. Both very distressing to hear and see. At such times Philippa was inconsolable. Could not bear to be touched. Sometimes when most disturbed she would feign attack on those whose presence distressed her. Veronica, Elizabetha and he, Timothy. But never Bannion. Bannion was inexplicably the one to whom she most responded. Sometimes when distressed her eyes would light up at his approach. She would cease whining, cease jerking her neck.

He would kneel by her. Philippa would explore the features of his face like a blind person trying to see through the touching tips of her fingers. Bannion never feared to approach her. Never failed to come when she was most afflicted. Foregoing whatever pleasures might await him elsewhere. He thought nothing of being roused from his sleep in the dead hours of night. Early morning. Going to crouch. Or sit by Philippa's bed. Holding her hand in his. Gently stroking Philippa's. He never spoke but gazed lovingly at the tormented woman with his eyes, which had all the ineffable beauty of Bridget's.

Veronica would surreptitiously drop a piece of sweet-wrapping she herself had scavenged. Hoping that Philippa might find it. 'There,' she would say. 'There's a beauty just there, Birdy.' Squealing with pleasure Philippa would swoop upon the paper. Retrieve it. Place it in the shopping bag made of plain cloth where she kept all her papers. Pieces of material. And which Veronica called her 'Gatherum'. Like Elizabetha she also gathered material. Papers. Was much more frugal in dispensing them. Too many gifts were apt to overwhelm Philippa. Confused. Pained her. She would suffer extreme bouts of excitability rather than acute anguish which was the most remarkable feature of her illness. The tide in time would recede leaving her more spent, more broken than before.

Their visit to Tibraddenstown was intended to cheer Philippa. Already there was a hint of frost in the air. The sun was setting. Dark steel-blue streaks were encroaching everywhere in the evening sky. The evening star was brightly visible. At one time Veronica would have attracted Philippa's attention to its presence but she did not do so now. The beauty of that brilliant solitary body entranced Philippa. She would stare intently at it. Claiming to distinguish it easily even when night advanced. The sky was a mass of stars. Though it was still early November some of the shops had their windows gaily decorated. Bright paper chains. Other gilt and silver cut-out decorations which helped make their windows attractive. Festive. Glitter lay everywhere on gloves and woollens of all kinds. On soaps. Boxes of powders variously scented. All contained in the packets and tins which showed drenching sprays of lilacs. Lily-of-the-valley. Roses or orange blossoms. So reflecting the particular scented powder inside. Expensive fountain-pens. Not so expensive broochs. Sometimes a small gold object. Every imaginable item was on best display. All failed to catch Philippa's attention. She gazed at the gaily decorated windows without showing the slightest interest in them. They passed on, Veronica despondent that what had been intended as a special treat for Philippa had turned into a rather dismal walk about town. Timothy, however, experience almost childlike delight in the window displays. The bright lights. Decorations. Soon it would be Christmas. To his astonishment he found himself looking forward eagerly to the festivities. He would soon have his school holidays. Would not have to worry for some weeks about the examination he would have to take in June of the following year which would help decide his future.

He had not made any friends with any of his school companions. For reasons he could not quite understand himself, he had responded coolly to the friendly overtures of some of the fellows. Why, he simply did not know. It was he thought some sort of mechanism with which he sought to protect himself. Exchanging at all times the civilities whenever they arose. He had struck up a friendship of sorts with one of the teachers. A Brother McNally. A gaunt thin figure of medium height whose natural colouring was so pale the man looked as if he were recovering from a recent illness. They met frequently in the school yard during the dinner break. Unlike the others Timothy brought a thermos flask of strong sweet tea. The others drank milk from bottles. All ate sandwiches. No one now jeered him as being a 'slum rat'. Nor did they strike him. Or pushing against him seek to bring him down. Murray, a senior student, a bully disliked by all, had once provoked him beyond tolerance a few days before the past summer's holidays. Possibly to impress the new juniors who according to custom were admitted to the school before rather than after the summer holidays. They had fought. After school. It had been a long, bloody fight. Murray dismayed at encountering any resistance whatever had panicked. Fought foully. Savagely striking out at him, Timothy, with his booted feet. He, Timothy was struck several times on the shins and legs. There were derisive jeers from the onlookers in the lane. The greater part of the school was there. Several of the older fellows threatened to take on Murray if he refused to fight cleanly. Just when it seemed to him, Timothy, that he could no longer withstand Murray's onslaught, Murray dropped his defence. His enormous hamsized hands fell slack for one brief moment. Timothy was on him and as Alexander had shown him, he moved in pounding Murray's face without restraint. Murray failed to protect himself. Timothy continued to pound him in the face. He, Timothy, attacked Murray's upper body with all the strength he could muster. His, Timothy's teeth bared in sheer savagery as he sought to beat Murray into submission. Momentarily, he, Timothy saw Alexander as Alexander pounded Flannery in a similar fight. Timothy's lust was aroused. He exulted. He continued to strike out at Murray who was offering little resistance. Murray fell to the ground. Despite taunts from the onlookers remained where he had fallen. Inexplicably Murray began to weep. Not in fear. Or frustration. But as if from some curious inner pain. Everyone fell silent. Timothy remained taut. Tense. Ready to resume the fight whenever necessary. They jeered Murray without pity.

Some spitting in contempt at the weeping fellow. Several times they cheered Timothy loudly. Raucously. He, Timothy paled with excitement. Stunned that he loved such acceptance. Adulation. Had unconsciously sought it. Impelled by misplaced sentiment. More truthfully by the fact that what he did struck the others as something noble.

He offered his hand to Murray. Murray grasped Timothy's hand, pulled him to the ground. Straddled him while pounding his, Timothy's face, with his bony fists. There were cries of rage. Efforts were made to get Murray off. They succeeded. Not before Murray had struck a few hard blows to his, Timothy's face. Willing hands helped him, Timothy, to his feet. Timothy happened to glance at the school building, part of which housed the brothers who taught there. McNally stood at a large landing window of the Order House. Which overlooked the lane. He, McNally, stood stock still. His feet characteristically apart under his long cassock. Like someone intent on barring the advance of some horde at the cost of his life. If, at all, necessary. The window, large. The still figure readily visible. Word that they were being observed spread quickly. Everyone snatched up their heavy schoolbags. Left as quickly as possible. Some thought the figure at the window was a Brother O'Sullivan known to all as Orange Billy because of his nationalist sympathies. Hatefully expressed at every opportunity. Who taught Irish. Was somewhat offended that Timothy was more proficient in the language than anyone might have expected, thanks to O'Neill his Dublin friend who was a fluent Irish speaker.

The morning following the fight Orange Billy, who took the class in Irish and Latin, swept into the classroom, his black robes billowing about him. Always florid in complexion, he was livid. He demanded to know who had disgraced the reputation of the school by brawling in the back lane. He demanded that they come forward. Timothy thinking that Orange Billy was using incorrect English. It was, he thought, a fight rather than a brawl. Refused to stand up. As did Murray. Billy pointed a finger at Timothy, calling him to come out in front of the class. Orange Billy smiled in delight. 'Ah our refugee from the slums of Dublin is showing his true colours at long last. Being what he is we could expect no better.' He, Timothy, knew that he should split in the brother's face. Was not too afraid to do so. Or otherwise antagonise the mean-minded man. Who was delighted at the opportunity afforded him to indulge in self-righteous anger. Murray with a bruised face. Two black, swollen eyes followed him, Timothy, to the top of the class. He was slow. Reluctant to do so. Orange Billy struck him, Timothy, forcefully in the face with the broad of his open hand. He reeled under the impact of the blow. The class gasped at such behaviour. The strap alone was the usual way of punishing any pupil. Direct street force was never resorted to under any circumstances. Eyes wide with anger Orange Billy ranted at him, calling him an upstart to whom the school authorities had granted a place in the already overcrowded school only at the intervention of some influential friends. Had dragged the good reputation of the school into the gutter. Such behaviour might be tolerated in a city whose slums were notorious the world over. Not in St. Patrick's Secondary school in Tibraddenstown. There were standards to be kept up. One could not allow any conduct of any of its pupils to afford the Protestants an opportunity to jeer at the school. The Protestant Grammar school was an establishment of some two hundred years standing. The Brothers school a mere matter of some sixty years. Rivalry between the schools was intense in all matters.

The brawl, Orange Billy asserted, was the talk of the town. A matter of glee to the Protestants. Orange Billy used the old Gaelic term of contempt. Na Preachain. The crows. Everyone sat in shocked silence. Orange Billy was shouting. Almost roaring. Foam flecked about his mouth. His face deeply flushed running with sweat. He ordered Timothy to hold his hand out at arms length. He, Orange Billy took a leather strap from the sleeve of his cassock. It was in fact two short lengths of leather sewn together with a thin strip of lead between. He, Orange Billy, struck with delight. Zest. Putting the full force of his considerable body into each stroke. He, Timothy, cried out involuntarily. Orange Billy's eyes gleamed with malicious pleasure. He followed the first stroke with a further three in rapid succession. No one heard the classroom door open quietly. Certainly not Timothy. Smarting with pain. Tears in his eyes which he sought to staunch. 'The other hand,' Orange Billy ordered. He, Timothy did as he was told. Held out the other hand. McNally entered the room spoke quietly in Gaelic. 'Don't Brother. I'll see to that.' Orange Billy flushed. Then paled. Since he took the class in Irish, Latin, he had the right to correct. Punish any member of the class for misconduct. He, Orange Billy, stared at McNally in disbelief. Then in rage. Humiliation. He was being publicly corrected for what Brother McNally thought improper conduct. Such a thing had never before happened. Generally all the Brothers carried straps. Used them according to their nature. Those who were essentially brutal used it savagely. As often as they could. The others seldom used it. Their strokes were meant not to inflict pain but to shame. McNally rarely used the strap. Was never known to use it viciously. Now he stood in characteristic stance. Feet planted widely apart. Hands stuck deeply into the pockets of his trousers under the cassock. Orange Billy spluttered. Attempted to speak but was too flustered to do so. Fell silent. McNally spoke quietly. 'I'll take care of it, Brother O'Sullivan, if you have no objection.' Orange Billy spoke with great difficulty. 'If you insist, Brother.' McNally retorted sharply. 'I do insist, Brother. This is my class now. These boys are my pupils.' Orange Billy inhaled deeply. Exhaled deeply. Turned sharply. Left the room. Slamming the door behind him.

McNally took Timothy by the arm, squeezing it painfully. Led him to a deserted corner of the room. McNally turning him back to the class. 'I don't wish to witness again what I witnessed yesterday. However understandable or just it might be. You have been sufficiently punished. Now return to your place.' Timothy did so. McNally beckoned Murray forward. Again turned his back to the class as he spoke at length.

Murray paled. McNally gave him a few sharp strokes of the leather. Ordered him back to his place in the class. To his astonishment Murray was closer to tears than he, Timothy, was. McNally spoke to the class. To them in particular. 'I expect both of you to shake hands and forget this unfortunate episode. If there is any repetition of what I saw yesterday those concerned will pack their bag and baggage and leave the school. I'll personally see to it. And I'll see they stay out of the school.' All knew it was no empty threat. McNally glared at both of them. Then lightly on his heels turned to face the shrine of Mary Immaculate which was on a high ledge on the front partition of the room. Round the foot of the statue was a cluster of vases of flowers. At its feet a small votive lamp in a globe of bright blue glass burned continuously. All classes throughout the day began with three Hail Mary's and school ended with the 'Salve Regina'. A prayer, he Timothy, particularly loved.

Timothy later heard it from the boys who sat at the front of the class that McNally had said quite definitely to Murray. 'Fight clean or I'll play dirty.' The exact meaning of the phrase was not immediately obvious. It was clear that McNally did not approve of Murray's tactics when fighting. Timothy took heart. McNally did not take classes the following day. Or for some days after. It was rumoured that he was being disciplined for his action of the previous day. Orange Billy took all the classes for the days McNally was absent. The man was plainly miserable. Whatever the facts might be it was clear he was not rejoicing in McNally's humiliation. He dealt gently with the class. His old bluster and bully having altogether vanished. McNally appeared some mornings later while Orange Billy was taking the class. Orange Billy greeted him, McNally, jovially. Apparently sincerely. 'You are welcome, Brother,' he said. McNally nodded his head. 'Thank you, Brother O'Sullivan,' resuming his position at the head of the class. Orange Billy withdrew quietly. Quietly closing the door behind him. Of the two he, Orange Billy seemed the most chastened.

One dark afternoon when darkness was closing in McNally asked him to remain behind which Timothy did. McNally left for the Order House but soon returned with some books which he handed to Timothy. They were Dante's *Inferno*, Turgeniev's *Fathers and Sons*. A slender volume of the Sonnets of Gerard Manley Hopkins. 'Take these,' McNally said. 'You may like one or two. Possibly all three. Read them for pleasure. Not because they are books by famous writers, but because they are splendid works of considerable beauty.' He, Timothy, was astounded. He had never heard of McNally or any other of the Brothers lending books to a pupil. He, Timothy, was both touched. Grateful. McNally he realised was lonely. He always would be so. He had been given the books 'not to further any friendship between him and Brother McNally', but because McNally wished to pass on his love of literature. McNally shortly, almost curtly, dismissed him. He, Timothy was grateful. The books were delightful, not as much as they affected him, Timothy, great pleasure, but because each was in its own way an attempt on the part of the author to rise above the limitations of their human state. Capture for all time their particular vision of what might be called the sublime. So began a friendship which was essentially distant. Disciplined. McNally showed him no favour in the classroom. Though it became known that McNally lent him books. Chose Timothy to walk in the yard with him during the morning and afternoon breaks more frequently than he did with any of the other boys. The term 'snitcher'. A term of utmost contempt, was never levelled at him. Over the year McNally lent him a number of books all of the highest quality. Covering an astonishing range of interest. Plainly literature sustained McNally.

Timothy was pleased, curiously humbled by such generosity of spirit. Veronica, seeing him with some books she knew had not come from the library at Farrighy enquired about them. Timothy explained. For an instance even as he spoke a shadow crossed Veronica's face. She was disappointed that the book didn't come from one of the boys at school. She had been anxious that he met someone who would share his interests. With whom Timothy could form a friendship. She had more than once suggested that he invite a friend to Farrighy for a weekend. For some days during the summer holidays. Timothy thanked her but could not bring himself to say he had made no friends at St Patrick's. The shadow passed. Veronica's eyes shone. She was impressed. Pleased. That she didn't say but Timothy realised as much. 'Not bad for a clod hopper,' she said blithely. She saw Timothy's reaction. 'I'm sorry that was wrong of me and obviously unjust. McNally seems a good fellow. A man with a well rounded mind. I think perhaps you should write to him and ask him to come and dine some Sunday evening with us. I'll see that transport is provided.' He, Timothy, was not particularly anxious to share a table with McNally. Not for any snobbish reasons. But he felt he would be very uncomfortable with the Brother at the same table. McNally replied politely declining the invitation. The rules of the Order would not permit him to accept. He was restrained in his thanks. Timothy believed McNally was pleased to have received the invitation. Veronica saw that some fresh fowl, wild and domestic, some fish, were delivered to McNally during the summer. She did meet McNally for a cup of tea in a small cafe in Tibraddenstown. Though she never said as much. She was impressed by him. Accorded him a respect she rarely accorded the clergy. Devout and pious she, Veronica, might be, but clerics she usually disliked. What she and McNally said was never discussed.

Continuing their afternoon walk they reached the Railway Arms Hotel. Veronica: 'I don't expect any of you would care for anything. Some food perhaps? A cup of coffee?' All declined her invitation so unenthusiastically made.

Veronica tossed her head. 'Perhaps it's just as well. They serve sludge as food and slime for wine. God knows what they serve as coffee.' They turned and began to retrace their footsteps back to where the pony and trap was tethered to a large iron ring, set into one of many granite blacks on the river wall. Timothy saw how some of the passers-by watched Philippa's odd behaviour with amusement. Some with glee. Others respectfully raised their hats while others — women and girls, nodded their heads and smiled. Veronica noticed also. Was very saddened by the bad manners of some. She was visibly grateful for the courtesy shown by others.

They arrived home to find Nora excited and agitated. 'Oh Miss Veronica the Sergeant is waiting to see you,' said Nora .... Something to do with Master Flannery.' Veronica paled. Appeared to stagger slightly. 'Timothy,' she said, 'Please take everyone to the dining-room and see they get their dinner. I'll attend to this.' Flannery had been absent for some days. His absence was readily accepted. Flannery was frequently away sometimes for weeks on end. He came and went. Only the foolish would even ask where he had been. 'And Timothy. See that Nora brings some whiskey and some tea in case the Sergeant wishes to have something to drink. We'll be in the parlour.' The parlour was a small joyless room off the hall used to receive strangers or acquaintances. It was furnished with a large round table surrounded by stiff-backed chairs. He, Timothy, was pleased Veronica had given him the responsibility for the care of the others. He gave instructions that dinner should not be served until Veronica was free to join them. Meanwhile they took their places at the dining table. Waited silently. It became evident that Veronica was not about to join them for some time. For the first time Timothy realised that something serious had happened. He rang for Nora. Asked that dinner be served. All were hungry. All ate well in silence. As the meal progressed it seemed a great bank of clouds of the deepest black was gathering above the house. Each realised that something extraordinary had occurred. That Flannery and therefore everyone at Farrighy, was implicated. Coffee was served. Elizabetha smoked heavily. Philippa sat still and unmoving. Her restless hands betraying her inner agitation.

Veronica summoned Timothy to the parlour where she

introduced him to Sergeant Deasy and two Civic Guards. All of whom he had never met before. Pale and stricken Veronica informed him that a tinker child of twelve or so had been brutally murdered after being sexually assaulted. Her naked body had been found some ten miles away in wild bogland. The police wished to question Flannery. If Flannery was not to be found to search his place. They had a search warrant not only to search Flannery's place but if necessary to search Farrighy itself. Veronica was shaken. 'Please escort the Sergeant and the Guards to Flannery's place and give them every assistance. The wretched murderer of this young child must be brought to book.' It was plain from the tone of her voice and the expression on her face that she believed Flannery not just to be deeply implicated but possibly that he was the murderer.

Neither Timothy nor the Sergeant spoke as they passed through the yards on their way to Flannery's place. Behind them trailed the two Guards, both of them silent also. Hoar frost was settling on the tufts of wild flowers high on the yard walls and on the high weeds and grasses which grew in profusion about Flannery's place. To their astonishment a light showed in one of the upstairs rooms. The front door was wide open. From inside came a peculiar noise, like that of infants weak with hunger, crying as they slowly succumbed to their starvation. 'Rats,' the Sergeant said grimly. He turned to the two Guards. 'Draw your batons and take up positions behind the house. Stop anyone trying to escape. Use fair means if possible. If not, use foul.' His voice was merciless. His jaw jutting forward in grim determination. His eyes gleaming with brutality. There was little doubt that the Sergeant considered Flannery the murderer also. 'If you have any feelings young fellow prepare to forget them. I've never seen a body so mutilated in such an unnatural way. The man, if man it was, was no man. He was a beast of the lowest degree. A fit of madness maybe. Maybe just lust. It's not for me to judge but I saw that child in death. I saw the pain in her face. The terrible state of her body.' He sighed. Drew deep breath. 'You needn't come in with me if you don't like, but since Miss Phipps chose you to represent her I want you to accompany me. I need the two men at the back to stand guard and I need you as an impartial witness to what we see. Or fail to see. Take a deep breath and take hold of yourself. Follow me — quietly.' They entered the house. They heard distinctly what he, Timothy could describe as the voice of infant children crying weakly.

The Sergeant flickered on the torch he was carrying and for good measure drew his baton. 'Is there anyone there?' Silence descended on the house and all in it. The Sergeant flicked the torchlight about. Everything appeared normal. The remainder of a meal half eaten and left on the table was the only thing noticeable. They heard the excited piping upstairs. The Sergeant called out. 'Is there anyone there?' There was silence. Then the scurrying of many feet. Before they could properly prepare themselves a hoard of rats came running down the stairs. Squealing excitedly they dashed by. They went scampering through the doorway out into the night. They were, Timothy had noticed, very fat with sleek shining coats which shone in the torchlight. Their faces like those of cunning, cute infants. 'Mother of the divine Jesus what the hell was that,' the Sergeant exclaimed. 'Rats,' he said unconsciously replying to his own question. 'Rats .... But why. Why so many?' He mustered self control. Again took charge of things. There were pieces of mud lying on the stone floor. Each in part imprinted by the sole of a wellington boot. Flannery he realised rarely even in the worst of weather ever wore wellington boots. 'Don't step on them,' the Sergeant snapped. Timothy snapped in return. 'I wasn't about to walk on them.' The Sergeant breathed deeply. When he spoke there was an edge to his voice. 'Boy I want you as an impartial witness. For the love of Christ don't panic.' The Sergeant was quite unaware that his own voice was sharp with panic. He went to the table. Yelling and shouting he pounded on the bare boards of the table. There was scurrying. A few more rats dashed down the stairs and out the door. 'We had better go up,' the

Sergeant said. 'Keep a tight hold of yourself. God knows what we're going to find.' They climbed the wooden staircase quietly, each dreading in his own way what lay before them in the lighted room above. 'I smell blood,' the Sergeant murmured as if to himself. 'Human blood.' They gained the doorway to the bedroom.

The scene registered acutely and with such totality that Timothy would never forget even the smallest of details. There was a jam-jar on the window sill by the bed. It contained bluebells which had blanched. Withered with time. The lower half of the jam-jar was stained a bright green where the foul water had stagnated before fully evaporating. Remarkably the bell shaped flowers still adhered to the main stalk though one would have thought they would have fallen and withered. Timothy found himself thinking. 'They have been transformed into glass. If they were to fall they would shatter tinklingly on striking the window ledge. I'll remember these flowers,' he thought. He saw Flannery's body. Naked, it lay on a pile of bloodstained sheets. The head had been severed from the body. Had rolled aside. The body itself had been disembowelled. The entrails spilling from behind the retaining bulwark of the stomach muscles. Huge rats feasted on what lay before them in such abundance.

'Jesus, Mary and Saint Joseph,' muttered the Sergeant as he kicked out at the scavenging rats. They squealed. Fled. With the exception of two or three who were determinedly nibbling on one or other of the body's inner organs, openly displayed. The Sergeant swiped at them with his baton. Struck one a heavy blow. The others fled. He, Timothy, screamed. Not consciously. He was simply aware of someone in the far distance screaming wildly. The Sergeant struck him a blow. He, Timothy, saw the Sergeant strike out. Felt the blow of the open hand on the side of his face. Was glad that the person screaming in the distance had stopped. 'Go back to the house. Say nothing whatever about what you've seen. Say Mr. Flannery is dead. Leave the details to me. Now send up Mullins or McCarthy to me.' Timothy was aware he was being spoken to. He nodded stupidly. Very carefully made his way downstairs. Then, he, Timothy bowed his head. Was violently sick. Hardly had he ceased vomiting than he again heard that fellow in the far distance screaming again. Wishing someone would relieve his misery, he, Timothy, lapsed into unconsciousness.

It was, Veronica later admitted, stupid of her to send one so impressionable on such a mission; but she herself was so disturbed at the Sergeant's visit, she had not been thinking straight.

Timothy had been confined to bed on Veronica's instructions. The servants were strictly forbidden to discuss what had happened though Farrighy and all in it was immediately brought to the attention of the world or rather to the attention of those many thousand who relished a sensational murder. The death of the tinker child allowed them to indulge their morbid interests and self-righteousness. A hoard of reporters, journalists and photographers descended on Carra village and the neighbouring district. Spent their time attempting to photograph and interview anyone let through the police cordon around the house. A boy delivering a telegram, itself of no importance, was pleased when his photograph appeared in a national newspaper. His broad oafish grin, his ill fitting uniform, his decrepit bicycle, were immortalised in the few seconds it took to take the photograph. The photograph was titled 'More Bad News?' in at least one newspaper. Journalists and some who insisted they were reporters interviewed anyone who had the slightest connection with Farrighy. All who lived in the house, Veronica in particular, became the object of their attention. Photographs of her wedged into her old Sunday tweed costume, wearing her old but lovely headscarf with its pattern of magnolias both in bud and blossom, appeared in many papers. Her jaw tightly set. Eyes direct. Angry. There were even 'newsreels' of her leaving the house to attend Sunday mass. Tan barking excitedly. Dancing about at her feet. Dozens of motorcars and whatever other means of conveyance they could procure, even an inglorious donkey and cart trailed behind the pony and trap. Bannion as angry by all the attention and every bit as tight-lipped as Veronica who firmly refused to forgo daily mass despite the conduct of the newspaper people. Attention as such didn't particularly worry her but the means by which they tried to imbue the most trivial of matters with monstrous overtones disturbed her deeply. 'They,' the press were not behaving decently. 'They,' weren't playing fair. Veronica disapproved. Strongly. Their conduct towards Philippa revolted, angered her, in the extreme. Philippa could not be denied her daily walk. To do so resulted in agitation. Restlessness which in time gave way to anger. Inevitably resulted in what Veronica termed 'difficult conduct'. Philippa therefore continued to take her late evening walk with Bannion. Her eccentric dress, her even more eccentric behaviour made her immediately interesting to reporters and photographers. Photographs of her appeared even in European and North American newspaper. The reporters told her so as if she were being honoured by such worldwide attention. Some hinting darkly that because of her illness she might in some way ... however obscure ... be connected with the murder of both the tinker child and Flannery. Veronica was outraged.

She was grieving at the death of a relative for whom she had felt little sympathy during his life. His death was so foul and hideous she experienced excessive guilt and remorse. She therefore saw that Flannery was buried according to the rites of the Church of Ireland to which he had at one time adhered rather nebulously. His funeral was solemn. Well attended. Some came to simply stare but there were those who had to some extent liked Flannery. Felt he had the right to decent burial. Veronica received and entertained the 'Protestant Crowd' as she invariably called those who belonged to the Protestant branch of the family. Their sympathy had been more marked than at Peter's funeral. Which they had attended to ensure that their side of the family was not outnumbered. After Flannery's funeral they returned to Farrighy where

Veronica provided a light luncheon. Some drinks. They seemed in some way grateful that Veronica had not insisted on a Catholic burial for Flannery. His mother after all was known to be Catholic. She had been known to very few. Had she presented herself at their homes they would not have received her. Veronica was touched by their fidelity to the unhappy man whose sexual desires marked him among men, and whose extremely unpleasant behaviour was largely due to head injuries received during the war. Veronica could have insisted on Catholic burial. They would have been in no position to stop her if the Church had permitted such a burial. Veronica for her part had no wish to keep a cricket score of weddings, births and deaths as they occurred in one branch of the family or the other. She was touched by their solicitude for Flannery. They had been far more kind, attentive, to him in his illnesses than she, Veronica had been. They had never refused him help nor did they always wait until asked for help. Timothy realised for the first time where Flannery went when he was not to be seen at his place at Farrighy. He doubted that all the time was spent with those of the family who knew, understood him better. They treated Flannery decently. That mattered very much to Veronica. Something of a thaw occurred at the luncheon following Flannery's burial.

Philippa was a great concern to all. Veronica feared that details of the murder might penetrate her consciousness, that the presence of so many people about the house might frighten, perplex her. Such didn't prove to be the case. She remained as ever calm. Distant. Quite unmoved by events about her. She appeared preoccupied with an inner life which excluded all other things.

On a very wet afternoon she approached Elizabetha, requesting drawing paper. Pencils. She spoke clearly. Her voice even. Controlled. Elizabetha who cared for her when Bannion was not about, was astonished. Pleased. She at once told Veronica of what had happened. Both experienced a surge of hope that Philippa had recovered to some extent. Would hopefully in time recover altogether. She drew innumerable sketches of small exquisite birds. The drawings were minute but perfectly detailed. All had full feathered tails rather like strutting peacocks. It was clear that whatever Philippa had lost, she had not lost her artistry. When questioned about her drawings she simply stared unseeingly at whoever addressed her. As soon as each piece of paper was completely covered with drawings on both sides of the page she abandoned them. They fell from her hands like leaves from an old, stricken tree unaware of its extreme state of decrepitude. She continued to collect wrapping papers off sweets, chocolates. She thrust them into her cloth bag which she always carried. In a short time she had vast amounts. At night after dinner she retreated to the library. Squatting before the fire she carefully smoothed out the balled pieces of paper with the nail of her right forefinger. She carefully stored the smoothed papers in one of many empty chocolate boxes. Each night she took leave of everybody. Allowing herself to be led off by Nora to a night of drug-induced sleep. All without protest. Like a lamb, Timothy thought, like a lamb she goes to slaughter and like a lamb she utters not a word. Holding close to her breast the chocolate box she was currently using. Her two arms folded about it like the arms on the effigies of virgin martyrs with their hands folded about their breasts to signify their unviolated state. A state they chose above the very gift of life itself.

She no longer gathered flowers. Was quite unmoved by the most impressive array of flowers in the garden. In the ditches. Hedgerows of the fields about the house. She showed no emotion when presented with bunches of flowers by Veronica or Bannion or Timothy. Whoever gathered them. Hoping they would arouse in her the delight she once beheld at the sight of flowers or blossom of any kind. She smiled enigmatically from time to time. There was something chilling to those who saw her smile so. She was silent also. She no longer croaked as she used. Nor did she laugh. Or scream with terror during the night marking the total collapse of her mind. Her final descent into madness which all felt instinctively would come sooner or later. She took a walk each evening, irrespective of the weather, with Bannion in whose company she was least strained. Veronica did not fully approve and at times seemed to resent the state of affairs but she had been advised not to defy Philippa in all but the most serious matters. To do so might precipitate a further bout of illness. They walked very far. Sometimes being absent from the house for close on two hours. Or more. Veronica was extremely tense during their absence. Smoked a great deal. Fell silent. Savagely kicked the burning logs in the fire. Bannion returned Philippa safely on each occasion. Veronica relaxed. Brightened perceptibly. Was grateful to Bannion for such staunch devotion. Striking fidelity. As with Alexander, he, Timothy, was jealous at the fact that Bannion had in this matter displaced him in Veronica's affections. He knew it wasn't so. Certainly not at the level which most mattered. Nevertheless he suffered jealously.

The inquest into the death of the tinker child was conducted in Tibraddenstown Courthouse. Evidence was given as to the true extent, the nature of the assault on the child. The major assault which had resulted in her death. She had been battered to death with a blunt instrument. For the first time the public received details regarding the sexual assault prior to her death. The details were sickening. So much so that a detailed account could not be published in the newspapers, Irish or international. Forensic evidence showed that some of the blood in the child's clothing was of the same blood group as Flannery's. More conclusively it was proved that some of the blood found on the discarded clothing in Flannery's bedroom was that of the child. The evidence seemed conclusive. The child had been sexually violated in an inhuman manner. A short stave had been inserted in the vagina. Driven upwards with great force. Then the child already dying was battered about the head with unbridled savagery. Death had resulted but there was no doubt the girl had suffered greatly. How greatly, for how long, could not be established. Veronica had cried aloud when the evidence was presented. She was led from the court weeping. Showing signs of collapse. Elizabetha and Timothy sought to sustain her. He, Timothy, felt as before ... that should Veronica falter. Fail. All at Farrighy would fail with her.

Father Doran was a blunt bullet headed man with unruly grey hair on his head. In his nostrils. Ears. Called at Veronica's request to see her at Farrighy. The man was dour. Harsh in his treatment of people. Veronica had shown no liking for him in the past. Now it was to him. Her parish priest she turned to. He was her confessor. Must have shown in the confessional qualities which were otherwise not obvious. He, Timothy, had rarely confessed to him, preferring to go to one of the priests in the priory in Tibraddenstown. Father Doran who was not noticeably pious. Yet Veronica who loved the works of great Catholic mystics found in him a source of comfort. Support. He gave her hope where no hope had hitherto been forthcoming ... the grace to hope in hopes to come. Timothy thought the man a lout.

Attention was once again focused on Flannery's death. It had been thought that both murders had been the work of one maniac. Now that it had been established that Flannery had murdered the child, the question then arose, who had murdered Flannery?

It had been established that both murders had taken place on the same day or night. Oates was immediately suspect but Oates was behind bars in Tibraddenstown gaol where he was being held pending a court case involving two factions of the tribe who had met in the town the night before the murders were discovered. Both factions had engaged in bloody fights with clubs of wood or iron bars. The better part of his tribe were therefore witness that Oates was not directly involved in the murder of Flannery. The suspicion lingered that Oates was deeply implicated. Nothing could be proved — a search of his encampment some miles outside Carra yielded some results. In a decrepit caravan a small hoard of jewellery was discovered. The couple living in the caravan swore they were innocent of all knowledge of the hoard. Knew nothing whatever of its existence. The police inspector conducting the search believed them. What better place to hide something. To ensure its safety. Than under the feet of someone totally unaware of the hoard's existence. Police enquiries readily established that Bobo and Skipper were both abroad at the time of the murder. They plainly indicated they would remain there indefinitely.

Veronica was deeply distressed when confronted with the items discovered. A cigarette case of Sterling silver. A gold signet ring. Both engraved in the name: John Gerald Phipps. She recognised immediately as having belonged to her father. Her father had on a number of occasions been robbed. Robbery was in a sense an inevitable consequence of his way of life. More than once he had been robbed by one of the ladies he had entertained in the room of some of the smaller hotels in the province. During the civil strife of nineteen-eighteen to nineteen-twenty two Farrighy itself had been frequently raided by both the British auxiliaries and the more notorious, undisciplined Black and Tans. On every occasion some items of value were stolen ... the spoils of war as Veronica termed them rather grimly. Though deeply grateful that all in the house had survived unmolested. Uninjured. The house not burned down about them. All the family valuables including the house silver had been lodged in the bank at Tibraddenstown. Except for some household silver that had remained there since. They were valuable though not extremely so. Comprising for the most part of objects which had belonged to her father. Her father. Not her mother. Was the one who delighted in personal decorative objects. Cuff-links. Tie-pins. Rings. A number of cigarette cases. What distressed Veronica deeply was that the pieces found in the caravan had never been lodged in the bank. They survived in a small box in which Veronica kept all the readily available money in what was known as the strong room. Over the years items belonging to her father, some few pieces of jewellery, disappeared. There at one time had been an incident in which one of the servant girls had all but been accused of stealing from the strong room though she had no means of access whatever. The girl had left of her own volition to seek work in a factory in England. The thefts continued. Had then suddenly ceased.

It was now quite clear that Flannery had been the thief though how he obtained entry to the strong room was something Veronica was at a loss to explain. There was a small amount of money in bank notes which was kept for emergencies. Household expenses. Flannery could easily have taken the money. But Veronica concluded grimly Oates would have preferred valuables rather than bank notes. Oates denied any theft, freely admitting that Flannery had given gifts to him. When asked what he, Oates could have done to receive such generous payment Oates cooly admitted that he had brought young tinker girls to model for Flannery's drawings and sketches. When asked if he had ever seen any of Flannery's oil paintings, he answered 'No.' The paintings were in the view of the police inspector conducting the case, of the most obscene kind. They were he asserted, vile beyond belief. Young innocent children were depicted in a manner which would shock.

At his suggestion Veronica had destroyed all the paintings. Most of the drawings. Sketches. She believed they were not without merit of some kind but were nevertheless vile and calculated to pervert rather than edify. Accordingly they were destroyed. Though he, Timothy never saw them he had seen sufficient of Flannery's sketches. Watercolours he had done over the week he had spent with them when they had been harvesting the turf a year previously to realise that those sketches were undoubtedly the work of a first rate artist. He, Timothy could only regret very much that he had not been permitted to see the paintings. Veronica refused to allow him to make a selection of the more 'innocent' watercolours. Nor would she allow Elizabetha select some. Elizabetha had seen the obscene paintings. Rated them highly as paintings but also undoubtedly obscene. The work of an indisputable degenerate. There was every reason for preserving some of the less offensive works but Veronica was adamant. What paintings, sketches, drawings were in Flannery's place were burned by Veronica herself. She alone. Carried them from the house. Piled them on a bonfire in the wild overrun garden of Flannery's place which yielded such perfect roses with the minimum of care and attention from anyone. Satisfied that she had heaped all the paintings together Veronica carefully standing down wind set the heap alight. It blazed immediately. Spectacularly. The leaping flames must have risen to a height of some ten feet. There were minute explosions as taut canvas strips ripped apart. Tubes of paint burst. Not only was Veronica burning Flannery's paintings she was also burning all his oils and brushes. Every piece of canvas in the place. Used. Unused. All over the fields of Farrighy and on the house itself floated soft pink coloured ash which fell. Turning grey. In some instances white when it landed. Some had lighted on Timothy's bare arms burning them faintly, very faintly. He was to remember the white ash that showered down about Farrighy that day some ten years later when Jewish survivors of concentration camps described how the white ash of their cremated fellows had fallen on fields of Edelweiss. The ash that day Timothy had seen disappear like melting snow. It had burned faintly. Very faintly. The ash from the 'Factory' chimneys had not faded .... It burned very deeply on contact with living tissue. It scarred Timothy's consciousness, the consciousness of all mankind. Reading the terrible reports of the attempt to murder Jewish people, he, Timothy, was deeply moved ... and thought ... I still love Alexander .... Standing there in a London street in bright sunshine remembering the white ash that had fallen on Farrighy ... and still remembering with love. Loss. Alexander who had little pity for anyone else ... and still he thought with love. Loss .... 'I love Alexander ....' Did he survive the war? Yes he did. Was he implicated in the mass murders? ...?

Standing near the bonfire, Timothy thought the ashes are still burning ... they could start fires if they alight on bare dry timber. On the dry grasses. Wheat fields nearby. No such thought occurred to Veronica. If it did, she didn't allow it to disturb her, deflect her from the task. She worked hard and it was twilight when she was done. A great scorched circle of twinkling ash marked the spot where Flannery's paintings, his every belonging, had burned. Veronica deep in thought stood staring at the circle, hands thrust deeply into the pockets of her cardigan. Her lips parted, her teeth gritted. She remained looking for some time, then rain began to fall. It fell lightly at first. Strengthened. Fell with some ferocity drenching everything. Veronica remained. Her bow backed figure awash with rain. Timothy already drenched could no longer stand it. Ran to the shelter of the house. The following day Flannery's place was boarded up. Sealed. Isolated. All access to it barred. As far as Veronica was concerned it had ceased to exist.

Few considered Flannery deserving of any pity despite the fact that his imbalance of mind was due to wounds sustained in the war. He was not altogether responsible for his actions. Timothy did pity. Veronica did not. Flannery was never likely admitted to her 'canon of the dead' which she so esteemed. Venerated. Before whose souls she laid her many petitions.

Alexander returned from Germany quite pleased with himself. He had been accepted as an extra-mural pupil by the University of Berlin. They went to extraordinary lengths to accommodate him. Lectures would be mimeographed. Forwarded to him weekly. He would be set exercises which he would have to complete. Return to the University for correction. He would in virtually every respect be a participating student without however having access to a science laboratory for research. It was by no means the best of solutions but it was the best Alexander could attain. He would not have succeeded to such an extent had he not met a former lecturer of his from the Gymnasium he had attended who attested to his undoubted brilliance. The expectancy of great accomplishment in his chosen field. The question of military service had been postponed until he returned to Germany. It was hoped, his health would have improved sufficiently to allow him to serve his term. Elizabetha was not noticeably elated at what Alexander had achieved. She feigned satisfaction because it was the least Alexander could expect of her in a matter which would determine the future course of his life.

He expressed horror, dismay at Flannery's death. Elizabetha had kept him informed at all times. He had written a short note offering his condolences to Veronica. Now offering his condolences in person. Veronica received his expression with noticeable coldness. Alexander suggested that he and Timothy resume their daily swim.

His confessor held his breath on hearing him speak. Had stumblingly asserted that his, Timothy's, unnatural state, might be the means by which Timothy could attain grace in his life. Salvation in the next. Homosexuality he took great pain to stress was not sinful. Homosexual acts were most certainly so. One of the most bestial sins there was. Particularly repugnant to God. The Priest, Father Cotter whom Timothy had found sympathetic, understanding in the confessional, had ended what for him must have been one of the most embarrassing consultations of his life as a priest offering Timothy a miraculous medal on a blue thread to wear about his neck as a safeguard against all temptations of the flesh. Timothy declined gently. But determinedly. He felt not without reason. He was never again to seek help in a similar way. It seemed it was not believed that the homosexual state, and any sense of personal honour were compatible. He, Timothy, believed that this was not so. Was determined to prove so.

He accepted Alexander's offer to swim. He was rising earlier than usual because of the long slow cycle to Tribraddenstown. Now he rose even earlier to swim with Alexander. For what Timothy believed was the first time in her life, Veronica did not rise for Mass. Her declaration that she could not risk the life of what she called Bannion's old nag did not ring true. To his astonishment her failure to attend daily Mass saddened him deeply though he had long ceased to attend Mass with her.

It was the severest of winters. Hard frost occurred in the hours of darkness. Persisted throughout the day. Cycling to Gerrard's Cross was dangerous. Sometimes the roads were so bad Moss Twomey could not make the journey to Tibraddenstown by lorry. To do so would endanger the life of those travelling in it. On such mornings, he Timothy was compelled to cycle the entire journey to school. The journey took some two hours to complete. He persisted because the following June he would have to take his Leaving Certificate examinations. Soon after, the Civil Service examinations. The results of both examinations would determine his life. His standard of living. His social standing. The life-long company of those whose standard of behaviour, moral beliefs, he would be expected to accept. To honour. He persisted in attending school when he could honestly plead exemption on the grounds that the weather conditions made such a daily journey all but impossible. Because he felt gathering in him in the sense of strength. Determination he had hitherto lacked to a marked degree. He was, Timothy realised, maturing. Could soon expect to enter a man's estate. What precisely life would entail for him as a homosexual, which he now realised he, Timothy, most certainly was, he could not imagine. He had sought the counsel of his confessor at St. Patrick's Church in Tibraddenstown. And the advice of one of the town's two doctors. Both of whom happened to be Catholic. Priest and doctor had been acutely embarrassed by his admission of homosexuality. The possibility of a cure for his condition. The doctor had been blunt. Cure? There was no known cure for his ancestry. History. Timothy heard in the dark cold distance a Mass bell calling the faithful to their prayer. Those hearing that bell. Refusing to respond.

He, Timothy, experiencing the sorrow of the remaining faithful.

The morning was freezing. The cold soon penetrated their layers of clothing. Chilling them to the bone. Even before they reached the river, Timothy's fingers and toes were numb as he imagined Alexander's were also. They stripped quickly. 'Don't hesitate,' Alexander shouted plunging into the black river banks on which stood the rushes, sedges and other weeds. Rigid with frost. He, Timothy, saw that Alexander was wearing a bathing slip. Stunned, he hesitated for a second then plunged into the water which wasn't quite as cold as he expected it would be.

'Just a few strokes,' Alexander called out, 'until we get used to it again.' The waters proved numbing. They had to climb out after a few minutes. Both feeling frozen to the marrow. They ran up and down the riverbank shouting. And yelling. Leaping. And jumping to accelerate the circulation of the blood. Generate some warmth. He, Timothy, looked hard at Alexander when he believed Alexander wasn't aware. Alexander was if anything more beautiful than Timothy remembered him since that day Alexander had arrived at Farrighy. Stepping forward, crunching the gravel beneath his feet, extended a hand in greeting while smiling warmly. Alexander aroused his love, affection. As had no other living person, but now lust was inextricably entwined with his love. Affection. As it had been before. Timothy realised it was all futile. Alexander had told him as much by wearing a bathing slip whereas before they had both swam naked. Alexander, Timothy realised, had consciously or unconsciously Alexander placed him, Timothy, beyond the pale. The limits of their friendship deep though it was, had now been clearly demarcated. Some evenings later Alexander came to Timothy's room after he had gone to bed. Timothy was reading by candlelight. A detective thriller he had borrowed from Veronica. Alexander greeted him. Sat on the side of the bed. They spoke of nothing in particular. Alexander had long exhausted the topic of the miraculous recovery of Germany under the National Socialism. On his return from Germany he could speak of little else. To the despair of all who had to listen to him. That night, sitting on Timothy's bed Alexander had paused, looking directly at him, said sadly. 'Timothy, you have lost your innocence.' He, Alexander. Flushed red. 'I do not mean, well — your sexual innocence. I mean rather that peculiar innocence of both body and spirit I sensed you to possess when first we met. Now it's gone.' Timothy replied coldly. 'I think you imagine things, Alexander. I doubt if I ever possessed such innocence. If I have lost it I am unaware of any sense of loss.' Alexander again flushed. 'If I've offended you I'm very sorry. I simply meant ....' 'I know what you meant,' Timothy interrupted coldly. 'There's no need whatever to explain.' Alexander smiled wryly, 'Perhaps'. Alexander left the room. What Alexander had said disturbed him .... He, Timothy, was acutely aware of a sense of loss. A loss which was partially though not principally a loss of sexual importance. He was aware of a religious sense of loss. He felt that a slender thread had been broken. In his case forever. But such loss he believed was experienced by all on reaching adolescence. It had to be born. It was the price of adulthood. There was little to be gained by dwelling on the fact. He continued to read a little. Could not continue. He rose, took a cigarette from his bedside table. Lighted it. Sat smoking.

The house was perfectly still. The dynamo had ceased to throb. Outside the countryside was white and still and frozen. On impulse he dressed. Made his way to the kitchen. The tray prepared for Veronica every night. Left for her on the kitchen table wasn't there. It usually consisted of some thin sandwiches of cheese. White meat. She took Ovaltine which was made in a stout brown mug for her. More oddly, a small bowl of jelly. Or custard. Or some other after dinner sweet. She had as she said 'a sweet' tooth. Hence like a dessert of some kind last thing at night. During the lenten fast she did not take her 'night-tray'. Nor did she take it if she were praying for a particular intention. Seeing the tray wasn't there, he assumed Veronica had long gone to bed. The kettle on the range was cold to touch. Had been last used quite some time ago. He raked the fire in the grate. Put the kettle on. Taking a blanket from a nearby chair draped it about his shoulders. The kettle boiled. He made some strong tea. Sat. Thinking.

The blanket had belonged to Bridget. She used to drape it

about her shoulders while she sat musing. Praying quietly before she retired to her bed in Philippa's bedroom. Sometimes to her own bedroom in the small house by the orchard. Timothy, had seen her room a few times as he helped her with her chores about the house. A double bed in an attic room. Bareboarded. Frugally furnished. The bed was large. Sharply defined by its austere white linen. Above hung a detailed engraving of the Disposition of Christ from the Cross. A washing stand. A large blue bowl. Pitcher of the same delicate colour. Resting on the washstand. Completed the furnishing. A recessed window looked out over the orchards to the fields beyond. Far. The grey mountains. He had always thought how marvellous it must be to wake in such a room. He thought of her now. His 'Mary of the Gaels' an old Irish name for Saint Bridget which placed her on the same high level of affection as Mary the mother of Christ. How he wished she was alive. He remembered her. Aged. Bowed. Blue eyes. Very beautiful in the way old people sometimes are. Lips parted in prayer as she moved about with a bunch of mint in her hands as she shuffled about replacing the mint in the jam-jars which she had positioned on various window sills about the house. There they remained fresh. Green. Smelling sweetly in the hot summer air. The cuttings rooted readily in the jars sprouting long white tendrils. The bunches of mint seemed to last forever. One could be forgiven for thinking they took care of themselves. One day, one passed a window. Noting that the bunch was withering. Then there was the mint, again. Green. Sweet smelling as if by the grace of God. Bridget who said so little. Did so much. Praying with her Rosary which was in a pocket deeply hidden in her long black dress. As she climbed the staircases to see that the oil lamps were all properly trimmed. Always had plenty of oil. Particularly the one by the window which was referred to as the 'night lamp'. Burned all through the night. She looked so unsubstantial. So unaware of the world in which she moved. Had her being. Yet knew all there was to be known about those in the house. A great many outside the house as if by extra-ordinary dispensation. It was to her they all turned in their hour of need. She in her hour of need made her way to the small kitchen of her own house by the fruit laden apple trees. Where in the dim light of the votive lamp she kneeled. Prayed before an oleograph of the Christ. His exposed heart. There she kept vigil of her own. Laid all her pleas. Made all her intercessions. He, Timothy, wished she were alive. Though unaware of having transgressed in any way he felt the need to confess. Receive absolution. 'Oh Timothy, love .... How innocent you are.' Bridget had murmured more than once.

He rose. Ferreting in the large clothes press at the far end of the kitchen in which was kept woollens. Coats. Mackintoshes. Together with boots of all sizes. Innumerable pairs of socks. All of them unmatching, which were the common property of anyone who chose to use them. He put on an extra pullover, a pair of socks. Boots. Finally a scarf. A heavy tweed overcoat which didn't quite fit. Quietly he lifted the latch of the kitchen door and stepped outside pausing briefly to see if Tan had heard the sound of the door being unlatched. No sharp yelp disturbed the sleeping house. The ground outside was treacherous with heavy ice. He could hardly gain a foothold. Slipping slightly with each step he took. The open fields he knew would not be dangerous. Patience. Concentration would get him there. He kept his hands thrust into the pockets of his coat. If he fell he wanted to land on his side rather than impulsively try to break his fall by putting out an arm which would most likely be broken. He made his way through the yards. Round by the side of the house. Gaining at last the open fields. His boots crunched the prickly grass underfoot. Each time he stepped in a frozen hoofmark, the ice crackled and broke with a sharp snap. Thistles, ragworth, sorrel, sedges, rushes. All were stiffly white. Striking in a way not noticed before. The air sharp and cutting. It hurt his lungs to inhale for some time. His breath vaporised in white gusts of steam like large billowing clouds virginally white against an ink blue sky. Which usually augured rain. The dark sky was thickly studded with stars. All shone with extraordinary clarity. In the far distance a dog yelped as if in sudden pain. His bark carrying clearly on the clean cold air.

Timothy made his way to the riverbank. Watched the smooth black waters moving silently by. Shining in the starlight like an unending ribbon of darkest velvet. He no longer rose early to swim as he had once done with such delight. Alexander still swam. On his own. Irrespective of the weather. Since the rift in their relationship Alexander had been less expansive. Less exuberant than before. He seemed preoccupied. He smiled considerably less. Was less prone to enthuse about things which had once seemed of great importance. He rarely visited the dynamo relying on Bannion to care for it as he had long before Alexander had arrived at Farrighy. Bannion maintained it in the near state of disintegration which he considered the dynamo's natural state. Was well pleased with himself. Chugg, the Hungarian car Alexander had worked on for long a time, had gone to great lengths to restore to running order, remained in the garage, its chassis resting on wooden blocks. All but forgotten. Veronica had used it occasionally when Philippa had come out of the nursing home but preferred a jaunt in the pony and trap ... which she found so much more bracing. Since it was so rarely used Alexander advised that it be kept on wooden blocks rather than simply garage it. This was done.

Elizabetha returned to her former stage of isolation. Asserting herself far less than when Philippa had been first ill. She herself seemed beset by problems smiling vacuously when spoken to. Not always replying. She ate little. Made brittle metallic statements about nothing in particular from time to time. She read with an appetite which bordered on the voracious the newspapers which continued to come from Germany as frequently as before. She sat in various little-used rooms. In the corner of the library. Morning rooms when they were otherwise vacant. She and Alexander quarrelled bitterly and loudly. Usually at night. Sometimes Elizabetha wept audibly. Timothy realised as did Veronica, that inwardly

Elizabetha was crumbling. Lapsing into a state of despair. Which might prove total. Irreversible. Neither he nor Veronica knew how to help her. She spurned their approaches. Smiled. Deflected their questions concerning her state. Withdrew. Further despaired.

Philippa had obtained a large spool of strong. Pliable copper wire. Together with a pair of snips which enabled her to cut the wire as required. She most likely discovered them in the garage. The dynamo-house. With the wire she began to construct the framework of scores of birds of the kind she had been drawing so obsessively for months. It was of the utmost importance to establish if she had asked anyone specifically for the wire. Snips. Had she done so the fact that she had spoken rationally might have indicated that areas of the brain thought dormant had in some extraordinary manner been reactivated. But she had not spoken to anyone. Apart from her continuous construction of her birds she remained as remote. As inaccessible. Veronica who had hoped so much was bitterly disappointed.

To the south the lights in the windows of the cottages. Cabins. Set in the low hills fringing the lowlands range beyond gleamed in enticing beauty. Timothy thought. How beautiful. How memorable. How many walking the streets of New York or Chicago drew a sharp breath when they remember such a sight. How lonely they must be remembering the place of their birth. He stood looking intently at the scene before him and thought ... and later he, Timothy, was to remember thinking. How terrible to die. Never seeing such a scene again. He walked on curiously at peace with himself. Alexander and he had ceased to be friends. Alexander still aroused in him, Timothy, the deepest love. And affection. But Timothy no longer liked Alexander. He knew he would never love again with such innocence and the possibility of such betrayal. And he, Timothy .... Would he betray others during his life? And how often? He heard the old interior voice tell him that he Timothy would betray many people. Many times. With little reason. He would not be spared that .... Mankind's terrible blight.

~

He moved quietly not with any intention of doing so. Because his sense were curiously altered. He was aware of the heightened sensibility one experiences on rare occasions. His movements were fluid. His shadow darkening the white frosted glass by his side. He turned from the fields close to the main road at the end of the long avenue which led to the house. Above him tree branches were entwined like hands. He began to make his way on the frozen churned-up slush below the trees. Everything was so still. He so utterly a part of the scene it seemed to him that he was a dream figure moving silently across a dream landscape.

He had only gone a short distance when he heard a cry of pain. Quickly muffled. Ahead. Against a tree he saw two figures locked in sexual embrace. Astonished. He stood still not daring to move. He instantly recognised Bannion whose companion's head, shoulder. Long white arm. Hung about Bannion's shoulder like a broken body of a swan. The figure he saw was Philippa. He realised with drawn impact that Philippa, Bannion. Were lovers. Their love was carnal. Had been so for many years. He realised that the true nature of their relationship had been known to Veronica. Possibly from when it first occurred. This, he Timothy, realised, he would have considered some short while before. As sinful lust. A grievous sin causing grievous pain to the heart of God. Now he saw it otherwise. It was an act of love. A very deep, affectionate act of love. It denoted the presence of grace rather than establishing its absence. To what extent Philippa responded to the act of love, Timothy could not imagine. It was possible that she was quite unaware of the act. Or it had no significance for her. She might well be aware of the act at a very deep level of consciousness. Be revitalised by it. Strengthened. Made braver. Sexuality could, he, Timothy, knew, be what he had once considered the grace of God. Carefully he turned. As silently as possible made his way back down the drive. Unable to completely avoid the crunch of frozen gravel beneath his feet. He regained the fields. Circling about to avoid Philippa, Bannion. Arrived soon at the house. He shed some of the additional clothes. Hurriedly made a mug of tea which he would have by his bedside as he read in bed.

At the landing window the lamp about which Bridget had been so particular. Attentive to. Shone brightly, its long elongate flames unstirring. Casting shadows everywhere. Silence enfolded the house. All in it, Timothy thought, are sleeping, but no sooner had he so thought that he sensed the presence of someone in the shadows of the attic staircase. He sensed it was Veronica. She stepped from the shadows. Came halfway down the short attic staircase. Now more fully visible in the light of the oil-lamp. She seemed more bowed. More aged than before. Timothy knew that she, Veronica, realised that only death lay ahead of her. Until she did die, her life would be one of unremitting drudgery as it had been since she was a very young woman. Philippa could not long survive outside a custodial institute where she would become one of those broken-backed people with fractured eyes. Beat low by life. The vicissitudes of life. Soon. The land about Farrighy would be repossessed by the institutes to which it belonged. It would cease to be. The House. Would very shortly fall into disrepair. Inevitably. Ruin. Veronica, he sensed to be deeply saddened. A lighted cigarette hung from her lower lip. Its smoke spiralled upwards behind the protective lens of her glasses which so distorted the damaged retina of her left eye much.

'Did you chance to meet Philippa and Bannion while out walking,' she asked hesitantly. 'Yes,' Timothy replied. 'I saw them at the end of the long drive. I expect they walked further than they intended and are therefore a little late.' 'Yes,' said Veronica in a leaden voice. The voice of one who would welcome the soft approach of death. 'I expect that's what happened. I worry about them so,' she continued. 'Philippa of course in particular. But thank God there is Bannion. If I die Bannion will not forsake her. He is touchingly faithful to her in his own way.' 'Yes,' Timothy agreed. 'Bannion is very faithful.' He now knew that Veronica was aware of the nature of their relationship. Was profoundly grateful things were so. He no longer wished to prolong their discussion. He wished Veronica 'Good night'. She returned his good wishes. Hoping that he would sleep well. Then as he took his leave she asked quietly 'do you no longer pray Timothy?' It was a brutal question. Struck Timothy with brutal force. He turned. Faced her. 'No Veronica, I no longer pray.' 'At all,' she asked. 'Never,' he replied. He was about to take his leave again when she asked sadly. 'May I remember you in my prayers?' It was he knew, the greatest gift of her keeping. Rarely given. Never lightly. He bit his lower lip. Tried to staunch the rising tide of long repressed emotions. Suddenly, he Timothy was aware of a desire to wound her, Veronica, deeply. By refusing her prayers. 'May I remember you in my prayers?' How sadly she said it. As sadly when once intruding on him while he was at prayer. 'I'm so sorry. I thought perhaps you had difficulty in sleeping and thought to bring you some crystallised fruits.' 'Yes Veronica. Please remember me in your prayers.' 'Thank you,' she replied simply. He knew everything between them was now ended. He gained his room, distressed. Disturbed. He, Timothy reflected. I saw those mountain cottages as through the eyes of an exile. But I am an exile. Ever have been. Ever will be.

Some mornings later he rose before dawn, took what money he had. Cycled to Tibraddenstown. Caught the first train of the day to Dublin where he embarked on the night boat to Liverpool. The life which awaited him in England. He left Veronica a short, kind note. Knew that it would hurt that Timothy to whom she had been so kind would appear so ungrateful.

About the Author

Liam Lynch was born in Dublin in 1937. He lived in Cork, Limerick, Birmingham and Manchester before returning to settle in his native city. During the 1960s and '70s Lynch's plays — including *Do Thrushes Sing in Birmingham?*, *Strange Dreams Unending*, *Soldier* and *Krieg* — established his reputation as a playwright. Lynch's first novel, *Shell, Sea Shell*, was published by Wolfhound in 1982, followed in 1985 by *Tenebrae: A Passion*. He was nominated as 'one of the top Irish Contemporary Authors' in 1984. Liam Lynch died five years later, aged fifty-two. *The Pale Moon of Morning* is his last work.

Also by Liam Lynch

Shell, Sea Shell

Someone mentions the sea . . . and Anna's odyssey begins. Shaped
by love, torn by wartime tragedy, this is the story of a young Jewish
girl's life. Her flights from Holland to England and finally to an
Irish island, move through relationships that form and reform her
person and her outlook on life.

*'The poetic romanticism of plot is exonerated by the author's ability to lift
events out of cliché to almost unnerving heights.'*
In Dublin Magazine
ISBN 0 86327 030 1

Tenebrae: A Passion

Tenebrae is the forceful, passionate record of a priest's struggle
with his own inner demons.
Canon James Fitzgerald's loss of faith, coupled with an
arrogant contempt for his parishioners and the memory of youthful
thwarted affections, is precariously countered by his awareness of
religious grace in a dying young woman with whom he shares
a supernatural experience.

An unforgettable evocation of a man's failure to recognise his need
for love.
ISBN 0S 86327 036 0

More Fiction from Wolfhound Press

The Hungry Earth

Seán Kenny

Turlough Walsh is a high-earning yuppie accountant — nice car,
nice kids, nice Dublin house. The boss admires his cutthroat
approach to personnel management — squeezing the utmost from
'human resources'. He's getting places — some call it succeeding —
and this involves keeping others down. Not that it bothers
Turlough. Guilt and remorse just aren't his way of thinking.

Things start to change when he inherits a rural stone cottage, and
cracks his head falling drunk through the open half-door. He
awakes in the throes of that human catastrophe, the Great Irish
Famine. Here he meets people who are suffering, people he grows
to love and care about. Suddenly he's asking himself questions. His
suburban complacency begins to crumble.

In this stunning first novel, Seán Kenny fruitfully combines realism,
history, and time-slip sequences with the shocking flavours of a
psycho-thriller. Macabre humour leavens the spiritual bankruptcy
and quest of a very contemporary character, whose routine work,
social life, and extra-marital affairs with young women are about to
turn round forever.

ISBN 0 86327 479 X

More Fiction from Wolfhound Press

Breakfast in Babylon

Emer Martin

They're enmeshed in a bad luck union . . . .

Isolt is a young Irish drifter, catching the magic bus from Tel Aviv to Paris, floating down to the South of France, trapped in drugs and dreaming of Dublin.

Christopher is the Hoodoo Man, dealer, king of petty crime and collector of refugees and winos, on the run from the police and the Detroit bikers.

'Heaven is a rainy Sunday morning in Clontarf, a bottle of Jameson and
Breakfast in Babylon *to read again. I loved it from start to finish.'*
Niall Quinn, author of *Welcome to Gomorrah.*
ISBN 0 86327 483 8

More Fiction from Wolfhound Press

Welcome to Gomorrah

Niall Quinn

*'Lia gave me a smile from her repertoire of smiles. It had that touch of fear
and bashfulness, like the mountain cat's.
She was all of smiles, of hues of smiles, all the tropical colours of happiness.
I began to tell her of a mountain cat I had once known, that spoke to me in
English, Irish and Latin. A trilingual cat. Her face snapped into open
bewilderment, and then she listened. And with disbelieving eyes
she believed all.'*

Set mainly in Brazil, with forays into Europe, Niall Quinn's brilliant
new novel is a love story driven by the pulse of obsession and the
primacy of survival.

'[Niall Quinn] is the spiritual successor to Kerouac and Burroughs.'
Die Rabe, Germany

'These stories at times ignite with fury at a single spark of
illumination. Demanding and rewarding.' *Library Journal*, USA

Quinn's skill at evoking atmosphere is often tremendous. His sense
of poverty and of the oppressiveness of work is of rare depth.
Above all, there are few writers who have captured so well the
disintegration of Irishness in the birth of a new international
underclass.' Fintan O'Toole, *Sunday Tribune*
ISBN 0 86327 469 9

More Fiction from Wolfhound Press

The Café Cong

Niall Quinn

The interrelated narratives of the Café Cong are voyages of
discovery; the narrator is a traveller whose destination is unknown.
His journey through the Caribbean and North America ends in
Paris in 1968, the turning point of that most exuberant
yet violent decade.
Gathered in the Café Cong, a shabby meeting/sleeping place, are
the young whose gods have failed.
Political, philosophical and personal ideals are in turmoil
— a crisis of faith.
To this era and its generation belongs the 'we-shall-not-be-moved'
ethos, and the nurturings of modern terrorist groupings. And in
their midst, the narrator of *The Café Cong* survives against the
political backdrop of the Vietnam war and the Paris negotiations.

Niall Quinn's first collection, *Voyovic*, showed his adherence, as one
reviewer put it, 'rather to the East European tradition of spiritual
opposition to the easy virtues than to anything we have had on this
side of realism and naturalism.' *The Café Cong* further illuminates
Niall Quinn's original vision of human beings and the webs
entangled about them.
ISBN 0 86327 303 3